THE WAY TO GAME THE WALK OF SHAME

JENN P. NGUYEN

Swoon Reads   New York

A Swoon Reads Book

An Imprint of Feiwel and Friends

Our books may be purchased in bulk for promotional, educational, or business use. Please contact your local bookseller or the Macmillan Corporate and Premium Sales Department at (800) 221-7945 ext. 5442 or by e-mail at MacmillanSpecialMarkets@macmillan.com.

Library of Congress Cataloging-in-Publication Data
Names: Nguyen, Jenn P., author.
Title: The way to game the walk of shame / Jenn P. Nguyen.
Description: First edition. | New York : Swoon Reads, 2016. |
    Summary: "After a drunken night, Taylor's perfect reputation is ruined
    unless she can convince bad boy surfer Evan to pretend to be tamed"—
    Provided by publisher.
Identifiers: LCCN 2015030156 | ISBN 9781250084071 (paperback) |
    ISBN 9781250084088 (ebook)
Subjects: | CYAC: Love—Fiction. | Dating (Social customs)—Fiction. |
    BISAC: JUVENILE FICTION / Love & Romance. | JUVENILE
    FICTION / Social Issues / Dating & Sex.
Classification: LCC PZ7.1.N52 Way 2016 | DDC [Fic]—dc23
LC record available at http://lccn.loc.gov/2015030156

Book design by Ashley Halsey

First Edition—2016

10 9 8 7 6 5 4 3 2 1

swoonreads.com

To my dad, my number one biggest fan.

I miss you every single day.

Con thương bố nhiều lắm.

1

{Taylor}

Before I even opened my eyes, I knew something was wrong. I wasn't in my bed like I should be, surrounded by the cream duvet comforter that Mom and I had gotten from Macy's last month. The fabric under my fingertips was cool and kind of scratchy.

Evidence number two: It smelled different. Not in a *bad* way. Just not like the apple-cinnamon air freshener that Mom loved and sprayed all over the house, despite the fact that Dad and I hated cinnamon. I usually countered it by walking around the house with vanilla candles. As a result, our house smelled sweeter than the largest bakery in town. Ironic, because none of us could actually bake.

I sucked in another deep breath to be sure. Nope, there were no apples, cinnamon, or vanilla of any kind here. Instead, it smelled like cotton with a faint touch of pine and grass.

But the most damning evidence of all was the muscular,

bare back of a half-naked—at least I hoped it was just half, since I couldn't see beneath the navy blanket wrapped around his hips—guy lying beside me. Who definitely should not be in my *bed*.

"Oh god. Oh. My. God." My voice came out in a hoarse squeak. I squeezed my eyes shut before opening them again. Once. Twice. Over and over until fuzzy stars appeared on the pale-blue ceiling—a ceiling that was also not mine—but he wouldn't disappear.

And the stars didn't help my throbbing head. Why hadn't anyone warned me that drinking would make me feel like crap the next day?

With shaky hands, I peered beneath the covers, and—*whoosh*—a sigh of relief escaped. Thank god I was fully clothed. If you could call the lacy black tank and capris that Carly had stuffed me into the night before fully clothed. But besides that, everything else looked normal. Except for the strange room and the half-naked guy I was in bed with.

I was in a crapload of trouble. Why had I let Carly drag me to that party last night? (Note to self: Nothing good ever comes from listening to that girl.) But she'd caught me in a weak moment. Granted, I had a bunch of weak moments after I got my wait-list letter from Columbia.

But seriously, me, Taylor Simmons. Wait-listed! I still couldn't believe it. Didn't they know who I was? Did they even *look* at my application, for god's sake? It was impeccable, *and* I turned it in extra early. I even had to add an extra page for my list of accomplishments. I should have been a shoo-in.

But the months passed, and no acceptance letter. And they didn't respond to my e-mails and phone calls to check if the computers were down. Or if the acceptance committee was all sick and hospital-bound. Nothing. Until finally, a measly wait-list letter last month.

Anyway, that wasn't the point. Not really. The point was that I'd been dragged to the party . . . and then I'd left. Obviously. But where was I now? And how did I get here? Where was Carly, and why hadn't she stopped me or—

"*Hmph.*" The guy flopped over onto his stomach, away from me.

Heart racing, I could barely move. My chest tightened, but I didn't breathe, didn't blink, until the soft snoring from his side of the bed resumed. And even then, I could only let out short half breaths.

That was close. Too close. I needed to get out of here. *Now.*

I cautiously eased off the mattress, inch by inch, wincing as the slight movement made my head pound harder. My toes touched the soft carpet, and I pushed myself upright, freezing for a full minute every time the bed creaked. *Only a bit farther.*

After what felt like hours—although it was probably only a few minutes—I slipped off the edge of the bed and took a step toward the door. Big mistake. The floor's creak was like a shot-gun blasting across the room. The guy stirred, and I dove toward the ground, landing on the maroon carpet with a soft thump. My head smacked against my forearm. *Ouch.*

What the . . . ? A name was written on my left forearm in my curly handwriting. My name. *Taylor Simmons.* How hammered had I been to scribble my own name on my arm? Seriously, what the hell happened last night?

There was no time to think about it now. Still on my hands and knees, I stumbled around the dark room for my silver sandals. The only noise was the soft snoring from the lump on the bed.

Still...who *was* my partner in crime? Could it be someone I knew, or was it—*holy crap*—a random guy I met at the party? Was I a harlot like in those Regency romance novels I hid in the back of my nightstand?

Or was *courtesan* the right word? It *sounded* classier, at least.

"Oh god." I shook my head and resisted the urge to smack my palm against my forehead. Now wasn't the time to get technical.

A sliver of sunlight shone through the top of the window shades, casting a shadow over his face, which was still partially buried in the pillows. I peered over the edge of the mattress but couldn't see more than his muscular, deeply tanned back. I *thought* his hair was dark, but I couldn't be sure. Even though I knew I should get the hell out of here, a part of me—probably the part that was still drunk—hesitated. I had to know who he was. But each time I tried to get closer, the damn floor kept creaking.

Jeez, what kind of house was this?

Against my better judgment, I snooped around the room, careful to crawl on my elbows and stomach like a soldier on enemy territory. Tennis shoes, video games, textbooks with crisp pages that hadn't been used very often, an admirable collection of old-school comic books...*Bingo!* I hit the jackpot when I tossed a dirty magazine out of the way and found a stack of pictures. I shoved my tangled, dark hair out of my face and moved a little closer to the light.

Cars and girls. Loads of them. Girls, I mean. And there was a *lot* of skin in most of them. My cheeks flushed hotly at a picture of a girl and the minuscule bikini that could barely restrain her large boobs, which she thrust toward the camera with a coy grin. I couldn't even tell if she was a redhead or a brunette. Just teeth, lips, and boobs. *Flip.* A blond with boobs. Another blond with boobs. A picture of someone's legs on the beach.

"Come on. Show your face," I muttered with a quick upward glance to make sure my unknown partner was still sleeping. He was.

Finally, I found a picture with a guy in it. He was standing in profile, but his face was turned toward the camera, dipped down toward—what else?—more boobs. His nose was pretty straight, aside from the teeniest bump at the bridge. Slightly spiky dark blond hair. Laughing dark-gray eyes that glanced to the side. His jaw was sort of large, which could be from an under-bite, but it suited him. Especially when he smiled. So very hot.

And familiar.

My head jerked to the smooth, lounging back. Then I focused on the tiny glimpse of black Chinese characters trailing down his left forearm. I'd seen that tattoo close-up once before. Everyone claimed it meant "Just live." But for all I knew, it actually meant "Gum lover."

A low groan escaped my lips. No, no, no. Not him. *Anybody* but Evan McKinley, Nathan Wilks High School's very own legendary manwhore. Said to have screwed so many girls that he had to get a new surfboard, because his old one was full of nicks in memory of each new conquest.

Killing any remaining traces of hope that I was wrong, he stretched out his left arm, and I could see his name written on his skin. *Evan McKinley.* In *my* handwriting.

WHERE WERE THOSE DAMN SANDALS?

I crawled around so fast, I was pretty sure I'd have permanent carpet burn on my elbows. I didn't care. If anyone caught me within a yard of Evan, the rumor mill would explode. It had been hard enough to squash the gossip that spread last year when I'd nearly drowned in the Harrison Parks community pool and he'd saved me. Since then, I'd steered clear of anything that had to do with him.

Which would really suck if anyone knew I'd spent the night *in his bed*.

Shoes, shoes ... maybe I didn't need them. Dad had bought them for me when I became editor of the school yearbook. He probably wouldn't even notice that they were missing, but Mom definitely would. She'd been the one who persuaded him to get them for me despite their ridiculous price—you would have thought the crystals were real diamonds—instead of the modest black pumps I needed for my internship at his law firm next year. "You need something pretty! Something fun!" she kept saying over and over. Weird how I was more like Dad, even though I wasn't his biological daughter. The only thing I'd gotten from Mom was her brown eyes.

And she would give me hell if I didn't have my shoes. Besides, I didn't know how far from home I was. And I already wasn't looking forward to the walk of shame I had ahead of me. I wiggled even more beneath the bed, arms spread out in search.

A sleepy male voice laced with amusement suddenly drifted over my head. "They're under my desk."

"What?" I scrambled out and shot upright, smacking the back of my head against Evan's jaw. He must have been leaning over the bed, watching me. A loud crack echoed through the room before we both sprang apart, each groaning loudly. *Gah*, his jaw was as hard as a hammer, and I was the screw he'd nailed. Not exactly the best metaphor, but he'd knocked whatever literary sense I had out of me.

When the pain finally lessened, I glanced up. Evan was turned to the side, slightly bent over, both hands massaging his cheeks and jaw as though checking if anything was broken. With a mind of their own, my eyes slid down his body. I'd seen him at the pool and gym before, but I'd never actually *looked* at him. At least, not this closely.

Light freckles were sprinkled where his very tan shoulders and back came together. Thank god he was wearing a pair of wrinkled khaki shorts—although they rode pretty low on his hips. On one side, a pale line peeked out beneath his tan. A spot that was probably never in the sun and no one ever saw. At least no one he wasn't sleeping with.

"Uh…" My head nearly burst from the instant heat that sprang to my cheeks. I tore my eyes away and focused on a tropical postcard hanging on the edge of his mirror, squashing the unwanted yet not unreasonable disappointment that he was wearing clothes. This was *not* the time to be ogling Evan McKinley.

"So, I guess I should say good morning." He stretched his arms over his head and grinned down at me, enjoying my discomfort. I saw his lean biceps ripple distractingly out of the corner of my eyes. "Isn't that what people are supposed to say first thing in the morning?"

Look away, Taylor. Look away. I shaded my eyes against the tantalizing view and focused on the lines on my palm. "I don't know. Shouldn't you know the morning-after protocol better than me?" Damn, I shouldn't have said that.

To my surprise, he threw his head back and laughed. "Yeah, I guess there's no denying *that* truth."

I clamped my jaw shut before anything else inappropriate slipped out, and my eyes longingly glanced toward the door. I should have slid out when I had the chance.

Did we have to go through the polite pleasantries? Couldn't we just forget about each other as though last night (and this morning) hadn't happened? Like we didn't know each other?

Oh god. He probably *didn't* know me. Just because *I* knew who he was didn't mean *he* knew who I was. Aside from my choking out "Thank you" after he'd saved me at the pool, we'd never spoken to each other before (or since). Not to mention, I had looked like a drowned rat that day, so I kind of hoped he didn't remember. Besides, he must have saved hundreds of girls in the past year. I'd even seen a girl pretend to drown in front of him just to get some lip action.

Nah, Evan couldn't possibly remember. I was just an average one-night—wait, we hadn't slept together, so scratch that. I was a random, strange girl in his room. And it was going to stay that way.

I climbed to my feet, intending to make a quick escape, when a wave of nausea caught me by surprise. My mouth filled with a bitter taste. *Urgh.* I pressed a hand against my lips as my vision blurred.

Evan reached forward as though he was going to catch me. Either me or my vomit. I automatically backed up a few steps until my back was pressed against his desk chair.

"The bathroom's over there," he said with a jab over his right shoulder. "I guess you're a bit of a lightweight, huh?"

Pride made me swallow back the bile that struggled to climb out of my throat. "No, I'm all right," I choked out.

"Are you sure? I mean, you really shouldn't be keeping it in. Especially if you're going to eat breakfast. You know, eggs, cereal, or bacon. Or sausages, if you prefer that. Me, I like the crunchiness of bacon. Especially when paired with some warm pancakes, gooey butter, and syrup that drips all over the place and runs down—"

The images he painted made me want to give up the fight and hurl on the carpet right there. "No, just—stop. I can't—" I stopped trying to breathe since the air was making everything worse, and I clenched my lips tightly together instead. I squeezed my eyes closed. *I will not throw up. I forbid myself to throw up.*

My eyes popped open again when Evan pried my fingers away from my face. I was too surprised by his touch to react. His laughing gray eyes twinkled down at me. He placed an unopened water bottle in my hand and wrapped my fingers around it. "Here, drink this. You'll feel better."

"I can't."

"Trust me. I know how to handle hangovers better than you." His hands moved up to my shoulders, and he pushed me down on the plush leather chair. "Seriously, just drink it. It's not poison. I promise."

I eyed the water. "And I'm just supposed to take your word for it?"

"No, you'll take my word for it because you don't have a choice," he said with a snort. "Besides, if you throw up in here,

I'll have to clean it up, and you can bet your ass I'm not doing that."

Hmm. He had a point. I took the bottle and forced myself to drink. It threatened to come back up, but I didn't stop until it was empty. My full stomach bounced uncomfortably, but I didn't feel like I was going to die anymore.

As Evan watched me, his brows furrowed together until they were practically one dark-blond line. Suddenly, he reached out and touched my forehead.

I jerked my head back and batted his hand away, despite the fact that it was nice and warm against my clammy skin. My fingertips massaged my forehead, and I willed the whole situation to go away. More than anything, I wished this was just a bad nightmare and that I was actually all snug in bed. "Shit, I'm in so much trouble. I'm supposed to meet Brian about the alumni speech. But not before I KILL Carly and—why are you grinning?"

"Nothing, it's just..." His smile grew so wide that his eyes became slits. "You don't look like the type of girl who curses much. It's sort of weird."

I stared at him. My life was turned upside down, and *that* was the most important thing on his mind right now? "Well, I do when the situation calls for it. And believe me, *this* calls for it. Shit. Shit. Shit." I actually wasn't used to cursing, but this was a special occasion. And I was offended by his comment. Like I was some type of Goody Two-Shoes. I would have thought waking up in his bed should have eliminated that possibility.

And why did I even care what he thought of me?

Evan let out a low whistle. "Okay, I get it, Taylor. You're a badass. Don't make me have to censor you."

"Whatever. I'm sure you've said much worse—" Wait a second, did he just . . . "You called me Taylor."

"Um, yeah. That is your name."

"But how do you know my name?"

"Because it's written on your arm?" He pointed at my left arm just as I tried to cover it up. "Besides, we *do* go to school together."

My jaw dropped. Crap, he knew ME.

I leapt to my feet. The nausea and headache suddenly vanished. It was as if the fear and anxiety had absorbed all the alcohol. Best cure for a hangover? Imagine your reputation tarnished in an instant. Better than tomato juice; or whatever people drank to sober up.

"Listen, Evan. You have to promise me that you won't tell anyone about this. Ever." I said the last word as firmly as I could, channeling my dad in the courtroom when he intimidated a witness. "No one can ever know that I spent the night here. Especially with you."

His forehead wrinkled. "And what's so bad about me? You know, it *may* be hard to believe, but girls are usually pretty happy when they wake up in my room. Perky, too."

"Uh, hello?" I grabbed the picture of Boobs Girl off the ground and shoved it in his face.

Evan stared blankly down at the photo and scratched his head, making his hair even more disheveled. My stomach flopped.

"I don't get it."

Even though it wasn't possible, I could practically *feel* my blood pressure rising. I ran my fingers through my own hair, jerking a bit at the clumpy tangles. "Look, I'm sure you're right. Plenty of girls would love to be here right now. Anyone but me. Seriously. I'm not that kind of girl! I'm a Columbia girl. A future lawyer like my dad. I don't want be lumped in with a group of bimbos who give pictures of themselves in tiny string bikinis to random guys."

Evan narrowed his eyes, but I could tell that he was hurt by my rant. A pang of guilt hit me. "That's not—"

"I know I'm being a jerk." My hands dropped to my sides. Who was I to judge *them* when I was in the same position? Although technically, *he* was the one sleeping around, not them. So if there was finger-pointing, it should be at him. "They're not bimbos. I'm sure they're all very nice. And *pretty*, from the . . . little that I can actually see. Maybe their cameras slipped and they accidentally took a picture of their boobs. How do I know? Water can be pretty slippery."

"No, I mean, *this* is a picture of her in her bra." He leaned toward me and tapped the picture still in my hand.

I dropped the picture like it burned and watched it flutter to the carpet—thankfully, face down. "So, like I said, we should just forget about last night. Not that I actually remember—I mean, it was nothing."

Evan clenched his fist to his bare chest and doubled over. "Ouch. And here I was pulling out all my best moves for you."

My cheeks burned. "Sorry, I didn't mean—"

"I was joking."

"Oh."

"You're right, though. We should just forget this," he continued, gesturing toward the bed and then at me. "Whatever *this* was never happened. We don't even know each other. Hey, do you need a ride home?"

I shoved him back when he took a few steps toward the door. "No, I don't need a ride! What part of *this didn't happen* don't you understand? There will be no rides, no talking, not even a glance between us in the future. Got that?"

"But what if I need to return your underwear or something?"

"You don't have my—" My hands lowered to my hips, and I almost checked in front of him. "Ha-ha, very funny."

The corners of his mouth jerked up into a smile again. "I try."

"Well, from now on, there will be no more mention of my underwear or any other undergarments to anyone." I held out a hand to him. "Deal?"

Was it my imagination, or did his eyes drop to check me out? His gaze was back on mine in an instant, so I couldn't be sure. Still, I tugged at the thin straps of my tank top and wrapped my arm across my small chest. I nodded toward my outstretched hand. "Deal?" I repeated, louder this time.

His hand grasped mine, practically dwarfing it. His thumb grazed my knuckles and sent shivers up and down my spine. I forced myself to stand still and stare up at his face, hurting my neck in the process.

"Deal."

2

{Taylor}

The two-mile walk home took forever. Within minutes, I regretted not accepting Evan's offer to drive me home. I knew *why* it would have been a bad idea, but with each painful step, the reasons disappeared.

One thing's for sure, these sandals were definitely *not* made for walking.

Finally home, I barely had time to sneak into the bathroom to throw up before my parents caught me. Kimmy, my nine-year-old baby sister, was sitting at the top of the stairway when I rushed past. She started to call out my name, but I motioned for her to shush. The sweetheart nodded solemnly and mimicked zipping her lips shut.

There was a knock on the bathroom door a few minutes later. "Taylor? I didn't think you'd be home so soon. I called your phone earlier, but you didn't pick up, so I called Carly and she told me you were still asleep."

My hands automatically flew to my pockets, even though I knew my phone wasn't there. I must have left it at the party or something. "Yeah, sorry, Mom. I think the ringer is off or something," I called out, trying to sound as normal as I could.

"It's okay. So did you have fun at the party? Did it help take your mind off things?"

That was an understatement. "Yeah, I can *honestly* say it really did."

"I knew it would!" I could hear the glee in her voice. "Do you want some breakfast? I made your favorite. French toast with a side of mushroom hash browns. Heavy on the mushrooms."

Urgh, more food talk. I plopped down next to the toilet again, feeling crappy both inside and out. "Maybe a little later? Let me shower first, okay?"

"Sure."

Yeah, there was no way I could hide this hangover from Mom and Dad. Especially Dad. That man could detect any hint of weakness and lies. Which is why he's a great lawyer. Although right now, I wasn't so proud of those skills.

Once the coast was clear, I poked my head out of the bathroom to check. The hall was empty. Only Kimmy still sat by the top of the stairs, like a guard dog with braids.

I cleared my throat and motioned her forward. "Can you let me know when Mom and Dad are gone? I don't want to see them right now."

"But—"

"If you help me and keep this a secret between us, then you can have my French toast with extra syrup. Deal?"

I don't know if it was the thought of keeping a secret from

our parents or the French-toast bribe, but her smile widened until all you could see were her shiny teeth. "Deal!"

After she left, I hopped into the tub. Well, not so much hopped as stumbled around with my head held between my hands in an attempt to make the throbbing stop. Thankfully, the steaming-hot water eased my headache, making everything feel better. Not *perfect*, but better.

I stayed in the shower for ages, until the hot water turned warm and finally piercing cold. Not wanting to turn into an icicle, I finally got out. My fingertips were already wrinkled prunes.

Wrapping a thick cream towel around myself, I wiped at the condensation on the mirror and stared myself down. "So you had a minor setback with Columbia yesterday and Evan this morning. Big whoop." I narrowed my eyes at my own reflection. "It doesn't mean anything. *You're* still Taylor Simmons. You're still you. You're still awesome. And this time next year, you'll be sitting on the Columbia campus thinking, *Evan who?*"

"Tay, Mom and Dad left. Can I eat the French toast in your room?"

A horrified denial automatically sprang to my lips at the image of crumbs and syrup all over my sheets, but I pushed it down at Kimmy's earnest tone. I owed her one for helping me out anyway. "Sure, but uh, make sure you get extra napkins."

"Okay!"

I let out a slow, deep breath and pointed a wrinkled finger at the mirror to continue my pep talk. "So pull yourself together. Tomorrow you're going to go to school and pretend nothing happened. Actually, not even pretend. Because. Nothing. Happened."

Evan's grinning face popped into my head. His dark-gray eyes twinkled with amusement like he was listening to my speech. I shivered and swiped at the mirror again, hoping it would help clear my mind. "Nothing."

⌒•⌒

Thank god I had Sunday to lie around and sleep, or I doubt I would have ever made it to school. Kimmy and I hung out in my room and watched movies all day long. After she finished the French toast, I brought the dirty plate out myself and pretended I'd eaten it. Luckily, Mom had errands to run that day, so she couldn't ask me too much about the party.

I wished avoiding people at school on Monday were as easy as avoiding my parents. Everyone's eyes were on me as I walked to class. Seriously. Heads turned, and people whispered behind their hands with every step I took. And the worst part was they weren't even *trying* to be subtle about it.

There had to be another reason—any reason—that they would be looking at me. Maybe I had won some sort of an award. Or Brian failed a test or something, and I was the valedictorian now. (One can dream.) At this point, I wouldn't even mind being the one who failed the hypothetical test. Anything would be better than the truth.

I fumbled with the combination on my locker. Out of the corner of my eyes, I saw a brunette girl in a black sophomore sweatshirt turn to some guy beside her and point at me. At first I couldn't hear what they said, but my ears perked up at Evan's name. Straining to hear, I leaned in closer.

"I think she's the one who went home with Evan McKinley after the party," she said in a hushed tone.

"No, way. Isn't she like a nerd or something? Like a teacher's pet?"

"Everyone calls her the Ice Queen. Now she's just another one of his flings."

He snickered. "Guess even queens can't resist Evan McKinley."

Party. Evan. Fling.

No, no, no. This had to be a dream. A really sucky, horrible nightmare.

Even though my hangover was gone, I suddenly felt like throwing up again. Forgetting why I was even at my locker, I stumbled away without opening it. Everything in front of me spun. The lockers. The other students. This couldn't be happening. This had to be some type of *Twilight Zone* or something. Or a bad romance novel where I was the gentle, well-bred, titled daughter who had her reputation ruined because of a scandalous, notorious rake.

Reading about it was way better than experiencing it.

But damn it, how could everyone know already? And what exactly *did* they know?

It was the longest walk of my life. Like someone had decided to build an extra mile into the hallway over the weekend just to torture me.

Even Faith Watkins, whom everyone at school nicknamed the Reincarnated Mother Mary, gave me a sympathetic look when I passed her. The little Catholic girl with the white sweaters and JESUS LOVES ME stickers on her backpack knew. And if *she* knew, that meant *everyone* knew.

Once I was finally able to reach the safety of first period, I plopped onto my usual seat without looking at anyone around me. They were still whispering and pointing, but at least now there were only twenty-five of them instead of the entire school.

My forehead dropped into my hands, gripping it tightly as though that would help shrink my headache. God, could this day get any worse?

Mr. Peters strolled into class and closed the door behind him with a loud bang. "All right, did everyone finish the report on a significant event of the 1900s?"

There were moans and groans, and a couple of students immediately started rambling off excuses why they didn't do their homework.

Glad for the distraction and to finally have things back to normal, I let out a sigh of relief and opened my bag to get the red folder I stuck the report in to keep the pages fresh. It took me less than a minute to realize it wasn't there. Where was it? When I had finished, I had immediately put it in my folder . . . and left it on my desk at home.

Crap.

I shuffled through the loose papers in my bag again, even though I knew that the report was at home, neatly stapled and ready to go. I had finished it days ago but forgot to put it in my bag yesterday because I was so sick.

After making a couple of notes in his binder, Mr. Peters moved around the classroom to collect the papers. As he got closer and closer to my seat, the panic in my stomach grew. I prayed for a miracle, an earthquake or tsunami to suddenly hit, even though something like that had never hit Wilmington before. Or anywhere in North Carolina. But that's what miracles were, right? I mean, if Evan McKinley and I could hook up—or whatever we did Saturday night—then that was proof enough that the impossible could happen!

Heck, I wouldn't even have minded a meteor right now.

"Ms. Simmons?"

"Uh, yes?"

With a frown, he waved the papers in the air. "I need your report."

My eyes lowered, and I traced the old P ♡ Q carving on the corner of my desk. "Well, you see, it's funny. Kind of. The thing is . . ." My voice lowered into a half whisper. "I think I left my report at home."

"You think?"

"I mean, I know I did." My attempt at an apologetic smile felt forced and weird. But it wasn't my fault. I'd never been in this position before. I didn't know what to do.

He blinked at me like he still didn't understand. "You don't have your report?"

"No." Why did he keep making me repeat myself?

"You can't blame her, Mr. Peters," a loud voice suddenly called out from the back of the room. With a smirk, Lauren Tillman leaned back in her chair and swept her fiery-red hair over one slender shoulder. "Taylor had a really *busy* weekend."

My weak smile melted like an icicle on the sidewalk in the middle of summer.

Even though we'd gone to school together forever, I could barely count the number of times Lauren had talked to me. Or even about me. I didn't even know she knew my name.

Mr. Peters shook his head. "Still, this isn't like you, Taylor. Your record is usually so impeccable."

"Oh, don't worry. Little Miss Perfect blemished a lot more than just her record at the party. And after," Lauren loudly continued.

At that, the whole class snorted with laughter. A couple of guys in the back row winked and made kissy-faces at me.

"All right, that's enough." Mr. Peters had to smack his binder against the side of my desk to get everyone to shut up. "Let's just start class."

He leaned down and lowered his voice a bit. "You can bring it to me tomorrow, but I'm disappointed in you, Taylor. Really. I expected more from you. If I can't trust you to hand in a simple paper on time, how am I supposed to let you plan Career Day? Or give the alumni presentation?"

It was as though all the blood had drained from my face. I could feel myself getting light-headed. "No, I swear I did the report. I did it on the first test-tube baby in the U.S. It was Elizabeth Carr in Virginia. If you want, I could run home and get it! Or my mom can bring it to school for me, or—"

He waved his hand to stop my defense. "Look, we'll talk about this later. Just see me after class."

"Yes, sir." I made the mistake of looking behind me and locking eyes with Lauren again.

She pursed her lips in mock sympathy and wiggled her fingers at me in a half wave.

Cheeks flaming, I whipped my head back around. My fingers dug into the sides of my chair. *Gah.* I wanted to crawl beneath my desk and die. The mockery and gossiping were one thing, but I had never had a teacher be *disappointed* in me. Much less a teacher who had connections to the alumni and faculty at Columbia. This was the worst time to get on Mr. Peters's bad side. A good word from him to the guest speaker could make all the difference in the world. Could turn my being wait-listed into an acceptance.

And now it was all slipping down the drain.

Double crap.

⁓･⁓

"You!"

I didn't look up. Not even when Carly tapped the top of my head with a binder. Twice. Though it throbbed, I buried my head even deeper in my arms, trying to disappear. I didn't want to see all the eyes around the cafeteria staring at me, like they'd been doing all morning. I thought it might die down a bit by lunch, but I couldn't even eat my barbecued meatloaf and steamed vegetables in peace.

"First you don't pick up my call, and now you won't even look at me?" Carly's voice got more high-pitched with each word. From previous experience, I knew this wasn't a good sign. She was like a ticking time bomb, and if I didn't respond, the lunch ladies would be scraping pieces of me out of the gravy bin. She was my best friend and I loved her, but her nosiness and booming voice were probably going to kill me. "How could you ditch me at the party?"

I turned my head and wiggled my nose when my hair flopped over my face. The strands parted with my loud sigh. Her face hovered over me with a scowl.

"Oh, hi. How was civics?"

"As exciting as a class taught by my mother could be. She

called me sweetie pie and fixed my hair in front of everyone."
Carly slumped into the seat across from me and rolled her dark
eyes so far back, I worried they'd get stuck. "I was tempted to
stab myself with a pen just to have an excuse to leave."

I usually didn't bring up her mom, but I needed something to distract Carly, at least for a bit, and her mom was her
kryptonite. She could complain about her all afternoon if she
wanted to.

Carly's mom was a substitute teacher, and although she
promised her kids she'd never work at their schools, the econ-
omy was so bad that sometimes she couldn't help it. It was still
money, after all. This was the first time she'd taught one of Carly's
classes, though—something Carly had been dreading all week.

I liked Mrs. Winters, but that was because she spoiled me.
Carly swore her mom would still love me even if I egged their
house weekly, because she approved of "my career choice." In
Mrs. Winters's mind, doctors, lawyers, and dentists were the
way to go. Either to become one or to meet one—like Carly's
older sister, Nancy, did. She married an optometrist. The crème
de la crème.

So her younger daughter's love for drama and music was a
touchy subject between them. Although with Carly's over-the-
top theatrics, theater was the obvious choice.

Carly opened a bag of veggies, once again on her never-
ending quest to lose weight. "I'm asking again. Why did you
ditch me at the party? And why did you lie to me?"

"I don't remember leaving the party." I squinted up at her in
confusion. "And when did I lie?"

"Uh, after you disappeared, I texted you a gazillion times, and finally you texted back that you were already home, remember?" She waved a carrot stick in the air like a sword. "Imagine my surprise when your *mom* called me the next day asking about you. You're lucky that I'm brilliant at improv and was able to cover for you."

Chewing on my lower lip, I tugged on my ear and tried to remember texting her, but I couldn't. I still didn't know what happened that night. "Sorry."

She let out a heavy sigh and poked me with her carrot stick. "Seriously, though, do you know how worried I was? Don't disappear on me like that again! And could you please sit up? I feel like I'm talking to a corpse."

"Sorry," I said again, pulling myself upright and propping my chin on my palm. "But you know, none of this would have happened if you hadn't dragged me to that party. And gotten me drunk."

Carly scoffed and rolled her eyes. "What else was I supposed to do, let you keep moping at home and camping out by your mailbox for news from Columbia like you've been doing all month? You'll get accepted. One little party isn't going to change that. This is our senior year! We have to experience it! And it was your own fault for not eating all day. That's why it hit you so bad. You barely drank."

Really? I swear I must have drunk a lot more to have felt that crappy. Maybe Evan was right. Maybe I was a lightweight.

My fingers tapped against the table. I was irritated and wanted to blame someone. Anyone. But I couldn't blame Carly. Mainly because I knew she would blow up at me if I did. But she was right. It's not like she dragged me kicking and screaming to the party. Or poured the drinks down my throat. The wait-list letter had made me panic, and I was stupid. Really stupid.

"Sorry," I finally said.

"I forgive you." She dusted off her hands and picked up her Diet Coke. "So now that we're done with all the apologies, you have to tell me. What *did* you do after you left the party with Evan?"

"I don't know."

"Don't know or won't say?"

"I don't *know*. Seriously."

"Hmm." Carly continued munching on another carrot stick. *Crunch. Crunch. Crunch.* "As your friend, I know I'm supposed to believe you, but seeing how you and Evan were making out at the party in front of everyone makes it kind of hard. Especially when you both disappeared together afterward. It was all anyone could talk about."

Great, my first time making out with a guy, and I can't even remember any of it. At least now I knew how everyone found out.

My head flew up, and I winced. Oh god, what if I was awful? Like too-much-saliva, garlic-breath horrible? I'd only kissed three guys in my life, and none for more than ten seconds. And barely any tongue. I wasn't exactly experienced. Then again, since Evan ended up taking me home, I guess I couldn't have been *that* bad, right?

Not knowing the inner turmoil her comment caused, Carly picked up my unused fork and stabbed at the cold mystery meatloaf on my plate. "Are you sure you guys didn't do it?"

"Carly!"

"Come on! You have to at least tell me if you did. Remember,

I lied to your mom for you." She waved the fork at me. "You owe me some details."

"I told you. Nothing happened."

"Seriously?" Her eyebrow rose. "You went home with the dude, and you guys didn't *do* anything? How is that even possible? He's Evan McKinley, for god's sake."

I looked down at my half-eaten plate. The memory of waking up in his bed was still fresh in my head. And the image of a nearly naked Evan was practically seared into my mind. "I don't know. It's complicated."

Her dark eyes brightened with excitement. "All the best stories start off that way. Spill it."

I let out a halfhearted laugh. No matter how hard the day was, I was glad to have Carly by my side. Loud and bossy as she was. "Well, it all started when I woke up and didn't smell any apples..."

3

-Evan-

McKinley!"

Figures. I'd been here for less than an hour, and Aaron had already found me. Did he have some sort of sensor on me or something? Usually I would be happy to see him, but lunch with Mom and Brandon had made me want to punch someone, and I was pretty sure Aaron wouldn't want to be that someone.

Pretending I didn't hear him, I ducked my head lower and wove my way through the crowded hall. But he wasn't Nathan Wilks's second-string running back for nothing. He could have easily been on the first string if he gave a shit about the team and went to practices like he was supposed to.

He dove between Lucy Kim and her group of flag-team members to grab the back strap of my bag, yanking me backward. "Sorry, ladies. We've got urgent business to talk about. Where were you all morning, man?"

I glanced at the group of girls, who were obviously eaves-dropping, and brushed him off. "Just busy," I said, deliberately sounding mysterious as I winked at Lucy. She grinned and motioned for me to call her before walking away.

Hmm, did I even have her number? At least *she* thought I did. Maybe she'd given it to me before and I forgot.

"I'm sure you were." He shoved my left shoulder. "So tell me, what was it like?"

"Huh?" Great, now I sounded like an idiot. So much for being mysterious.

"You know." Instead of explaining, he wiggled his eyebrows and grinned down at me.

Not up for another one of Aaron's guessing games, I walked toward the vending machines by the cafeteria. "What the hell are you talking about?"

"Look, I don't know why you're trying to be noble. Everyone saw you leaving the party with her the other night." I didn't have to look up to know he had a sneer on his face. It was evident in his voice. He moved forward until he blocked the drink machine in front of me with an outstretched arm. "Don't be shy."

"I'm not being shy, I just don't know what the hell you're—" An image of Taylor smiling up at me as we swayed to the fast-paced music popped in my head. My hands were wrapped tightly around her waist. Us laughing and plastered against each other as we walked around the block to my house. It had been like this all weekend—just brief flashes of us in my head. But as much as I tried, I couldn't figure out what hap-pened once we *got* to my house.

Judging by the dopey smile on Aaron's face, I can imagine what everyone assumed happened. "You're an asshole. Now either move or buy me a drink."

He laughed and dug into his pockets for some change. "Fine, I'll just imagine it on my own." Aaron snorted and shook his head. "Dude, I still can't believe you were able to hit that Ice Queen. You, my man, are a god. A modern, womanizing Zeus."

At his words, a broad smile crossed my face. It was wrong, since technically I didn't "hit that," but who didn't like being called a god? On any other day, I would have happily obliged Aaron's request. Hell, I was usually the one to start bragging about the chicks I hooked up with. In detail. But lunch with Brandon earlier still left a sour taste in my mouth. I shouldn't have taken up Mom's offer and had lunch with them. I didn't know what I was thinking. Usually I'd rather mow the lawn with my teeth than eat a meal with my stepdad.

It was bad enough that they showed up unannounced for my drug test, something Brandon—the dickhead—insisted on when he found drugs in my room once. They weren't mine, but he didn't believe me.

Mom knew the drugs weren't mine. I would never touch the stuff after my cousin Stacey died from an overdose. We were pretty close. She used to watch me whenever Mom went to work after Dad went to jail. That was before Mom met Brandon Willard.

But instead of sticking up for her own son—and, god forbid, getting in a fight with her saintly new husband—Mom would rather make me suffer the embarrassment of getting a professional monthly drug test. Brandon suspected I would somehow tamper with the home tests. Mom even spoke to the principal and the office about my "appointments" so I could be excused.

Someone deserved the Best Mom of the Year award.

I was tempted to fail the drug test on purpose just to piss off Brandon even more, but I settled on cutting school whenever I could. The school calling him at work to tattle on me always embarrassed the hell out of him, and that was more than enough satisfaction for me.

I had almost chugged down half the can of Sprite when hoots and wolf whistles filled the air. "What's going on?"

Aaron shrugged and stepped toward the cafeteria. I followed him and stopped when I spotted Taylor sitting with her friend Carly a couple of tables from the entrance. There was a crowd of jocks surrounding them.

"Well, look who it is. Anyone ready to party?" some dude asked. I think he was a junior or something. He braced his hands on the edge of the table and sneered down his pointy nose at the girls. "Dang, Simmons, I should have introduced you to tequila a long time ago. Especially now that you dropped your good-girl front and acting like you're better than us all the time."

I expected her to explode, but to my surprise, Taylor just bit her lower lip and turned away from him. Her cheeks burned, but she still didn't say anything in response to the jerks around her.

This was a far cry from the girl I'd danced with at the party. And especially from the one who woke up in my bed yesterday. That girl smacked my jaw and made me swear not to tell anyone about what happened. Not that I could have if I wanted to. But the point was that *that* girl was fierce. My jaw still ached.

Her hands clenched and unclenched, but she still didn't say anything. Suddenly, Taylor looked up, and our eyes met across the room. Pursing her lips together, she lifted her chin and looked away. Her face was still red, but she looked a little scared. Not of the guys around her, but of . . . *something*.

Something in me snapped, and I automatically grabbed Aaron's arm, ready to beat the crap out of those guys.

I had barely taken three steps forward when Carly whipped around in her seat and glared them down, despite the fact that they were all twice her size and could probably squash her like a bug. "Oh yeah, Todd? If you want to talk about fronts, why don't you tell everyone again how you wet the bed until you were twelve? How many mattresses *did* your parents have to throw out before you finally learned how to use the toilet?"

Todd's face grew blotchy. But she didn't even bat an eye and continued to stare at him. Hell, she even leaned up so she could be more in his face.

To my surprise, he muttered something low under his breath and jerked his body away to storm off. His cronies snickered behind their fists and followed.

Taylor slumped forward onto the table and whispered something to Carly. She just snorted in response. "Don't worry about it. I guess now that he can use the big-boy potty, he thinks he's all badass," Carly said, not even bothering to lower her voice.

I couldn't help laughing. Man, if anyone was a badass, it was Carly. Right now I kind of wanted to go over there and give her a hug. And Taylor, too. But judging by the way she was glaring at me now, she'd probably scratch my eyes out if I tried.

Seriously, I just didn't understand that girl.

Carly waved at me as Taylor dragged her past us through the doorway. I turned my head to watch them leave.

Aaron pulled his arm out of my grasp and crossed his arms. He had a goofy look on his face. "Interesting."

"What?"

"Nothing, it's just interesting. So that's why you don't want to tell me anything? 'Cause you have a thing for her?"

I gaped at him. "That's stupid—I don't know what you're—" This time I was the one to chase Aaron down as we walked to our lockers. "Are you kidding me?"

He stooped down to tug on his combination lock. "Hey, it's cool if you do. The Ice Queen's not as hot as the girls you usually date, but she still ranks pretty high. I mean, talk about untouchable."

Of all the crazy things Aaron was saying, the fact that he kept calling her the Ice Queen irritated me the most for some reason. "Her name's Taylor."

"Oh, I guess you two are on a first-name basis now that you're so close, huh?" he said with a wink. "Anything else you want to tell me about her?"

There was a loud bang as someone slammed a locker shut.

Aaron glanced past me and froze. His eyes grew wider with each second. I followed his gaze and saw Taylor standing behind us with crossed arms and a huge scowl on her face. Perfect.

With a cough, he bounced upright with the agility of a bullfrog just as the bell rang. He shook his head until his dark hair covered his eyes, shielding himself from her wrath. For a big guy, Aaron was always uncomfortable around angry women. And the one in front of us was so pissed, I wouldn't be surprised if her ears started steaming. "Er, I'll leave you two alone. I'll see you in PE, Evan."

I nodded, although I couldn't help feeling as though he were ditching me at my own execution. The traitor. I crouched down to shut his locker for him.

When Aaron followed the moving crowd and turned the corner, Taylor shoved my right shoulder. Hard. My left hand shot back to hit the ground so I wouldn't fall on my ass. "Hey! What was that for?"

She glanced around, but the hall was already more than half empty. The few people who lingered were slowly moving away, already pulling out their phones to text about our sweet encounter. "Why didn't you say anything? Now he really thinks something happened between us," she hissed.

I stared up at the bumpy white ceiling. Damn, this really wasn't my day. "I tried. You could see that he doesn't believe me."

She snorted and rolled her eyes upward. "It didn't look like you were trying *that* hard. I guess you can't help it. With your reputation, no wonder nobody believes anything you say."

Being called a liar was one of the less offensive things anyone could call me. Hell, it was more like a fact.

When it was obvious that Taylor wasn't going to leave anytime soon, I sighed and plopped on the ground to get comfortable. I leaned against Aaron's closed locker, one leg pulled up against my chest, and crossed my arms around my left knee. "Probably. So tell me again, how many people believed *you* when you told them what happened?" I asked with a raised eyebrow, already knowing the answer.

Her mouth opened and closed, but nothing came out. Instead she chewed on her lower lip and turned away. "Never mind. Sorry, you're right." She rubbed both sides of her forehead. "It's been a really long day. Not to mention I have to get a new phone now because I lost—"

Before she even finished her sentence, I dug in my bag and whipped out the cell phone I had found stashed in my shorts pocket yesterday. I leaned forward and tucked it into her hand. "Your friend called a lot."

"So I heard. Thanks." After she stuck the phone in her back pocket, Taylor finally looked at me again. Her eyes slowly trailed from my face down to my scruffy gray sneakers. I raised an eyebrow at her. If I didn't know any better, I would have thought she was checking me out, but girls don't usually check me out with frown lines on their forehead.

I climbed to my feet and stared back. Was this girl really the same person who had danced in the streets with me? It was hard to believe now that she was in front of me. Her long, dark hair was pulled back from her narrow face with pins. She wore casual jeans and a loose T-shirt, nothing low-cut or tight. Her left arm was piled high with books and binders. Aaron was right. She definitely wasn't my usual type.

I couldn't help thinking that she still looked pretty, though. Even with the dark, irritated look on her face. I moved a step closer to her.

As though Taylor suddenly realized what I was doing, she jerked her entire body to the right. A bright blush crept up her neck. "I have to go. There's a quiz in my next class that I should study for, and I don't know if I—"

I felt guilty for messing with her. Maybe it was the shadows under her eyes or the way she kept chewing on her lower lip, making it even pinker and puffier than usual against her pale face. I wanted to press my index finger against her mouth to make her stop, but I doubted she would appreciate that very much. And I didn't want to get bitten.

It wasn't her fault that she was tangled up in this rumor with me. I might be used to the gossip and lies that flew around— mostly because I encouraged them, just to piss off my stepdad— but Taylor wasn't. And she definitely wasn't handling it well.

"—never drink like that. Ever. But did we—I mean, I'm positive we didn't, but I just wanted to make sure . . . because you know—" She breathed heavily through every couple of words as though they were being wrestled out of her.

"Nothing happened. Between us, I mean." My voice sounded confident even though I didn't really know myself. But I was *pretty* sure nothing happened. My body would have been way more relaxed yesterday if I had gotten some action the night before. "We just slept. Or at least I tried to. You snore pretty loud for a little girl."

Judging by the way her body slumped forward with relief, that was exactly what she wanted to hear. "Thanks." Taylor fumbled with her blue backpack strap and cleared her throat. "For letting me know. I guess I'll see you around."

When she turned away to leave, I reached out to touch her arm. It wasn't a grab or even a pat. It was a light touch, but I could feel her skin beneath my fingertips. Soft and warm. A warmth that seeped into my skin. If just a fingertip could make me feel that way, what would it feel like if I curved my entire hand around her wrist?

Despite my curiosity, I shoved both hands back in my pockets before she fully turned around.

"Look, I know this probably sucks for you since you're, you know, Miss Perfect and everything." I waved a vague hand in her direction. "But don't worry about it too much. People will get tired of this and move onto something new eventually. Trust me." I gave her my best innocent, everything-is-perfect smile. "I mean, who would know more about this stuff than me?"

"You're right. It'll be fine." She turned away, and I could hear her mutter under her breath, "Hopefully."

— • —

People continued to point at me as I walked to PE, but I didn't care. In fact, it was fun to pop in on a strange group or even lock eyes with people and watch their conversations fade into awkward silence. The simple joys in life. It certainly made the school day go by quicker.

I stretched out on the patch of lawn behind the cafeteria for a quick nap. Coach Jill used our PE class after lunch to practice with her cheerleaders before football games. As long as we stayed in sight, she didn't care what the rest of the class did.

With my left arm cushioned beneath my head, I was about to doze off when a shadow fell over my face. I pried an eye open but could only see the outline of a figure peering down at me. Judging by the red hair and the mouthwatering curves on the figure, I could guess who it was.

"Looking for me so soon? I thought you're supposed to wait an hour after you eat before you have sex?" I closed my eyes again. "I think I heard that somewhere."

There was a low chuckle, and Lauren flopped down on the grass beside me. "You and I both know that's not true. We certainly tested that theory out enough times last year."

A grin stretched across my face. "Right, I guess we did."

Despite our big talk, Lauren and I weren't dating. We did last summer, after she grabbed hold of me at the beach to introduce herself in the most exciting and memorable way possible. It was fun, but we broke up a month after that. Now we were friends who just hooked up once in a while.

I usually made it a rule never to date or even sleep with the same girl twice. Somehow Lauren was the exception. She always had a way of getting under my skin. Or rather in my pants. Besides the awesome sex, she was pretty cool. She was different from the other girls I knew. I liked having her in my life. And this worked for us.

"What are you doing here?"

Instead of being deterred by my casual tone, she rolled over until she was squished against me, not even caring that the damp grass was probably making green smudges on the back of her jeans. For a girl who cared about her appearance, she didn't think twice about sitting on wet grass. Hell, she'd go to school in a chicken suit if someone dared her to.

Lauren pulled my arm away from my side and laid her head on top of my stomach. She laced her slim, cool hand around mine. "I wanted to apologize for leaving the party early. Paul wanted to take me out."

"Paul?"

"You know Paul. That guy from the prep university I told you about?"

Ah, right. I shrugged. "It's cool. I found other people to hang out with."

"So I heard." She didn't say anything else, but I could tell something was bothering her. Lauren pressed my hand against her mouth. "You know, you could at least *pretend* that you're jealous about Paul."

That's weird. She never asked me about my girls, and I didn't ask her about her guys. It was an unspoken rule between us. "Sorry, so how is the prep boy doing? Did he get his fraternity's sigma tattooed on his ass yet?"

Her lips curved into a smirk against my palm. "That's better. And Paul's fine. I'll probably see him next week."

"Good to know that the tuition his parents paid for is being used wisely."

Lauren laughed, and the weight of her head disappeared as she leaned back on her elbows. She kept holding my hand, though. "So the funniest thing happened in class this morning."

"Oh yeah?" I played with her fingers, caressing her soft skin and smooth nails. "I'm surprised that you were actually paying attention in class."

Her grip on my hand tightened a bit. "Usually I don't, but I wouldn't miss the chance to see Taylor Simmons taken down a peg or two."

My hand froze. "What do you mean?"

"I mean, the princess didn't have her homework to turn in for once." Lauren giggled to herself. "You should have seen the anxiety on her face when Mr. Peters chewed her out. I could swear she was going to burst into tears or something."

With a frown, I let go of her hand and sat up. My arms crossed over my chest. "Uh, I don't see why the thought of another girl crying would be so funny to you."

She slowly sat up, too. "Because she's annoying. Every-body was glad to see her get yelled at for once." The expression on her face was curious as she watched me. Her blue eyes narrowed a bit. "And why do you care? She's just some random girl you screwed. You didn't even know her before the party."

The corner of my mouth jerked into a half smile as I re-membered the first time I actually spoke to Taylor. "Actually, that's not true."

It was last summer, after Lauren and I had broken up. I was working part time as a lifeguard at the pool when I saw some-one flopping around in the deep end. It took seconds for me to swim over and save her. After I carried her out of the water,

Taylor spit up pool water in my face and scrambled away after mumbling thanks. I was shocked. No girl had ever treated me that way before. I saved dozens of people in the pool—mainly girls—but she was the only one I remembered from that summer. "Taylor's not just a random girl. And to be honest, it's kind of bitchy of you to consider her misery *fun*."

Lauren's mouth dropped open. Even though everyone knew she was a bitch, this was the first time I had ever called her one. I felt kind of bad about it, but it was true.

She brushed her hair over her shoulder and shrugged. "Whatever, forget I even said anything." Wrapping her hand behind my neck, she pulled me toward her until her lips, her breath, was tickling my ear. "How about we get together tonight? My house? For old times' sake." There was smug smile on Lauren's face. Her blue eyes seemed to be taunting me, urging me to just give in.

I was tempted. Really tempted. Any other day and I wouldn't have even waited for tonight. I would have buried my face in her hair, pulled her into the locker room and locked the door for the rest of the period. God, I hated to admit it, but my emotions were usually controlled by my dick. But not today. I wasn't in the mood. "Sorry, as exciting as that sounds, sweetheart, I think I'll pass."

She shoved me away and rose to her feet. "Fine. But don't bother calling me the next time you want to hook up." With a huff, she stalked toward the parking lot, nearly knocking over Aaron on the way.

"Jeez, what's her problem?"

"You act like I ever know what she's thinking." I let out a

sigh and fished my keys out of the pocket of my gym shorts. "Come on, Jill isn't paying attention to us anyway. Let's get out of here."

Aaron was still watching Lauren as she peeled away in her car. "Okay, where do you want to go?"

"Anywhere but here."

4

{Taylor}

One day at a time. Until it all blew over and things got back to normal again. I repeated the same thought over and over in my head until I *almost* started to believe it.

When the last bell rang for the day, I jumped out of my seat with joy. Now all I had to do was go home and crawl into my bed, and this nightmare day would be over.

Just as I left my AP English class, some girl jostled my shoulder, making me fall back into the doorway. My books and binder smacked to the ground and flew open. Various articles for next week's newspaper edition sprinkled the floor. I cursed under my breath and knelt to pick them up, wincing as my shoulder throbbed. I turned to stare at her, but she had already faded into the hallway crowd.

"Seriously?" I muttered, stretching to reach my scattered books. My fingers had just closed around my blue binder when Todd Herbert, the unspoken leader of the pack of Neanderthals from lunch, smacked my butt.

I jumped to my feet, but he just smirked and gave his buddies a high five. I narrowed my eyes at him.

The reason people had never gossiped about me before was because I never gave them a reason to. I never did anything wrong. Unlike Carly, who never cared what people said or thought of her. Secretly, I envied that. I couldn't be like that. I preened with pride when people complimented me, and my stomach turned when I got a dirty look. Dad said what people thought of me affected the outcome. Granted, he was talking about court cases and the jury, but it's all basically the same. No matter what people said, appearances *did* matter.

But I was sick of it. Evan was wrong. Things didn't get better. My name was even scrawled on the toilet-stall door with Wite-Out, paired with the words WHORE + SLUT. I had waited until the bathroom was empty before attacking the door and breaking three nails in the process. And I was sick of everything. But most of all, I was sick of doing nothing. Screw appearances.

"Hey, idiot!" Without thinking, I snatched my binder off the ground and threw it at Todd. It hit his shoulder with a loud, satisfying smack. Score! I fist-pumped the air in celebration just as he turned around with a scowl.

Crap. Maybe I should have thought this through. I backed up a step when he stalked toward me, and—*whoosh!*—suddenly Carly flew in like my knight in a blue cardigan and jeans and shoved him aside with her shoulder. He stumbled backward against the lockers.

She groaned and rubbed her right shoulder. "Damn, that hurt!"

I grabbed her. "Carly! Are you okay?"

"Yeah." She turned to Todd. "But I swear you'll get a lot more than that if you bother either of us again." She waved her hand for him to come forward. "Try me."

His nostrils flared, and he lurched toward us.

With a yelp, I grabbed Carly's shoulders to pull her back and out of his way when a tall back obstructed my view of Todd. A very familiar back that materialized out of nowhere.

When did Brian get here? I peered up at him and poked the center of his broad back to make sure I wasn't imagining things. He turned to look at me, and his frown deepened. His hand lightly touched my arm. "Are you okay?"

I nodded. "I'm fine."

Carly cleared her throat. "I'm fine, too. Thanks for asking."

"I know you are. Nothing could bother you." Brian gave her a quick grin and turned away. "You know, Herbert, picking on two girls kinda makes you look like a wimp."

Cursing under his breath, Todd took another step toward us just as Mr. Peters stepped out of his classroom. "What's going on here?"

The hall had been crowded during our fight, but everyone faded backward and practically evaporated as soon as a teacher showed up. Our group remained quiet. Even if we didn't say anything, the evidence was pretty obvious. My books were still scattered on the ground. My binder was even at Todd's feet, and Carly was still rubbing her shoulder.

"Nothing, we just had a little accident, but everyone's fine now," Brian smoothly lied. He bent down to grab my books. "Nothing to worry about. Right, guys?"

"Right, it's nothing," Carly chirped with a beaming grin.

Todd's eyes flickered between each of us—lingering on me

for the longest time—before landing on Mr. Peters. After a long and agonizing minute, he shook his head. "Yeah, everything's good."

Mr. Peters didn't look like he believed us, but he nodded. "Then why don't you guys go home? School's over, you know. Ms. Simmons, can I talk to you again?"

"Uh, I guess so." I turned to Brian and Carly. "Do you guys want to wait for me?"

Carly frowned. "I have to go to theater practice. But I'll talk to you later." She gave my arm a tight squeeze and turned to Brian. "Take care of her, okay?"

" 'Course. I'll be here, Taylor."

With a nod, I let out a low, deep breath and followed Mr. Peters into his classroom. He sat down behind his desk, picked up a pen, and tapped it against the side of his desk. I shifted my weight side to side as I waited for him to speak.

"First the late report and now this *accident*."

I ducked my head a little. "I know. I'm sorry, it won't happen again."

"I hope not. But you're clearly too distracted these days. I think you should take a break from preparing the Career Day presentation. Drop off your materials tomorrow, and I'll have Lin take over."

And just like that, my dream of wowing the Columbia alumni—along with my chances of actually *going* to Columbia— faded away. "But—but you can't. I've been working on this for ages! You *can't* just give it to Lin. She'll mess it up."

He dropped his pen with a clatter and meshed his hands together under his chin. "I'm just helping you out, Taylor. I know senior year is tough and you have a lot on your plate, but that's life. Everyone has things to do. Obligations to fulfill. Families to feed. *Bills* to pay. This isn't easy for me, either."

His words made me feel like an idiot. And I hated that feeling. But he couldn't just take away my speech and give it to *Lin Cheng*. That girl had it out for me since we were in kindergarten. It wasn't my *fault* I colored inside the lines quicker than her. Or that she was always in second place. Now third, since Brian had moved to town and kicked us both down a spot. But you didn't see me being bitter about it all the time. Much.

Wringing my hands together, I tried to look contrite. "I'm sorry about your obligations and your bills, but I can handle it! I swear!"

"Then you'll have nothing to worry about. This isn't a punishment. Maybe later you and Lin can even work together on it. Help each other out." He leaned back in his chair and nodded toward the door. "That's it. You can leave now."

Yeah, right, she'd help me. More like help herself to all the credit and my hard work.

I wanted to argue with him, but to my horror, his face got blurry. *Damn it. Not now. Don't cry.* Maybe when I was safe at home in my soft gray sweater that fell past my knees, but I couldn't cry here. Not in front of everyone.

I don't know how or when I left the class, but next thing I knew, Brian was standing in front of me, shielding me from the other people still lingering in the halls. Without saying anything, he wrapped an arm around my shoulders and led me into the library's empty media room. I wanted to lean against his warm shoulder—god, I was so tired—but I kept my back stiff instead, determined not to show weakness. He shut the door and stood in front of it with crossed arms. I didn't know if it was to prevent me from leaving or anyone else from coming in.

I leaned against one of the bookcases and scratched at the fading blush polish on my nails. There was barely any trace left from the time my mom pulled me out of school for a mother-daughter manicure date. I was so annoyed afterward, because I'd missed the review session in calculus and ended up getting a B on the test. Especially since that was the first class that Brian had barely squeaked by with an A. If I had been at the review, I would have gotten an A+ and could have finally beaten him for once.

Ironic, since I would kill to get out of school now. Bring on the pedicures. Hell, I'd even perm my hair like a poodle to get out of here.

I let out a deep breath and rolled my tired shoulders before straightening up. "So thanks for, you know, before," I finally said to Brian and reached for the stuff in his arms.

"No problem." He released my binder and the papers before shrugging. "Sorry if I'm being nosy and overstepping my boundaries, but what the hell are you doing, Taylor?"

I glanced down at the folder of articles in my hands. "I'm going to organize some ideas I had for the next issue of *New Voices*. We should focus on the background people this time. Stage crew for plays, water boys in games. That sort of stuff."

"That's a good idea, but that's not what I'm talking about." He shoved his hands in the pockets of his jeans. "I meant about all this Evan stuff."

"I don't know what you're talking about."

"You're a horrible liar, Taylor."

Of course I knew what he was talking about. That's what everybody was talking about. If only Brian would be intuitive enough to get the hint that I didn't want to talk about it. For a smart guy, he could be really stupid sometimes.

We'd only been friends for a little over a year, but it felt like a lifetime. Surprising, since I'd despised him from the start. Brian transferred to our school early last year. And within one semester, I was shoved down from number one in the class—a spot that I had all to myself for the past two years—to number two. And the most infuriating thing was that he didn't even have to put any effort into being number one. He didn't wake up early each day to study in the library or come to school with dark shadows under his eyes from cramming all night like I did.

It was also pretty annoying that he was so darn *likable* to everyone. He did great in school and was average in sports. Good enough to have people invite him to games, but not good enough to be the star and have everyone hate him for being perfect.

Even though I hated him for stealing my spot, I liked him. He understood and put up with me. And he was perfect for me. I always figured that we'd get together someday. It just made sense that we would. Preferably after we were settled in college and on our career paths.

Brian wasn't in-your-face gorgeous like, well, Evan, but he was handsome in his own way—tall and lanky with broad shoulders and straight black hair that pointed in all directions. The disheveled look contrasted with his crisp, well-fitting clothes: He opted for dark dress jeans and button-down shirts rather than T-shirts and khaki cargo pants.

From the neck down, he looked like a *GQ* model. From the neck up, he looked like he'd just rolled out of bed. Yet he made it work. I loved a well-dressed guy in a tie. Add in a vest, and I was putty on his shiny shoes. Carly always made fun of the fact that while other girls fantasized about football players and firemen, I'd swoon over a businessman in a suit. What can I say? I had mature taste. He also had dark, soulful eyes that made my knees weak, although his were black rather than gray like Evan's.

I squeezed my eyes closed, determined to shake the images away. Why couldn't I get Evan out of my head? He wasn't my type. T-shirts and holey jeans were his uniform.

Although . . . I bet Evan would look smoking hot in a pair of dark-wash jeans and a casual pinstripe vest. Maybe paired with a dark-gray button-down shirt with rolled-up sleeves that perfectly match his stormy eyes and—*thwack!* I smacked my forehead with the palm of my hand. Why the hell was I dressing up Evan in my mind like he was my own personal Ken doll? Most girls would be doing the opposite.

A hand snapped in front of my face, breaking my train of thought. Brian stared at me with a worried expression. I didn't blame him. I didn't know what was up with me today.

I slumped down on top of the long table in the aisle, which usually held the projector. "You of all people should know not to believe rumors."

Both his eyebrows rose so high, they disappeared beneath the dark hair that fell across his forehead. "Yeah, everyone was really disappointed when I told them I didn't know karate when

I first transferred here. And that I wasn't related to Jackie Chan. Still, somebody had to break that stereotype." Something flashed across his face as he turned his head away. He was suddenly distant and a little cold. "So it really is just a rumor? You and Evan didn't . . ."

"No, we didn't."

He let out a loud sigh of relief. A quick half smile appeared on his face. He coughed in his hand before shoving it in his back pocket. "I didn't think so. I mean, he's not even your type or anything. And you're way smarter than that. I was just worried . . ." Brian shook his head and laughed. "Never mind. So what are you going to do about all the rumors, then?"

I kicked at the metal legs of the desk in front of me. "I figured I'd just lie low and stay quiet until they died down."

Brian snorted. "You? Stay quiet?" He crossed the room to perch beside me on the desk. His arm pressed against mine. "Come on, Taylor. You're the girl who refused to admit defeat during class elections last year. Even *after* you won, you insisted on another election with everyone's attendance so no one could accuse you of cheating. Even though nobody did."

My mouth quirked into a half smile. "Yeah. No one was happy about staying after school to vote, either."

Brian laughed and knocked his shoulder against mine. "No, we weren't."

We sat there in silence for a few minutes, both lost in our own thoughts. Finally, he straightened and stood in front of me, arms crossed as though he were a lecturing parent. "Look, I am just going to say it as it is. Staying quiet is a stupid idea. This isn't like you! You need to fight back." He bent forward until he was at eye level with me. "Seriously, show everyone out there who you are and that you deserve everything you've worked so hard for. Don't let this stupid rumor ruin things for you."

Brian was standing so close that I could see all the details on his face. The perfectly straight line of his nose, the crinkles around his eyes. He even had a small wrinkle over his left brow.

His words scared me, but I tried to laugh it off. "Aren't you overreacting a bit? I mean, it's just a tiny rumor, Brian."

He rolled his eyes and scoffed. "Oh yeah? Look at what it did already. I mean, come on, Taylor. Why do you think everyone's screwing with you out there? They're using this 'tiny little rumor' to yank you off the pedestal so they can stomp on you."

The images he painted were so vivid that I had to shake my head to get rid of them. Especially after my talk with Mr. Peters. It really did feel like everything was slipping out of my grasp. "So what do you think I should do?"

"Prove that they're wrong. Beat someone up. I don't know. *Something.*"

His words hit me like a bolt of lightning. He was right. I was tired of getting picked on. I needed to do something. My future, my life, depended on it.

But the question was, what could I do?

✧ ⋅ ✧

"So what do you think?" I asked Carly on the phone later that night. I balanced the phone between my ear and shoulder as I carefully slipped my report into my bag. There was no way in hell I was going to forget *that* again. "Short of having Evan

♥ 51 ♥

whacked, I don't know what could make everyone forget about this."

"Why would you want people to forget? This is the most exciting thing to happen to you all year. Actually, your whole life."

"But I don't *want* my life to be this exciting. Tell me what to do."

"Well, for one, I think you should have slept with him."

I almost dropped the phone to the ground. "Can you please be serious?"

"What? I just think it's a waste that you're going through all this suffering and you didn't even get any. Not even once. I mean, come on!" There was the sound of a door slamming, and I knew Carly had shut the door to get some privacy. Ironically, the door always got stuck, so when it slammed, her mom knew she was up to no good. She probably just had about a minute of talking time left before her mom popped in to "check" on her. "Seriously, if you're not going to sleep with him, then at least date him or something. People wouldn't care so much if the two of you were dating anyway."

"You're impossible." I rolled my eyes at my reflection in the mirror across the room.

"Impossibly lovable. Hey, I gotta go. I think I hear my mom down the hall. Just think about it. The innocent debutante always reforms the rake in the end, you know."

Even though she was crazy, Carly's words kept racing through my mind. *What if . . . ?*

Later that night, when everyone was asleep, I headed downstairs toward Dad's office. I don't know if it was the dark-green tweed furniture or the dusty shelves full of law books, but this was the only place I could think clearly. This was his domain that he had decorated himself. And by decorated, I mean, he drove to the furniture store, pointed to a couple of pieces, and told them where to ship it within five minutes, tops.

The rest of the house—besides my room, thank god—was decked out in bright, cheery colors and ruffles. It was like Barbie's Dreamhouse had exploded. And since Dad didn't care, I was outnumbered when it came to what color the curtains should be. Kimmy was still at the age where she loved pink and sequins. I'd hoped that she'd outgrow the girly stuff in two years when she turned eleven. I did. Of course, I outgrew a lot of things that year.

Even though I hadn't made any noise when I crept in, it was like Oreo, our dog, sensed there was someone awake who could feed him. Despite the fact that he was a dachshund who got fed three times a day, he was always hungry. Always.

I closed the study door just as his paws came scampering down the hall. His dark nose instantly poked under the door, and he whined. The high-pitched yips sounded like he was being tortured.

Afraid that Mom or Dad would wake up, I jerked the door open. Oreo was sprawled out on the carpet, nose down-turned as though he were still trying to get beneath the door. As soon as he saw me, he froze for a few seconds before slowly flopping on his back. His brown eyes stared at me, willing me to bend down and scratch his belly.

I snorted with laughter and rubbed his stomach for a few seconds before getting to my feet. "Come on, you can keep me company while I work."

Before I got started, I moved around the office and rearranged a few things. Lining up the books on the shelves so they all faced out. Adjusting the shades so the perfect amount of moonlight would stream through the windows. The usual stuff that would otherwise distract me.

I worked through the night. Sunlight was starting to peek through the windows when I finished printing out the final copy of the contract. I stretched my arms over my head and yawned. Finally, it was done. Now was the hard part—getting Evan to cooperate. And for that, I needed his number.

I immediately called Carly. That girl knew anything and everything that went on in that school. Too bad she was also too nosy for her own good. "Have you changed your mind about sleeping with him?"

My cheeks flushed hotly, and I thanked god no one could see me. I tapped my pen against the table so hard that the top flew off and rolled somewhere beneath the desk. "Carly, this really isn't the time." I dropped to the floor to search for the top. Capless pens were one of my biggest pet peeves. "Just get me his number, okay?"

"Already ahead of you. I messaged this girl who has it and already texted it to you. So are you going to let me in on this plan or what?"

"Let me figure it out first, and I'll let you know." I crossed my fingers. If things went according to plan, everything should be better by tomorrow morning.

"I guess that's good enough for now. Call me if you need any more hotties' numbers."

Mom and Dad had already taken Kimmy to school, so the house was pretty quiet when I crept out of the office. Oreo woke when I was nearly down the hall. He let out a sharp bark and chased after me, nipping at my ankles with every step I took. I dug a can of dog food out of the pantry, scooped a large helping into his bowl, and refilled his water. For myself, I got a large glass of orange juice and made a piece of toast from the bread bin on the counter.

Once the spoiled rat Oreo was fed and I had nothing left on my napkin except crumbs, I knew I couldn't put off the call anymore. I closed my eyes and counted to ten, then punched in the numbers before I lost my nerve. The phone rang twice before Evan picked up.

"Hello?"

My fingers traced the condensation on the glass. "Hi, Evan? This is, um, Taylor." Silence. "Taylor Simmons? You know, the girl who, hm, we—uh, we—"

A throaty chuckle stopped my stuttering.

I realized I was gripping the glass with both hands and forced myself to let go. *Just breathe, Taylor. You can do this.* I rubbed my palms on my jeans to dry them. "Listen, I think we need to talk about the other night."

"What happened to 'Don't talk about what happened to anyone'?"

Jeez, I could practically *hear* the smirk in his voice. "I... not just anyone," I said lamely, unable to think of a better comeback.

"That's for sure."

Was that a compliment or an insult? I shook my head even though he couldn't see me. "Let's start over. I need to talk to you. Now. Can you come to my house?"

"You're not at school?" The surprise was evident in his voice.

"No, I had a free period this morning." I shook my head, forgetting that Evan didn't take extra classes throughout the year like I did. He probably didn't have any free periods. "I guess I could meet you after school somewhere."

"That's all right. I'm not at school, either."

"Really? Why not?"

There was some rustling as if he was moving the phone around. "Let's just say you have your secrets and I have mine. I'll meet you at your house."

"Okay. Do you have a pen? I can give you my address."

"Don't worry about it. If I'm lucky and it's fate, I'll just find your house somehow."

I let out an aggravated sigh because he wasn't taking me seriously. Maybe it *would* be easier to just hire a hit man. I was sure Dad would be happy to defend me in court. If I was caught, that is. I'd learned a thing or two from watching *CSI*. "What do you—"

Evan snorted. "Keep your panties on, I was just joking. I know where you live, and I'm on my way now." I turned away from the phone to curse, but he must have heard me, because I ended up having to hold the phone several inches away before his booming laughter made me permanently deaf. "Sorry, I forgot that no underwear talk was allowed. I won't do it again."

Oreo nudged my leg for more food, and I sank down beside him on the cold tiles. My fingers played with his floppy ears as I stared at the silver fridge. "Uh-huh. So I'll see you in a half an hour?"

"Make it twenty minutes. And don't worry, I'll be sure to jump the fence so no one will see me." He laughed again and hung up without saying bye.

Evan was only five minutes later than he said he would be. And he did show up at my back door—although I'm not sure how he managed to jump my five-foot steel fence—with two large branches on either side of his head. Even his cheeks were streaked brown and black with mud and dirt for camouflage.

Despite my mood, I couldn't help but give him a reluctant grin. "I hope those branches didn't come from my yard."

"'Course not. Who do I think I am?" He grinned as he tossed the branches aside. His teeth seemed even whiter than usual against the mud. "I took them from your neighbor's yard."

"That's a relief."

As soon as I let him in, loud, fierce barking filled the room. Evan looked around, but Oreo was nowhere in sight. I smothered my snicker with a cough. He may have sounded like he was going to rip Evan limb from limb, but I knew he was probably cowering somewhere safe and out of reach. He was always like this whenever a stranger came into the house. The perfect definition of all bark and no bite.

I didn't tell Evan that, though. Instead, I wet a couple of napkins and handed them to him. "Here."

"Thanks." His eyes kept flickering around the room as Oreo's barking turned into a low, demon-from-hell growl. God, I loved that dog sometimes. "Okay, either your dog is really small and that's why I can't find him, or he's a ghost dog and I'm going crazy. Which is it?"

"What dog?" I asked with wide eyes. At his freaked-out expression, I couldn't keep the laughter in for long. "He's probably squeezed between the edge of the chair and the corner over there."

Evan dropped on all fours and ducked underneath the kitchen table. Immediately the room got quiet. "Oh, there he is."

I leaned against the counter and waited for him to get up so I wouldn't have to talk to his butt the whole time. It took a few minutes, but I didn't mind.

He muttered something to Oreo. I didn't know what he was saying, but it wouldn't have made a difference. Oreo never went to strangers unless he'd been around them for a few hours or they had sausages or bacon in their hands.

Of course, considering the disappointment of the past couple of days, it should have been obvious that the dog I'd had for over two years wouldn't do what was expected of him. It wasn't long before Evan was able to pull him out and settle him happily on his lap. I thought Evan only had a way with girls. I guess he had a way with dogs, too.

"So you wanted to talk?"

I crossed my arms, trying to look anywhere but at the gorgeous boy in front of me and my traitorous dog. The butterflies in my stomach multiplied. My mouth opened and closed, but nothing came out. Not because I didn't have anything to say, but because I was distracted. Again.

It really wasn't fair. Evan was a surfer, so he had the body. But did he really have to have the soulful I-understand-and-feel-your-pain eyes, too? I've always been a sucker for dark-gray eyes.

All my earlier confidence faded. I turned my head away to help lessen the power of his eyes. "Okay, so I thought about what you said after lunch, and I think you were wrong. About the rumor and everything. Because even if everyone forgets, it doesn't matter. The damage would have already been done. Memories can never be totally forgotten. So the only solution is to alter their memories into something you don't want to be forgotten. You know what I'm talking about?"

At the blank look on his face, it was obvious that he didn't have a clue. "Do you?"

To be honest, I wasn't really sure. "What I mean is that I think we should just roll with it."

"Meaning?"

I let out a deep breath. It was now or nothing. "Meaning I think we should start dating. What do you think?"

5

-Evan-

What did I think? My first thought was that she was crazy. My second thought? That she was super crazy. Knock-on-her-head, tripping-on-cracks crazy.

I held up a hand. "Hold on, just the other morning you were very, *very* insistent that we *didn't* know each other, and now you want us to start dating?" The dog on my lap let out a sharp bark and dug his claws into my shorts. "Ow. See? Even the dog thinks this is a stupid idea."

Taylor flushed and took him from me. "His name is Oreo, and that's not what I meant."

I eyed his two black ears and white face. "Clever name."

"Thanks. My little sister thought of it." She scooped him up and set him outside in one fluid motion. He stood at the door and stared at us for a minute or two before trotting off to lie on the deck and sunbathe, belly side up.

"So what did you mean about the dating?" My gaze ran up

and down her body, taking in her wrinkled, baggy, purple-and-blue-striped PJs. The pants were so long that they covered her toes and practically doubled as socks. " 'Cause, no offense, but you're not exactly my type," I said with a wink.

Her nose flared twice before turning as red as the rest of her face. She scooted around the countertop until the bottom half of her was out of sight. "None taken, because god knows *you're* not my type, either."

Ouch. Apparently the Ice Queen had claws like her dog. "You still didn't answer my question."

She leaned back and stared at her nails in deep concentration. "I just meant that we should *pretend* to date."

I lifted a hand to my chest and sighed with pretend relief. "Thank god. I thought you remembered how incredibly sexy I was and realized that you loved me after all. Or that you're pregnant and you want to raise this child right. You know, I think Elizabeth's a nice name for a baby. We could call her Lizzie. I dated a waitress named Lizzie once. Real sweet girl."

Her entire face was purple now. Taylor leaned forward. Her dark eyes seemed brighter than usual as she glared at me. Her hands gripped the counter to keep her balance. "I do *not* love you. And we do *not* have a baby. We didn't even have sex!"

"Ah, but you're not denying that you think I'm sexy."

Her mouth dropped open, and I thought she was going to yell at me again. Instead, she covered her face with both hands and laughed. A loud, uncontrollable laugh that was both deep and squeaky at the same time, weird as it was. Weirder was the fact that I liked the sound. It made me smile.

She laughed so hard that tears streamed down her face

and she was practically gasping for breath. Alarmed, I half stood up and reached for her, but Taylor just brushed me off and grabbed napkins to wipe her face. I couldn't help smiling a bit as I watched her. She was so different from all the other girls I dated. Fresh-faced, simple, girl-next-door.

I waited until she drank more of her orange juice and swallowed before continuing. No need for her to shower me with orange juice and spit. "Okay, now that I know you're not going to die from my one-liners, can you explain?"

"Well, it's a fact that everyone knows that we were together the other night. Even though nothing happened," Taylor quickly said when I opened my mouth with another pun about one-night stands. "Nobody's going to believe us. So to save our reputations, I thought we could pretend that we've been dating all along. That way they won't think there's anything wrong with the fact that we were together at the party and that night."

"Reputations? Seriously? Are we in the eighteen hundreds? Did my time machine finally work?"

To my surprise, she picked up a couple of stapled pages that I hadn't noticed on the counter and handed them to me. "Everything's listed here, so it'll be easier if you would just read it."

I flipped through the pages with wide eyes. There were freaking five typed pages. I repeat, *five* pages. She was kidding, right? What the hell did she need to talk about for this long? "You're very thorough."

She paced back and forth. "Thanks."

"That wasn't exactly a compliment." I skimmed the first

page. "So you want me to sign this contract and pretend to date you for the next couple of weeks?"

"It's not really an official contract."

"There's a line for our signatures."

"Well, it's really more of a formality, so we'll both know where we stand in this . . . relationship." Taylor stopped and faced me. Her hands were on either side of her hips in a defensive stance. "Come on, this could benefit us both."

I scoffed in disbelief. "Really? 'Cause all I hear is you, you, you. Honestly, I don't see why I need to agree to this."

"Because you're a generous and helpful person?" She snorted at the shocked look on my face. "I'm sorry, I couldn't even get through that. I don't know what I was thinking."

Hm, touché. Apparently her sweet exterior was just a front. I wondered what other secrets she was hiding from the world. "If this is how you plan to convince me, I'll tell you now that you're failing miserably," I said drily.

"You're right. I'm sorry. Again." She coughed and attempted to look serious. And failed. "Let's just think of it rationally. Think of how much respect you'd get from the teachers once they find out you're dating *me*. All the teachers at Nathan Wilks love me."

"Okay, first off, you better rein that ego back. You are not as great as you think you are. And secondly," I said loudly when she opened her mouth to respond. "Teachers like me just fine. I may not have a 5.0 or whatever crazy average you have with your extra classes and overachieving self, but I *do* have an average GPA. Above average, actually, since I usually get B's."

"You're lying, right?"

"Why would I lie to you? You're not my mom."

Her eyes narrowed in confusion. "But how is that possible? I heard you don't even go to half of your classes. You weren't even at school today!"

"Don't believe everything you hear. I only miss about a fourth of my classes. And the classes I do go to, I do damn good in."

"Well."

"What?"

"You do damn *well* in instead of *good*." She gave me a bright smile. "I guess English isn't one of the classes you have a B in?"

Huh. The more I was getting to see the snarky side of Taylor, the more I liked her. "I guess you can say that. So like I was saying before you rudely interrupted me for an impromptu grammar lesson, I don't need to be there to understand what's going on," I said with a shrug. I could probably homeschool myself, if I didn't have to worry about seeing Brandon's face all the time.

Taylor continued to stare at me with an uncertain expression, as though she wasn't sure if I was joking or not. I got this skepticism a lot when people found out that I was more than a playboy bum. I wasn't a closet nerd, either, but it wasn't hard to put a bit of effort into my schoolwork. Okay, a little more than a bit. I didn't want my stepdad's satisfaction regarding my bad grades to prove that he was right all along. That I was a no-good deadbeat like my dad. Don't know what's wrong with being a deadbeat, though. It sure beats being a pompous ass like him.

I leaned back in the chair, tapping the ground with my left foot. "So what else you got?"

She gnawed on her lower lip before snapping her fingers. "How about college? I could help you with your college applications. It's kind of late to apply, but with my assistance, you could still get into any school you want."

"Any?"

"Any . . . within reason."

With a smirk, I gave her a thumbs-down. "Sorry, as appealing as that sounds, that's not going to work. I don't care about college."

Her eyes widened in shock. "How could anyone not care about college?"

"I don't know. It all seems so far off."

"Uh, we're halfway through our senior year. There's barely any time left."

"It's not even February. There's plenty of time. And besides, I just don't think college is for me, so why bother?" I was lying. I had thought about college a couple of times. But I still wasn't sure what I was going to do yet. Going to college would get me out of my house and away from Brandon, but *not* going to college would infuriate him. Something that I had devoted years to doing.

It was a hard decision to make.

Taylor twirled her empty glass around in her hand and crossed out a couple of things on the list next to her. She gave me a quick glance and scratched out a few more things with a frown before crumbling the first sheet entirely. "No, that wouldn't—nah . . . how about . . ."

I was kind of curious to see what other reasons she'd put on there.

Finally, Taylor let out a sigh. "Well, this is a long shot, but aren't you getting tired of having girls throw themselves at you all the time?"

I snorted. "Do you really expect me to answer that?"

She looked a little uncertain, but she continued anyway. "Seriously, you've probably had a string of girls just chasing after you your whole life. And sure it's fun at first. All the sex and whatnot. But after a while, it has to be tiring. Every girl just like the last. Faceless conquests and sleeping partners." Her lips pursed together, and she gave me a pitying look. "When do you get to be alone? To be treated as a person instead of as a piece of meat all the time? To just be *Evan*?"

She had to be kidding. I swallowed back the laughter and struggled to keep a straight face. "And what do you think I should do about this problem?"

Her face lit up at my question like it was a green light of encouragement. "Well, if you had a steady girlfriend, you wouldn't have to worry about all those other girls anymore. Someone who could be a shield, a defense against getting hit on all the time."

Ah, there it is. "And that someone would be you."

"Well, I am here and willing." At her words, I couldn't help gazing up and down her body again. Nice and slow this time. Now, *there* was a thought. Even though Taylor was more sweet than sexy, there was something about her. I was drawn to her for some reason. Maybe it was like Aaron said. She was an untouchable ice queen, and I was tempted to know what I would have to do to make her melt.

Finally noticing where my eyes were looking, she snapped her fingers in front of my face before crossing her arms to cover her chest. "Not in *that* way, so don't get any ideas."

"Too bad. I was thinking that things could get pretty interesting."

And just like that, she was flustered again. God, this was fun. I grinned and scanned the document again. "Okay, let's say I'm considering it. It says here that while we're in this deal, I can't date or have any inappropriate interactions with the opposite sex unless approved by you." I couldn't keep the amusement out of my voice. "Is this a fancy way of saying that I can't cheat on you?"

Taylor moved away from me and back to the counter like it was her safe haven. One hand clicked her blue pen against the countertop while the other traced the flowers and leaves etched on the wooden edge. "Of course. I mean, that would just cause more gossip." *Click. Click.* "And the whole purpose of this arrangement is to lessen that. I promise I would do the same thing. It's a totally reasonable request."

Of course it was reasonable request. For her. If I agreed to this, I'd be living in my own personal hell for the next few weeks. She was crazy if she expected me to live like a monk. I dropped the papers on the tabletop, not even bothering to catch them as they fluttered off the edge. "And what happens in the end? When people stop gossiping about us and our *reputations* are restored?"

"Then we'll break up. Tell people that we decided we were too different and an amicable separation was the best result for everyone," she recited as though this were a divorce-court show. She handed me her pen as though that should have been enough assurance.

Amicable breakup? That would be a first. I'd had tons of breakups in my life, and none of them were ever amicable.

The most civil one was when I had a glass thrown at me in her parents' hot tub. Although I really should have gotten dressed before I mentioned seeing other people. She almost cut things that would have *really* hurt.

I uncapped and recapped the pen to make her squirm. "Hmm."

"Hmm?" Her eyebrows rose, making her face look elongated. "What does *hmm* mean?"

"It means I'll have to think about it first."

"You—" she spun around on her feet. Her jaw dropped so far, I could see the molars in the back of her mouth. "What is there to think about, and how long is that going to take?"

I struggled to keep the stupid grin off my face and stood up. She'd probably flip out if she saw how amused I was. But I couldn't take her seriously. She had to be kidding, right? A contract? "I don't know. I mean, you're talking about taking me off the market for god knows how long?" I shook my head with an exaggerated frown and handed her the pen. "That's a pretty big decision."

"But—"

"But I'll let you know when I do decide." On an impulse, I leaned down and kissed her forehead. Right where the vein was pulsing like crazy. "Don't worry, I don't think it'll take too long."

6

-Evan-

I made her wait three days. Like Jesus did before coming back to life. Well, barely three days. She gave me the contract Tuesday morning and started tracking me down by Thursday afternoon. And by tracking me down, I mean stalking me like a bounty hunter.

On the third day, I was late—as usual—so I didn't expect to see her until lunch. Five minutes after I parked the car and got to my locker, Taylor popped up like the Ghost of Christmas Past.

"Did you decide yet?"

My hand pulled off the lock but didn't open the locker. I peered around the halls suspiciously before looking back at her. Dark bags were under her eyes, matching her dark eyes and scowl. "Do you have a surveillance camera on me or something? How did you know I was here?"

Her nails scraped against the strap of her bag, and she looked down at her feet. "I didn't. I was on my way to the office and happened to see you."

"Sure you did." I grinned at her frown and opened my locker. A few folded papers fell out, all covered with neat, girly handwriting and exclamation points. "I see you had a pretty busy morning."

Blinking rapidly, Taylor snatched the papers from my hand and shoved them deep in her bag. "Momentary lapse of judgment. You weren't responding to my texts, so I figured I'd have to get your attention somehow."

"Mission accomplished." I watched her rock back and forth on her heels. How did anyone ever think she was an ice queen? The girl was like a whirlwind of emotions. On steroids. "Look, I know you're anxious, but I'm pretty sure this could count as harassment. Do you need me to put a restraining order on you or something?"

I meant it as a joke, but her gaze fell down to her feet. She looked vulnerable as hell. "God, you're right. What the heck is wrong with me? It's so stupid. This whole thing is. Just—just forget it."

My grin faded. I poked her shoulder. "Look, I didn't—I mean, it *is* pretty stupid, but it's, uh . . ." I didn't know what I was trying to say. I just didn't want her to burst out crying or something. I hated it when girls cried.

Eyes still downcast, she bit her lower lip like a little kid who was just told she'd never get dessert again. "Maybe I should just go."

I grabbed her arm before she could walk away. "I didn't mean—"

A group of girls passed us, and I automatically raised my other hand to wave. A couple of them gave me a half smile before turning to Taylor. Their smiles widened, but this time they were obviously fake.

"Do you think you'll be able to make the Honor Society meeting this weekend, Taylor?" a petite Asian girl asked, blinking innocently. "I know how busy you are these days, and I'd be glad to monitor the meeting for you instead."

Taylor swallowed and straightened her shoulders. Her chin rose so it seemed like she was looking down at the other girls, even though most of them were her height. "I'll be there, but thanks for asking, Lin. Maybe if you paid more attention to your classes instead of my social life, then you could have been the president of the club instead of just a secretary." Tossing her hair over her shoulder, Taylor turned away like she was dismissing them.

Lin gaped at her back for a few seconds before stomping away with her friends.

With an admiring grin, I gave Taylor a slow round of applause. "Nicely done."

She let out an unsteady sigh and shrugged. "I can handle a couple of girls. So don't worry. I have to get to class."

"Taylor—" I let out a loud sigh and banged my forehead against my locker after she left. Well, she just took the fun out of messing with her. Where was the sarcastic spitfire who was here seconds ago? I definitely would have preferred her pissed and hissing at me over sad and defeated any day.

A hand slammed against the locker next to me, making me jump back. "Dude, what'd you do to your new girlfriend? Don't tell me you kicked her to the curb already?"

I pulled on my ears to make them stop ringing. "No, we'd

have to be something first in order for me to kick her to the curb."

Aaron winced. "Ouch. So you're just going to pretend nothing happened? Damn, that's harsh, dude. Even for you. No wonder the Ice Queen looked like she was bawling when I passed her."

"Her name's—" I turned to stare at him. "Wait, was she really crying?"

He rubbed his chin. "I don't know. I mean, her head was down, so maybe? I do feel bad for her, though. A bunch of people are hating on her a bit," he said with a shrug.

"Really?" I hadn't heard anything. But then I never paid attention to what other people said. I thought back to the past couple of days. Those jerks in the cafeteria and the snotty girls just now. Maybe that was the real reason Taylor wanted to pretend to be dating. And why she was nagging me so much about it. I didn't actually understand what she meant when she said she wanted to save her "reputation," but maybe I should have asked instead of just laughing at her.

"Yeah, but you know how girls can get sometimes. All emotional and bitchy. Especially with each other. It's probably a good thing that you're blowing her off then, right? Just in case she goes crazy on you." His booming laughter echoed through the hall. "Dodged a bullet there. Believe me, having a real girlfriend is hard."

I couldn't laugh with Aaron. Hell, I could barely focus on him at all. All I saw was Taylor's disappointed face in my mind. Wide, sad brown eyes that glittered like the sea at night and defeated shoulders that made her look small and helpless. "Did you hear anything else?"

Aaron shrugged and looked uncertain. "There was also some talk in the locker room earlier about who could get her into bed next, but you know how those douche bags can be. That's why I don't want to officially be on the team. Spending too much time with them will kill my love for football. And life."

My hands curled into fists at my side at the thought of those punks laughing at Taylor. "We have to go."

"Where are we going?"

I wrapped my arm around his shoulder and started dragging him down the hall. "To the locker room to have a talk with some idiots and kick their asses. You're going to tell me exactly who said what."

— • —

"All right, you crazy girl, I'll do it." Even though I had made my decision once Aaron told me what was going on, I still couldn't believe the words that were coming out of my mouth.

Taylor stared at me and then around the room as though she wasn't sure this was real. That I was actually standing at her front door. Cookie crumbs were dusted all over her lips, while Oreo wagged his tail and scampered around our feet. "Uh, what?"

I pushed my way inside and pulled the stupid contract out of my back pocket. "I said I'll be your boyfriend."

Her brown eyes widened in shock. "Really? I mean, seriously? You're saying yes?"

God, how many times was she going to make me say it?

My hand scrawled a large, messy signature on the bottom line before I handed it over to her. "Yeah." I couldn't help but chuckle at the shocked look on her face and the way she clutched the sheets as though I'd take them back. It almost made my idiotic decision worth it. Almost. "I thought you'd be ecstatic that you're finally getting your way."

"I am, but . . ." Taylor stared down at the paper in her hands. "I didn't really think you'd agree to this."

To be honest, I hadn't thought I would, either. Still, I had nothing better to do—or rather, no one better to date—at the moment, so I had nothing to lose. Besides, I felt sorry for Taylor. And a fierce need to protect her. Like I told the jerks in the locker room, she wasn't someone any of them should mess with. Not if they didn't want to face the consequences. It only took a couple of punches at an empty locker for them to realize I was serious. I rubbed my sore knuckles against my palm. "Who knows? Maybe it'll be fun."

"Fun?" She repeated the word slowly, like she'd never heard of it before.

"Yeah, fun." I leaned back against the open doorframe, since she hadn't exactly invited me in. "It's what *Webster's Dictionary* describes as a way to make life enjoyable? Like if *I* wanted to have fun, I'd go to the beach, while *your* idea of fun would be to spend all weekend in the library polishing your pens and laminating your homework."

A glint appeared in her eyes, and she mimicked my stance, leaning against the wall facing the door. "But now that we're dating, that means *you're* going to have to come to the library *with* me."

I was starting to like the way she switched personalities so quickly. Hell, maybe I really *was* going crazy. "Why?"

"It's all here in the fine print." She waved the paper in front of my face before sticking it in her back pocket. "You should have read it before signing. Didn't anyone tell you that? Let this be a lesson for you in the future."

My eyes narrowed, but her face remained calm. A bit brighter from her gloating. "You're bluffing."

"Maybe. Maybe not."

Hmm. If we were going to do this, she'd have to understand who was in charge around here.

I leaned toward her. My left hand brushed the remaining crumbs off her soft lips before resting on the cool wallpaper on the other side of her waist so she'd be trapped in my arms. A flicker of panic crossed her face, but Taylor continued to stare up at me, not flinching or moving away. Not even when I bent down so my mouth would be right beside her ear. I let her take a deep breath before I whispered, "Then I'm going to need a copy of that contract."

Taylor let out another rattling breath and turned her head to face me. Her eyes were downward, so all I could see were her lashes. As though pulled together by some type of invisible force, our bodies angled even closer until her lips were barely an inch from mine. She touched my chest, and I could feel her hot hand through my T-shirt, making my body tense up. My gaze flickered down to her mouth for a split second before looking up again.

Right before I was about to dip my head to kiss her, Taylor smiled up at me. A triumphant smile. "I'll have a copy for you this weekend when you meet me for our study date." Before I could say or do anything, she laid her other hand on my chest and pushed me away.

Even though I was still hot and bothered by her teasing, I couldn't help chuckling as I walked to the door. "You know this will probably backfire on you."

"How?"

"You might fall in love with me and won't want to let go in the end."

Taylor snorted. "Yeah, let me know when you're done dreaming."

"Guess we'll just have to wait and see. I'm just warning you. It *could* happen." I winked at her. "I guess I'll see you tomorrow, then, sweetheart."

7

{Taylor}

Even though the meteorologist said it was going to be a crisp sixty degrees this morning, I still layered up in boots, an overcoat, and a scarf. I'd been played by the weatherman too many times to take the chance.

Sure enough, halfway to the bus stop I couldn't feel my fingers anymore. Sixty degrees, my butt. It had to be at most high thirties if you factored in the wind. If this crazy weather wasn't a sign of global warming, I didn't know what was.

A loud yawn escaped my mouth, piercing through the quiet morning air. I'd barely gotten any sleep, since Carly had kept me on the phone practically all night. After Evan left, I'd been in stunned disbelief for so long that I didn't call Carly to tell her about my new *relationship* until after dinner. My ears were still kind of ringing from her squeals and cheers. I swear, I hadn't seen her this excited since we sneaked backstage after the *Wicked* musical last year.

I was still pacing around the bench and securing my red scarf more firmly around my neck when a loud engine roared from down the street. It sounded like a large truck, but it turned out to be a slightly small, grayish-green clunker that pulled up beside me. There was a loud, clinking pop, and the engine died. The driver's-side window rolled down, and a tousled blond head popped out. "Come on, I'll give you a ride to school."

Evan.

I knew he was talking to me and not the two old ladies behind us, but I still had to look over my shoulder to make sure. Talking to him felt weird. Was weird. Like this wasn't real. "That's okay." I tucked my hands in my pockets and resumed my pacing. "I like the bus."

When it became apparent that I wasn't going to change my mind and jump in, Evan let out a sigh, rolled up his window, and climbed out of the car. Despite the cold, he just wore a plain blue T-shirt, jeans, and a dark gray and white hoodie.

Within seconds, he was in step with me, hands shoved in both pockets. Up and down the sidewalk we marched. No matter how slowly or quickly I walked, he would just adjust his pace. "Are we going to just pretend we don't know each other?"

I gave him a sideways glance. "Of course not. We *do* know each other."

"Yeah. Kind of a shame we don't remember exactly how much." My cheeks flushed hotly. To make matters worse, the wind carried his voice, and I swear, everyone at the bus stop grew quiet. Evan continued as though he didn't notice the two nosy old ladies obviously eavesdropping on us. "So are we only supposed to be *friendly* when we have an audience, or can we at least be friends? Real friends?"

"We are friends." The word sounded foreign on my tongue. Like *jabberwocky.* Or *hornswoggle.* I shook my head and tried again, stressing each syllable. "Seriously, friends."

"Okay, then as *friends,* we should go to school together." Evan touched my wrist to make me stop. "Come on, I said I'd take you."

Despite all the layers I was wearing, he managed to find the tiny slit of skin exposed between my mittens and coat. I don't know if this was an honest mistake or just a talent of his, but I could feel the heat radiating from his fingertips. How the heck did he manage to stay so warm in so few layers?

"And *I* said no thanks." The two old busybodies were blatantly staring now. I resisted the urge to shoo them away and softened my voice. "Like I said, I like the bus. It gives me time to . . . think."

To my surprise, Evan laughed like I had told him the funniest joke and pulled me in for a tight, one-armed hug. "God, you're stubborn," he muttered through beaming, clenched teeth. Shocked by his closeness, I blinked and stayed still as his breath tickled my ear. "Did you forget we're supposed to be dating now? How would it look if I let my *girlfriend* ride the bus when I have a perfectly good and comfortable car right here?"

Oh, right. Duh. I glanced over his shoulder and grimaced at the rust stains up and down the passenger door. "Are you sure you know the definition of *comfortable?*"

He let go of me, but not before he rapped his hand against the back of my head. "Come on, you can think in my car. Can't let you be late for class, now."

Ouch! I glowered at his back and rubbed my head as he walked away. It didn't hurt that much because my knitted hat cushioned the blow, but it *could* have. I crossed my arms and stayed right where I was.

Evan didn't get in the car. Instead, he jumped up and down and rubbed his hands together, blowing on them to keep warm as he waited. My annoyance with his arrogance slowly faded. He *was* making an effort. And it was sweet of him to even think about driving me to school. Especially when he really didn't have to. We could have started our charade when we arrived at school.

Despite the shabby exterior, the car's interior was pretty comfortable. And clean, too. I had to give him that. The gray seats enveloped me into the cushions. It reminded me of Dad's sofa in the study. A little lumpy, like it was homemade. It wasn't pretty to look at, but it was soft to the touch. At least to my touch.

And warm. Like I was sliding into a fire when I got in the car. My entire body tingled from the abrupt temperature change, but I didn't mind. I tucked my bag beneath the seat so only the top and the straps were poking out. Then I peeled off each layer of clothing, sighing with contentment.

For such a small car, the seats were abnormally wide. My legs stuck out awkwardly, like a kid with knobby knees who couldn't quite reach the floor. One glance at the rearview mirror and I grimaced. My baby hair beneath my hat stuck out of my braid. I tried to smooth them down for a few seconds before giving up. They just sprang back up again like prickly thorns. At least I didn't have to worry about Evan trying to seduce me. Hand me a lollipop, and I looked like I was in elementary school again.

Oh well. I tucked one leg beneath me and propped the other on top of my bag. "I guess we could use this time to get to know each other."

"Sounds like a blast."

Gotta love the sarcasm. I tapped my fingers against my thigh. "It would be pretty hard to convince people that we're dating when we barely know anything about each other."

The right side of his mouth quirked upward. "That's how most of my relationships are, but of course you'd want to be different. So what do you want to know?"

I never knew if he was giving me a compliment or an insult. "Do you have any brothers or sisters? What do your parents do for a living?"

"I'm an only child. And my mom's a nurse."

"And your dad?"

His smile slowly faded. "My—my mom's married to a doctor. An anesthesiologist."

"Your dad's an anesthesiologist, and you drive this old clunker?"

His jaw clenched, and his fingers tapped the horn at the center of the steering wheel, but not hard enough to actually make it honk. "First off, for your information, this isn't an old clunker. *This* is a 1989 BMW 325i."

I nibbled on my thumbnail, confused by the sudden rush of tension in the car. "Er, that literally means nothing to me."

"Secondly," Evan continued as though I hadn't responded. He flicked the left signal and moved around the silver car in front of us. "He isn't *my* dad. He's my stepdad. Major difference. And third, this classic car used to belong to my real dad, so no trashing it. I wouldn't trade Rudy for the world."

Oh. "Rudy?" I asked stupidly.

"Yes, Rudy." No explanations added. I could have sworn that he flushed before turning his head away. Subject closed.

"So your parents are divorced?" Why couldn't I stop asking the stupidest questions?

"Yeah, and my mom married a jackass."

I waited for him to continue, but that was it. No more talking. Apparently, my question had killed the conversation better than a nuclear bomb. *Boom!*

The layer of tension in the air grew until I actually felt suffocated. Evan didn't seem to notice, though. He just stared straight ahead and continued driving. His right hand gripped the steering wheel so tightly that his knuckles turned white. My curiosity made me want to ask more, but my nerves wouldn't let me.

Why didn't I just get on the bus?

He sped up, weaving around the cars instead of slowing down as we approached the Highway 8 Bridge. I nervously fingered the seat belt buckle to make sure it was secure. I had major acrophobia. Even a slight bridge incline was enough to make my stomach tighten in fear. Especially when combined with being in a speeding chunk of metal. "My parents are divorced, too," I blurted out to distract us both.

It worked. There was a slight squeaking noise as he released the gas pedal a bit. I could feel his gaze on me, but I didn't look up. I just concentrated on slowing my heartbeat. "Is your stepdad a jackass, too?"

My index finger tapped against the peeling plastic tint on the glass, and I stared at the small dog park across the street. Dogs playing tag and rolling green mounds dotted with yellow flowers flew by. "No, he's great. The title of jackass would belong to my real dad."

"Really?"

"Yeah."

We fell silent again. With nothing else to do, I started to arrange the CD cases stacked in the compartment on the side of the door. Rotating and stacking them neatly so all the names were facing the same direction. Finally, I looked up, and there was a confused frown on Evan's handsome face. I could practically see the wheels turning in his head as he figured out a subtle way to ask about my dad without seeming too nosy.

"What's wrong with your real dad?"

Forget being subtle. "It's complicated." I leaned forward and ran my finger along the dashboard, wiping at the thin layer of dust that clung to the plastic. Why couldn't I have brought up something else to talk about? School, books, even the dirty magazines in his room would have been better. I hated talking about Dad. Or even thinking about him. And that other woman.

"You don't have to tell me if you don't want to."

The fact that he was giving me a *choice* made me want to tell him. At least the short version. That and the fact that he had slowed down enough that I was no longer worried we'd die in a car crash. "Besides cheating on my mom every other month and forgetting he even had two daughters, he was perfect. A real smooth talker who always got his way." I let out a short laugh. "Then again, he wasn't a university English professor for nothing."

Evan let out a low whistle. "Yeah, he sounds like he'd win the Best Dad of the Year trophy. So where is he now?"

"I don't know, and to be honest, I don't care." My lower lip was starting to get sore from my chewing on it. I forced myself to stop. "The best day of our lives was when he finally did us a favor and walked out. Well, second best. The best day was when Mom married my stepdad."

"The hotshot lawyer?" Evan smiled at my surprised expression. "You mentioned him and your aspirations the morning we—well, you know."

"Right." I let out a deep breath and folded my arms together. "Any more questions?"

"Yeah, just one." He gave me a sideways glance and wrinkled his nose. "Why are you still taking the bus when you're seventeen? Can't you drive?"

I leaned back against the cushion, grateful that the interrogation about my dad was over. Just the mention of him brought back memories of my parents fighting every single night. And Mom's tears. "Technically, that's two questions, but I'll answer them both. Yes, I can drive, but I take the bus because I don't have a car. And I don't have a car because I decided to take the money my parents were going to spend on one and put it in my savings instead. To help with my living expenses when I go to Columbia."

"So you're trying to be a lawyer, too?"

"No. I will be one."

Evan let out a low whistle. "Wow, will be. Good thing I like confidence in my women."

It wasn't just confidence. There were just no ifs about it. I had to be a lawyer. I had wanted to be one ever since my stepdad married my mom. I didn't even know what I would do if I didn't get in. There was no plan B. There couldn't be.

Suddenly feeling fidgety again, I leaned forward to fiddle with the radio's plastic buttons, unable to find a good station. Or any station at all, actually. The only thing I heard was static. "So are you seriously not going to college at all? I mean, what are you going to do with the rest of your life?"

"Are you trying to test my criteria as a suitor?" He said the last word in a phony British accent. "I'm not going to be a lowly stable boy, if that's what you're asking."

I laughed at the hopeful expression on his face and sat back, angling my body to the left so I would face him. "Believe me, you've got a long way to go if you want to fulfill *my* requirements."

"Well, it's a good thing I'm not applying, then." He made a sad face and wiggled his brows until I laughed again.

I didn't know what to say. Everybody I knew was prepared for the future. Brian was still debating between being a doctor like his parents wanted or being a journalist, but he had already applied to a bunch of schools and was accepted to all of them. And even though Carly was going to take a break after graduation—something she was still hiding from her parents— she had already contacted several theaters for work in the meantime.

The thought of not knowing what to do in life, especially now, felt crazy to me.

He shifted back and forth in his seat, but I could have sworn he was avoiding my gaze. Finally, I had to smack his shoulder to make him look at me. "Maybe I could help you figure something out. Something for you to major in."

Evan laughed. "I forgot, because that's part of the deal, right? I pretend to be your boyfriend, and you straighten up my life and keep the horny girls away?"

"I just said I'll help you with college applications. I'm not making any promises after that." I smiled when his laughing got even louder. "Seriously, is there anything you're interested in?"

"Well, I like the sea," he said after a while.

"Right, 'cause you're a surfer." I tried to sound supportive but knew I failed miserably when he snorted.

"I mean, the real sea. The animals. The plants. You know, stuff like that. Did you know that most of the life on earth is underwater? Or that the sea is so large that we've barely discovered less than 10% of it? The rest is unseen and untouched."

I couldn't stop staring at Evan. Not because he was gorgeous (although he was), but when he spoke about the sea, his face filled with so much excitement that it practically lit up. He glanced over at me and I flushed, forcing myself to look away. "That's really cool."

"Yeah, well, that's what I like. Maybe I thought about being a marine biologist or something."

"Wow. A marine biologist?" I didn't mean to sound so shocked, but the truth was that I was. I didn't know what answer I was expecting from Evan, but a marine biologist was definitely not on the list at all. Catalog model would have been higher. "I didn't think that you would be—I mean, not that you're—"

"Why? Do I look like I'll be an accountant or something?" Evan flicked down the visor and pretended to fix his hair in the mirror. "It's stupid, though. I doubt it'll work out. I guess I'll have to settle for just being handsome."

"What I *meant* to say was that I don't know anyone who wants to do that. Everyone else wants to go into business. Or be a doctor or dentist or a—"

"Lawyer?" He laughed when I punched his arm, not flinching at all. "Like I said, it's just something I thought about. I haven't really decided on anything. For all you know, I might just become a typical doctor, dentist, or businessman myself. Not a lawyer, though. God, I can't stand them. Bunch of vultures."

Smack! I hit him again. Harder this time. "Anyway, I thought you said you never even thought about college or the future. That it wasn't for you." I couldn't keep the smirk off my face.

Evan grinned and shook his head in defeat. "Okay, you win. I have *thought* about it, but it doesn't mean I'll actually do anything about it."

"I don't know why. I think being a marine biologist would be awesome. I don't know what colleges have that major, but I think the counselor would know."

"Yeah." He shrugged as if he didn't care either way and slowed the car. "Well, like I said, there's still time to worry about that later. The only thing we have to worry about now is school, because we're here."

He was right. We were in front of the school yard. And early, too. None of the buses were even here yet. There were only a few students lounging around on the steps as they waited for their friends.

Evan concentrated extra hard on parking, as though he would win a prize if the car was perfectly straight. Finally, he killed the engine and turned toward me, touching my arm when I opened the door to get out. "Wait."

"For what?"

He leaned over my lap to pull the door shut. For a few seconds, his broad chest and arms were in full contact with my body. Even though we had at least four layers of clothes between us, I couldn't help sucking in my breath. My heart pounded so hard in my chest that I was sure that he would feel it. I pressed as far back into the cushions as I could.

Evan didn't seem to notice that anything was wrong. "I think we should go together. We could walk hand in hand to home-room. You could carry my books, buy me lunch, you know, all the things a good girlfriend should do."

"Ha-ha." Despite the books-carrying and the lunch, that was a good idea. He was really getting into this.

"Yeah, I know," he replied as though I had said the thought out loud. "Here, you should wear this."

It was a necklace. An old silver coin about the size of my thumbnail hung on the end. It had been twisted with pliers or something into a strange shape, vaguely resembling a number eight. He handed it to me to examine. "My dad gave me this."

I touched the smooth surface of the coin.

"I don't even wear it to the beach in case I lose it, so you better take good care of it. Even your life won't be able to re-place this. You can give it back to me when this is over." Without waiting for my answer, his index finger made a circular motion in my direction. "Turn around."

I handed the necklace back to him, but I didn't move.

Evan let out a loud sigh when I hesitated. "If I wanted to do anything to you, I would have done it when you were in my bed." He jerked his head away when my hands shot out to cover his mouth. "Sorry! I forgot I wasn't supposed to mention the *incident.*"

The chair squeaked as he leaned forward and draped the chain around my neck. He was so close that his breath grazed the back of my neck. It was . . . nice, even though my nerves practically crackled with electricity. Then his fingers were on my neck, gentle as he clasped the latch tightly. His fingertips traced the chain and my skin for a brief moment. It was warm and it tickled. I involuntarily shivered, and just like that, his touch was gone before the electricity could get out of control.

Embarrassed, I waited until he was settled back in his seat before I turned around. I occupied myself with putting on my coat and hat. "So . . . how many girls have seen this necklace?"

He peered out the window. "A lot. But the important number is that only one other person has ever worn this. And that's you."

My heart fluttered a bit at this revelation. I was surprised that he would go to such lengths just to prove to people that we were dating.

Evan brought me back to the present when he tightened the scarf around my neck for me. "Ready?"

I snapped out of my stupor, and his door was half open. Already people were circling his car, trying to peer inside. I knew the windows were tinted, but I didn't know if they could see me. Not that it mattered, since that was the point of this whole scheme.

It was now or never. I fingered the long chain, tracing the tiny links with my fingertips. It was cool and oddly comforting around my neck. "Let's do this."

8

{Taylor}

To say that we caused a bit of a commotion was putting it lightly. People actually stopped in their tracks as we walked down the hall together, hand in sweaty hand.

I am embarrassed to admit that the sweaty hand was mine. I'd been in front of crowds before, but it was usually at award ceremonies, where people barely paid attention to me. They were just glad to get out of class for an hour.

Everyone was definitely on full alert now. Although part of the staring might be because they'd never seen Evan early for school before.

It's like the dream where you arrive at school naked, except I wasn't. I even looked down to make sure my jeans were zipped. Yep, up and secure. I ducked my head down and self-consciously reached up to sweep my bangs out of my eyes, only to realize that my hand was still gripping Evan's. Cheeks blazing, I dropped our hands like a hot potato.

Evan, however, didn't even bat an eye at my awkwardness. In fact, he milked it for all that it was worth. He let go of my damp palm to brush my bangs out of my eyes for me. He even tucked a stray strand behind my ears before leaning in to kiss my cheek. You would have thought that pretending to be someone's boyfriend was just a daily routine for him.

There was a loud gasp behind us.

His lips curved into a smile against my face before he grabbed my hand again. His eyes twinkled down at me with amusement. I would have laughed with him if I weren't so nervous.

And just like that, I suddenly wasn't anymore. Especially when his hand—which was formerly on my waist—drifted lower. Way lower.

I shot him a glare. "What are you doing?" I hissed.

"Just making sure we know where the boundaries are." His hand zipped back up to my shoulders and hugged me to his side as he smothered his laughter. "Note taken."

The crowd moved forward with us until we were in front of the lockers. Evan let go of me and knelt down to open his. I took the opportunity to wipe my hands on the side of my jeans. Everything I needed was already in my bag, so I just tried to look casual as I waited. Like there weren't a bunch of students staring at us from every angle as if we were carnies at a circus. *A once-in-a-lifetime opportunity! Come see the nerd and the sex god!*

The only person who was more natural than Evan was Carly. Her acting skills came into great use. "Hey, Reformed Rake," she called out with a wink in my direction before giving him a high five.

Without missing a beat, he gave her a one-armed hug in greeting, like they were old friends. I noticed that she leaned into his muscled shoulder a few seconds longer than needed, though.

"Reformed Rake?" A confused expression crossed his face. "What does that mean?"

My face flushed, and I waved both hands at him. "Don't worry about it. She's crazy."

Just then Mr. Peters walked passed us with a stack of folders in his arms. "Hello, Taylor. Carly." He barely gave us a glance before he stopped short. He backed up a step and squinted at Evan like he didn't understand what was going on. I don't think anyone did. "Mr. McKinley. You're . . . here. Before the bell."

"I know, right? You're not the only one who's surprised." Evan laughed and wrapped an arm around my shoulders. "But I couldn't say no to Taylor. I mean, when she has her mind set on something, there's nothing this girl can't do."

"Hmm." Mr. Peters looked back and forth between the two of us a few times before shaking his head and walking away. "Well, it's good to see you. All of you."

I gave Evan a grateful smile. He didn't know about my problems with Mr. Peters or how much anxiety I'd been going through prepping for the fair, yet somehow he made everything better. I guess he really wasn't so bad after all.

He gave me a tiny wink like he knew what I was thinking. "I should head to homeroom. You'll probably want to hang out with Carly a bit, right, babe?"

"Uh, right . . . honey," I choked out the endearment as an afterthought, since it felt like he was waiting for something. "Meet you later for lunch?"

"Sure."

I expected him to hug me or even kiss my cheek again before he left, but instead he patted my head like I was a pet who deserved a treat for being good. My embarrassment went supernova, and I glowered up at him. Looking very pleased with himself, Evan chuckled and tweaked the tip of my nose before leaving.

Carly waited until he was down the hall before clucking her tongue at me. "So he drove you to school? You didn't tell me about this part of the plan last night."

"Because it wasn't part of the plan. It just . . . happened."

"Like a happy bonus?" she asked, still not taking her eyes off his retreating broad back. Neither of us did. "You can thank me for the idea later."

I rubbed my nose. It still tingled where he touched me. "Let's go to class."

⇛•↰

Carly was right, though. The Reformed Rake plan worked like a charm. It was amazing. Within hours, the girls stopped acting like I was the Whore of Babylon. In fact, they were a bit awed that I had bagged a steaming hottie like Evan. (Carly's words, not mine.) One girl even held the bathroom door open for me.

And the guys just stopped talking to me altogether. Not that I minded, since they didn't talk to me much before, either.

The students weren't the only ones who noticed. Mrs. Hines, the school's secretary, actually patted my shoulder when I came in to do the morning announcements. Not only was my reputation restored, but now I was on an even higher pedestal than before.

I didn't blame everyone for believing that we were a real couple, though. Evan's acting was so good that even I was fooled.

It was strangely natural when he sat beside me in the cafeteria. I did, however, smack his hand when he stole one of my sweet-potato fries. I made sure to smile lovingly at him when I did it, though.

Brian stopped in his tracks when he saw us sitting together. He gave me a questioning look, but I couldn't do more than shrug. Especially since there were a bunch of people surrounding us. Carly had to tug on his arm to get him to sit down. His jaw tightened, but he didn't say anything and sat down across from me, since Evan was already sitting in Brian's usual seat beside me.

Not noticing that anything was wrong, Evan munched on his barbecue chips and turned to talk to Carly about the drama club. Or rather, he asked what they had planned, and she started rambling a mile a minute about the upcoming musical they were working on.

"So, Brian, I think the original layout for the arts department is pretty good. But what do you think about the other clubs?" I asked, trying to act like having Evan sit with us for lunch was no biggie.

Brian gave another glance toward Evan. "What do you mean?"

"Well, the smaller clubs can't all be squished on only four pages. But there's no more space for them anywhere. We barely

have room to add a thank-you to the teachers in the end."
I chewed on my lip and tapped my pen against the table, trying to figure out a solution. The yearbook budget was already
pushed to the max, so we couldn't add even a single page.

Nodding to himself, Brian leaned forward on the table until
he was hovering over my notebook and wrapped his hand
around mine to guide the pen, drawing lines to connect certain
groups. "We could always move the Honor Society to the front
and combine the Poetry Club with the *New Voices* group. I
don't think they'd mind."

"But we still—ouch!" Someone kicked my knee underneath
the table, making my hand slip out of Brian's grasp. At first I
thought it was Carly, but she looked as shocked as I was. And
her eyes were glued to a certain someone, who was shaking his
bag of chips even though it was empty. I glared at Evan and
rubbed my leg. "What was that for?"

"What? I didn't do anything."

My gaze turned to Carly when she snickered, but she just
shrugged and gave me an innocent smile. Too innocent.

"Okay, so I think . . ." I trailed off, distracted as Evan picked the
mushrooms off his pizza with a fork. One by one. When he was
done, he laid the tiny pile on my own pizza like a peace offering.
"Now what are you doing?"

"Hm?" He took a big bite of his pizza before looking at me.

I jabbed a finger at my plate. "You don't like veggies?"

"Oh, I like them. But I know you like mushrooms the most."

That was true. I did. My mom used to say I was born in a
mushroom field, even though there isn't such a thing—is there?
I needed to visit if there was.

Either way—whether it was on pizzas, salads, or even in spaghetti sauce—I'd always eat the mushrooms first. It was just weird that *Evan* knew that. Nobody else noticed or cared. Until now. Which was both surprising and sort of creepy at the same time. Even Carly looked surprised at this revelation.

Brian jabbed at the list on the table with an annoyed expression on his face. I felt bad for him. Deadlines always stressed him out.

I didn't know what to say, so I offered Evan the rest of my fries. He gave me a wide grin and popped one in his mouth, making me wonder if that was his intention all along.

"How did you know I like mushrooms?"

Evan coughed and looked away. His hand swept through his dark-blond locks. They were less spiky and gelled than usual. Probably because he had to wake up early to drive me to school. There was even a little bit of a curl to them. "Uh, I saw you stealing them from Carly's plate once during lunch."

"You did what?" Carly glared at me.

"Oh please, you never even noticed they were missing." I stuck out my tongue at her before turning my attention back to Evan. "And why were you watching me at lunch?"

Instead of responding, he avoided my eyes and looked down at his invisible watch on his right wrist. "Oh, look at the time. Is that my class? I should go..." Within a blink of an eye, he jumped up from the table and practically ran out of the cafeteria.

My eyes narrowed. *Oh, he wasn't going to get away that easily.* "I'll be back."

Brian was already picking up my stuff for me, since we

usually spent the period after lunch planning the yearbook. "But Taylor, we were supposed to—"

"I know. I'll only be gone for a little bit." Before he could say anything else, I was gone. Darting around people, I finally caught up to Evan just as he got to the library at the end of the hall. He glanced over his shoulder and saw me, but he didn't say anything. Nor did he slow down.

Staying close on his heels, I glanced over my shoulder to make sure Mrs. Stills, the librarian and head of study hall, didn't see me. She was busy checking out books for some freshman. Hidden behind the large magazine rack, I slid into the seat across from Evan. He let out a loud groan and reached over my head to grab a random magazine, then began flipping through it. I knew he wasn't *actually* reading it, though. Not unless he really was interested in ten different ways to wear a scarf, as the cover claimed.

"Don't you have class?" he muttered without looking up.

"So you noticed me, huh?" I leaned on my elbows toward him. "Since when?"

Instead of making some smart remark like I expected him to, Evan ducked his head deeper into the magazine. "Since I saved you at the pool."

Okay, I wasn't expecting *that* answer. "Why?"

"I don't know." He purposely angled the magazine so I couldn't see his face anymore, but the tips of his ears were turning suspiciously pink beneath his deep tan. It was kind of endearing. "I guess you made an impression."

That was the nicest thing anyone had ever said to me. I knew I should meet Brian, but I couldn't make myself leave

Evan's side. I nudged his arm, poking harder and harder until he looked up. His eyes were wary over the pages.

"Guess what I did today?"

"You met Madonna? No, Bill Gates?" He snapped his fingers. "I got it! Jesus!"

I snickered. "How did you know? I had a near-death experience, and Jesus told me that Madonna and Bill Gates were looking for me in the backyard."

His eyes twinkled with so much amusement, they seemed to be a lighter shade of gray than usual. "I knew it."

Shaking my head, I pulled out the brochures and applications I had gotten from the counselor's office before lunch. All filed according to the difficulty of the essays. I spread them out in front of him. "I know you said you didn't care about any of this *stuff*." I made finger quotations when I said the word *stuff*. "But I figured it doesn't hurt to think about it, right? Just something to look at when you're bored. There were even some colleges with late application deadlines. Plus, I made some notes about which ones have the best marine-biology classes."

The magazine dropped, and his fingers flipped through the papers. "Does this obsession with me going to college have something to do with the Reformed Rake thing Carly was talking about earlier?" he asked, leaning forward until our noses were almost touching.

I sucked in a deep breath at his sudden closeness, but I didn't back away. In fact, I may have leaned in just a tiny bit. "I just had some spare time."

His lips jerked into a half smile, making my gaze slide down, and I couldn't look away. "Maybe we should be doing something else with our spare time instead of researching about a bunch of dumb colleges."

"Like . . . ?"

"Ms. Simmons?"

Rats. I had forgotten to stay hidden. I snapped back into my seat as though pulled by an invisible bungee cord. "Yes?"

Mrs. Stills frowned down at me. Even her wrinkles looked menacing. Unlike the other members of the faculty—who loved me—she never treated me with more than reined-in politeness. I never knew why. I wasn't proud to admit it, but I really was the biggest suck-up ever. In kindergarten, I would spend my recesses sharpening pencils for my teacher. Yeah, I was *that* student.

Still, the way Mrs. Stills treated me was actually a step above the way she talked to other students, so that was something to be thankful about. "I don't believe you're supposed to be here. Did you need my help with something?"

"Uh, no." I quickly got to my feet.

"Then I suggest you leave."

"Yes, ma'am." I stacked all the papers and brochures together, only stopping to fan my face with them to cool off.

Evan reached out and took my hand before I could dart away, squeezing lightly. "You could leave these here. I'll throw them away for you later."

Surprised, I stopped and stared at him, but he was glancing down at the brochures. His other hand shuffled through them a bit.

I bit back the smile that threatened to burst forth. The more I got to know Evan, the more I saw that the playboy facade was really just that. A facade. He really wasn't that bad. God forbid I ever tell him that, though. His head was big enough as it was. "If you're sure . . ."

"Yeah, thanks, though. And it was nice of you to get me all this. Even though I don't need it," he quickly added.

"No problem."

Not sure if it was the mushrooms or the college applications, but on an impulse, I peeked behind me to make sure Mrs. Stills was back at her desk. Once the coast was clear, I leaned over his left shoulder and gave him a quick peck on the cheek. He jumped and turned his head to look up at me. His eyes narrowed in question.

I gave him a wink. "See you later, sweetie."

9

-Evan-

Within days, we fell into a comfortable routine. I'd pick Taylor up for school, we'd go to class, we'd eat lunch together, and then I'd take her back to my place.

It was not as exciting as it sounds.

Like today, I was sprawled out on the couch as I battled aliens on my Xbox. Taylor sat in the kitchen working on her homework. I invited her to join me, but she declined. Without looking up from her report, she just asked me to promise to save her when there's an alien invasion or a zombie apocalypse. Whichever came first. The girl could be pretty funny when she wanted to be.

Going to my house after school was my idea, and it was a damn good one, too. Especially since my neighbor was none other than Alesha Brant, head of the school's gossip column. I'm pretty sure that's how our hookup came out so quickly.

Any doubting Thomases about our relationship shut up

the next day. I just had to take Taylor home by six thirty each day before my mom and Brandon came home.

Taylor did have one stipulation, though. Even though she'd been in my room before—obviously, since she woke up in my bed—she refused to go up there now. So we compromised—and by compromised, I mean, I was suckered into giving in—and I brought my Xbox down to plug into the living-room TV while she studied and did her homework in the kitchen.

I was seconds from taking down the mother ship when a car door slammed outside. It sounded like it came straight from my driveway. This wasn't good.

A feeling of dread swept over me. I put the game on pause and leaned forward on the arm of the couch to peer outside. No, not good at all. Through the large front windows swathed in cream lace curtains on either side of the front door, I could see two shadowy figures walking up the pathway, arms full of groceries. "Damn it!"

Taylor appeared at the door. "What's wrong?"

"My stepdad and mom are home."

Her eyes widened in her pale face. She stood frozen in the living-room doorway. "But—but you said they never come home before seven on a weekday!"

I turned off my game reluctantly. I had been so close to finishing the level, too. "Well, obviously today is an exception. And we're about to be screwed."

"Meaning?"

"Meaning that my mom is the biggest gossip at the PTA meetings, and if you don't haul your ass and get over here to cuddle with me, then our cover is blown!"

At my words, Taylor skidded over to the couch so fast that I half expected smoke to come out of her feet. *Jingle. Jingle.* The keys were unlocking the door. *Thud.* My arm dropped down around her small shoulders and pulled her close to my chest. She barely had time to curl her legs beneath her butt and drop her head on my shoulder when the door opened.

Realizing too late that we couldn't pretend to be watching TV since it was off, I turned my head and pressed my lips against hers. Her eyes widened, and she stared up at me, but she didn't move away. Even though I knew Mom was right there, I couldn't help noticing how soft Taylor's lips were. My fingers dug into the couch cushion, and I fought the urge to deepen the kiss.

"Honey, we're home. I'm going to start dinner soon, so I hope you remembered to put the chicken out to defrost—oh!"

I pulled away just as Mom stopped in her tracks. Brandon stumbled into her back and had to juggle the bags in his arms. "Oh, hi, Mom. Yeah, sorry, I forgot to put the chicken out."

Her voice grew a bit high-pitched. "That's okay, I can see that you were . . . that you're busy."

Brandon brushed past her and headed toward the kitchen without saying anything. Being a typical ass as usual. I thought he would have at least *pretended* to be civil with Taylor here. I guess that was just too much to ask of His Royal Highness.

I took Taylor's hand and pulled her to her feet before pushing her toward my mom. Her cheeks were still flushed from either embarrassment at meeting my mom or at being caught *kissing* me in front of my mom. "Mom, I want you to meet my girlfriend, Taylor. Taylor, this is my mom."

"Hi."

At the sound of her name, my mom's eyes widened with interest. "Taylor? You mean, Taylor Simmons? Aren't you the valedictorian?"

"Well, that hasn't been decided yet. The school year's still not over."

Mom snapped her fingers. "Right, you're still fighting with Brian Long for that position. But I heard that you're applying to Columbia. Have you gotten the acceptance letter yet?"

Taylor's eyes narrowed, but the polite smile on her face never wavered. "I'm hoping for it any day now."

"And how are your parents? Didn't your father graduate from Columbia, too?"

"They're fine. And he did." Taylor threw a panicked glance over her shoulder at me, and I just shrugged. I did warn her.

I don't know how or where Mom got all her information, but she always knew more about the kids at school than I did. Not so great, since that means she also knew way too much about my dating history. Although I was surprised that she was just finding out now that I was "dating" Taylor. I would have thought that she would have found out within an hour of that first day. She must be slacking.

"Simmons?" Suddenly Brandon appeared out of thin air like a freakin' jack-in-the-box. He hovered beside Mom. His eyes narrowed as he scrutinized Taylor. "You mean Cole Simmons from Winchester & Hewitt?"

"Yes."

And just like that, his nauseating, charming facade fell into place. *Urgh.* The wide phony grin that snared my mom was fixated on his face as he shook Taylor's hand, tugging her closer to his side. "I met him a few times at the Hope for Cancer fund-raisers. He's a brilliant man. Absolutely brilliant. I should have known you were his daughter. You're his spitting image."

"Thanks. He's my stepfather."

I snorted and had to play it off as a cough. That's my girl. I shot Taylor a proud smile that she returned with a small wink.

"Of course. Cole and your mother met after your father ran off with that—" Mom broke off her sentence. Her hand flew up to cover her mouth. "I'm sorry, I didn't mean to bring up the, well, the incident."

The expression on Taylor's face didn't change. "That's all right, Mrs. McKinley. It happened a long time ago."

"Of course." Mom shot a glance at Brandon. "And I'm actually Mrs. Willard."

Taylor blinked. "But Evan's—"

"My mom changed her name after she remarried, but I kept my name." I crossed my arms and nodded toward Brandon, who seemed to be trying his best to ignore me. His finger kept scratching at his leg, like I was an itch he couldn't get rid of. "I wouldn't want to contaminate the Willard name in any way."

Brandon didn't let that faze him. "So, Taylor, what's a smart girl like you doing with Evan?" He laughed as though it were the funniest thing in the world. "Don't you have enough sense to stay away? Some of us don't have a choice, but at least you do."

Mom laughed, too, but her eyes nervously flickered to me.

My hands clenched together into tight fists at my sides. I was about to tell him where he could shove it when Taylor spoke up.

"That's true. I didn't know what I was getting into when I met Evan." She gave me a genuinely sweet smile that made me automatically step toward her. I could feel my anger slowly fade as she reached out to take my right hand, gripping it tightly. "Or rather, what I was missing."

"That's . . . nice." The disgust on his face was evident. Probably couldn't believe how a deadbeat like me was able to get a girl like Taylor. Thank god he didn't know it was fake.

I wrapped an arm around her shoulders. "I must have brainwashed her or something. But hey, I guess I learned something from you after all, right?" Unable to help myself, I nodded toward my mom, who was studying the beige carpet beneath our feet, always conveniently turning deaf whenever Brandon and I fought. She was a pro at ignoring the truth.

Brandon's nose flared, and he turned an ugly shade of purple before stomping away. "I need to call the hospital to check on some patients. Let me know when you want me to help you with dinner, Eva."

Mom didn't look up or even respond until his study door slammed shut with a bang. She let out a deep breath and smiled at us as though the past three minutes hadn't happened. "I'm so glad to meet you. Evan never lets me meet any of his girlfriends."

"I'm sure he was just worried about bringing them home."

"Oh, I'm sure he brings plenty of girls home. I'm just saying he never let me *meet* any of them before."

This time Taylor's laugh was genuine. It got louder when

I sat down on the arm of the couch and dropped my head to my knees with a loud smack. Taylor patted my shoulder in sympathy.

"Did you eat yet?" Mom asked. "I can whip up a quick batch of chocolate-chip cookies. Or maybe you could even stay for dinner?" Her eagerness was obvious to everyone.

"I'm sorry, Mrs. Willard, but I should go home to eat dinner with my parents soon. I wouldn't mind taking those cookies home, though," Taylor quickly added when Mom's face fell. "My dad has a major sweet tooth."

"Wonderful! I'll make them right now. It won't take any time at all."

Unable to take Mom's fawning anymore, I grabbed Taylor's hand and pulled her toward the stairs. "Come on. We'll be back in a bit."

"Sure thing, sweetheart." Mom practically floated into the kitchen. If I didn't know that Brandon was an uptight ass, I would have thought they had stopped at a bar or something.

I shook my head. "You better run while you still can. If she could, she'd probably stuff you with cookies and food until you're too full to leave and will be forced to marry me."

Taylor stumbled and fell forward against my back, almost making me trip on the steps. I steadied myself against the wall and whipped around to hold her arm so she wouldn't topple over and hurt herself. Her cheeks were a bit pink as she moved a few steps down so I was no longer touching her. With one hand firmly on the banister, she waved her other hand for me to keep moving. I gave her a funny look before turning back toward the stairs.

"Your mom's not that bad," she continued as though we

both hadn't almost fallen off the stairs. "She actually reminds me a lot of my mom. Minus the baking. My mom can't bake to save the world." She stopped laughing when we reached the top and I headed toward my room. "Wait, where are we going?"

"Where do you think?"

"But . . . but we agreed that we wouldn't go into your room."

"Yeah, well, I just know I need to get as far away from *him* as possible." I waved my hand toward the stairs. "But if you want to hang out with them, then be my guest." I went into the room without seeing if she would follow.

She did. Slowly. As though she was worried that the door was going to snap shut and lock her in. I flopped on the bed and waited to see what she would do.

When Taylor was certain that I wasn't going to throw her on the bed and jump her bones or something, she edged closer into the room. Her fingertips traced the painted waves on my surfboard before she walked over to the dresser and bookshelves. She peered at each of the pictures on the surface, skipping all the pictures with the girls and lingering on the ones I'd taken a few weeks ago of a coral reef when I went scuba diving.

Finally, she sat down on my desk chair and spun the chair around and around. "Your room looks different."

"What do you mean?"

"I don't know. It's just not what I remembered."

I glanced around, but it looked the same to me. It's not like I had underwear and bras hanging around. In fact, I don't think another girl had been in here since Lauren a few months ago. Besides Taylor.

"So you were right." She finally swung the chair around to face me. "Your stepdad really is a jackass."

I laughed and shrugged. "Unfortunately, he treats my mom pretty well, so I can't kick his ass like I want to."

Her nose wrinkled. "Really? Because he seems like the controlling type."

"Oh, believe me, he is. But compared to how her life was before, living with him is like a fairy tale."

"Why? What was it like before?"

"Difficult." I leaned my body upward to settle my weight on my elbows and watched her closely for her reaction. "My dad was in jail a lot, so she had to worry about all the other stuff, like bills and taking care of me while she finished her nursing degree."

Taylor didn't ask me what he did time for like I thought she would. I couldn't have told her even if she did ask. I never knew why he hopped in and out of jail so much. It was probably for minor misdemeanors instead of something major, since he was never gone for too long. At least not until that last time nearly four years ago, when Mom finally had enough and divorced him. It wasn't long before Brandon swooped in from the sidelines to take advantage of her.

Still, Taylor wasn't reacting like people usually do when they found out about my dad. Pity. Disgust. Or even awe from a couple of girls who thought I was a broken boy who needed to be taken home and fixed. In fact, Taylor barely reacted at all. Her eyelashes fluttered a bit, but that was it.

"Where is he now?"

Clasping my hands beneath my head, I stared up at the ceiling. "I haven't heard from him in a while. But I think he's in Florida. Or at least that's what my mom says."

The edge of my bed dipped a little as she sat next to me. "I don't get it. It's just—you looked surprised when I said my dad was the jerk. But it sounds like your dad isn't that great, either. But you're not mad at him? At all?"

Mad? I had plenty of reasons to be mad, but I wasn't. Not at all.

It was stupid, but even though he was a horrible husband, he was a great dad. He took me to ball games and motor races. He listened to me ramble into the night about cartoons on TV or comic books that I read at the store. He even brought me to the aquarium for the first time when I was ten, and back every few months when he saw how much I loved it.

It's hard to be pissed at someone when all of your best memories are of him. *With* him. Even if he did leave us. And didn't bother fighting for us at all.

Okay, maybe I was a *little* mad.

I stared up at the plastic stars on the ceiling. My plastic stars. Dad bought them and stuck them along my doorway and ceiling moldings. When Mom married Brandon, I took them with me, even though they were hard as hell to pry off. Nor did they want to stick to the ceiling of my new room. But I needed them. I may be an unwelcome guest in this house, but at least the room would feel like home to me. They finally stuck, with the help of a portable hot-glue gun. And it gave me a sense of satisfaction to ruin Brandon's precious house.

"Evan?" I snapped back to the present when Taylor touched my shoulder. For a second, I had forgotten she was even there. "Sorry if I'm a little annoying."

I grasped her hand and pulled her until she flopped down on her back beside me. "You don't have to apologize. It's not your fault you're nosy."

She shoved at me but didn't pull away. We lay there side by side in silence. It was a comfortable silence. Our arms were inches apart. If I stretched out my hand, I could probably touch hers. I didn't, though. I didn't want to somehow ruin the moment.

"It's simple," I finally said. "He's my dad. The only one I'll ever have."

"Huh. I guess we think differently, then." Her voice was quiet and flat.

I knew I should leave it alone, but I wasn't going to. "Why did you lie about your dad leaving?"

Her hand rose toward the ceiling, and she used her index finger to trace connecting stars into invisible shapes only she could see. "I didn't. He did leave us. I just left out the part about who he left with."

"Who was that?"

"I don't know. Some waitress he got pregnant a few years after I was born. After Kimmy was born, she came back and told him about their kid. And he decided he'd rather play house with her than stay with us." The bed moved again when Taylor rolled over to face me. "So when it comes to our daddy issues, we're completely different."

I turned on my side, too, and tucked her hair behind her

ear. "He's an idiot. I would have chosen you in a heartbeat. And it's not surprising that we're different. I mean, I'm handsome, smart, funny, and heart-stoppingly charming, while you're—"

"You forgot delusional."

"For you? I'm getting to that."

She snorted. "Is this the charm you were bragging about? Because I think it could use some work."

I raised an eyebrow. "I'm going to make you regret that."

"How?"

In a blink of an eye, I rolled over and had her pinned beneath me. She squeaked and pushed me away, but my leg had her firmly secured while I planned my attack. My fingers slid down to her waist, and her squeals melted away to laughter as I tickled her. Tears quickly came to her eyes and streamed down her cheeks.

After a few minutes, I finally stopped, and we panted to catch our breath. It only took a few seconds for me to realize that we had never been this close before. Practically plastered against each other. Not that we could remember anyway.

And even more surprising, it felt good. Damn good. Taylor must have realized it, too, because she froze beneath me. Her eyes slid from my face to my chest. I could practically *feel* the heat in her eyes.

My stomach clenched at the feel of her body pressed against mine, her arms wrapped around my neck. Her heart thudded hard against me. Or was that mine? I wiped away the lingering tears on her cheeks. "So what should we do now?" I murmured, already lowering my head toward hers.

She let out a shuddering breath that made her body move up and down. "We—we should go downstairs and see if your mom needs help making the cookies." With that said, she scooted out from beneath me and hurried toward the door.

I froze for a moment. My elbows held up my weight as though Taylor were still there. For a second, I had forgotten about Brandon and my dad and her dad and basically everybody in the world but us. I even forgot about the fact that we were just *pretending* to be dating. All I wanted right now was for her to be back in my arms. Wide, brown eyes staring up at me.

With a groan, I collapsed on the bed.

10

{Taylor}

Today would have been another *Dear Diary* moment if I still had one. I did when I was younger. A navy hardcover spiral notebook with pastel-blue pages. The kind with a little metal lock on it and a key necklace. I wrote in it every day until I realized how easy it was to break the flimsy lock that was the only barrier to my innermost thoughts and desires. Then *bam!* Into the trash it went.

Did anyone even keep diaries anymore? Everyone I knew had a blog now—although in my opinion, that's even worse. Anyone could read it. Even the ones that are "locked" and marked private. You could even Google how to hack into it on the same web page. And if *anyone* could read it, there was really no use in making it private. Might as well put it in skywriting.

But that's beside the point. My point is that today was a *Dear Diary* day.

Carly was the one who brought up the problem first. She had overheard Lauren telling some other girls that Evan and I didn't look like a real couple. That there was no way he could keep his hands to himself at school if we had any real chemistry. And she gave us two weeks before we broke up.

Before I could even start panicking, Carly had an idea. "Why don't you guys have a big makeout performance at school and prove everyone wrong?"

Judging by her big smile, I'm pretty sure she'd been waiting ages to make this suggestion.

I was reluctant at first. Especially when Evan hesitated. Then I was a little offended. It didn't take long for him to get on board, though.

As we waited for the bell to ring and our audience to arrive, he stretched his arms overhead as though limbering up for a marathon rather than just a kiss. "Ready, Taylor?"

"Are you kidding me? I was up all night anticipating this," I said flatly, shuffling through the history flash cards I had made the night before.

"You don't know how much the thought of you in bed thinking about me warms my heart." Evan wiggled his brows at me. "And other parts of me, too, of course."

I rolled my eyes and smacked the cards against his shoulder. "Gross." I wasn't as offended as I would have been last week. Jeez, I'd even gotten used to his warped, dirty sense of humor. The best way to counter him was with sarcastic comments. Something I had plenty of.

My nonchalance was a front. Inside, I was a wreck. A big ol' fat mess. Every time I thought of kissing Evan, the image of that afternoon we almost kissed in his room flashed in my head.

I don't know what happened. Maybe my emotions had already been wired up because of my dad, and I had let down my guard. But I'd almost lost control. And strangely enough, the fear of losing control was what had snapped me out of it. Even though I had wanted to kiss him—really, really wanted to—I hadn't. I couldn't. Because I wasn't ready for it.

That was last week, though. I was fully prepared today. My emotions were reined in and I knew what to expect. I'd even read a couple of articles online on kissing in case my paltry experience wasn't enough. There was *tons* of stuff on the Internet. Thank god I clicked off the monitor before Kimmy and Mom came in, or I would have had a lot of explaining to do.

I shifted my weight from my left foot to my right. "Are you sure this is a good spot?"

"Trust me. This is the best place for our performance. Everyone knows this is the prime spot to get some action. And since it's behind the gym-room lockers, there's barely any teachers around."

"Hmm, I guess you would know."

"You can bet your ass I would." Evan slid down the locker until we were nearly eye to eye. "By the way, my mom wanted me to give you a basket of banana-apple muffins to bring home. Remember to get it from my trunk when I drop you off."

"Oh yum." I practically licked my lips at the thought. Every day, she gave Evan some new baked treat to bring me in case she didn't come home in time to see us. I had already gained over four pounds in the past two days. "Why didn't you tell me earlier? I could have eaten it in the car."

"Because I hate bananas. What if I tasted it during our kiss? I might throw up, and that would probably give people the wrong idea about you."

I raised an eyebrow at his look of horror. "Oh please. You don't see me complaining. I should have made you stop by the gas station so *you* could get some gum."

"Oh, you definitely don't have to worry. Carly gave me some. And I brushed extra long this morning for you." His pearly smile almost made me believe him. He gave me a slow wink, and my stomach fluttered in response. "But seriously, are you ready to give the kissing performance of a lifetime? I don't know how much experience you've had, but I have a reputation to maintain, so this has to look good. But then, you don't need to worry," he said as an afterthought.

"Why not?"

"Because you won't need to act. I'm sure you'll get too swept up in the moment to remember we're just acting." Evan let out a dramatic sigh. "I, however, will have to fake it the best I can."

I knew what he was doing. He was trying to keep the mood light so I didn't overthink this and get nervous. Too late. "Oh, just shut up and keep stretching." I shoved the flash cards in my back pocket.

"No need. I'm done." Evan straightened and motioned for me to come closer. I awkwardly placed both hands on his shoulders like we were ballroom dancing, and he smothered a laugh against his fist. "That's good, but I think we might have to get a little closer than that. I mean, unless you plan to telepathically kiss me."

"Ha-ha." I stepped closer and wrapped my arms around his neck. In response, he looped both arms around my waist.

"Much, much better. All right, Operation Makeout is about

to commence," he whispered when his face was mere inches from mine. He brushed my bangs off my forehead and smirked. "Showtime."

"God, Evan, did anyone ever tell you that you're a master at turning a girl on?" I muttered right before his lips touched mine, making him laugh.

Despite all his big talk, Evan was holding back. His lips were against mine, but that was it. It was nice—much better than the handful of kisses I'd had before—but something was missing. Like he was afraid I would run away if he deepened the kiss. I was still tempted to run, but now that we were here, my perfectionist nature was demanding to take over. If we were doing this, then this better be the best display of kissing this school had ever seen.

Deciding to take matters into my own hands, I wrapped my hand around the back of his neck and pulled him closer. His shoulders grew stiff beneath my forearms, but his lips pressed tightly against mine. I let out a soft sigh and touched the tip of my tongue against his. Evan sucked in a deep breath and hesitated for the barest of seconds before taking over. His mouth slanted open and over my own as his arms dropped down to my hips to hold me against his body, lifting me up. I had to tiptoe to stay on my feet. At least I think I did. I wasn't really sure, since I could barely feel the ground. My legs had turned to jelly. Mush. Ice cream on a sunny, ninety-five-degree day.

Hmmm. This was more like it. The kiss was turning out pretty nice. Okay, if pretty nice meant awesome, blow-your-mind-out hot.

It was . . . god, like nothing I had ever imagined. I'd read about kisses like this in novels, but I never thought that it was possible. Nothing can make the world melt away and make you forget about everything and everyone except the person in front of you. The way he smelled. His muscles and warm skin pulsing beneath your fingertips. The softness of his hair as your fingers ran through it. And his lips, soft but impossibly hot without burning as they pressed against yours, opening and moving to massage, to kiss, to taste . . .

The first thought that popped in my head was that Evan wasn't lying about his experience. In fact, he may have underplayed it. This was some damn kiss. And he didn't lie about the brushing. He tasted nice and minty.

I don't know how long the kiss was or how long it would have been if someone hadn't bumped into Evan, making both of us stumble into the wall. My head would have smacked against the bulletin board if his hand hadn't reached out to cradle it, blocking the impact.

Evan's breath tickled my left ear. "Are you okay?"

"Uh, yeah, I'm fine." I was barely able to pay attention to anything but the feel of his arms wrapped around me. But somehow, I pulled away enough to peer over his shoulder. Through the chattering crowd, I could see a slim figure dart through. Her curly red hair swung back and forth in its upswept ponytail.

Lauren.

Evan followed my gaze. "That's weird."

"What is?"

"That Lauren shoved us." He laughed and shook his head. "If I didn't know any better, I would have thought she was jealous or something, but that's impossible."

Noticing the familiar way he talked about her, the hazy feeling of the kiss vanished. "Are you—did you two used to date?"

"Well, yeah, but it's been over for ages. Now we just hook up every once in a while."

His casual admission hurt. It reminded me that he would have never been so honest if we were really dating, which we weren't.

For a moment, I had forgotten that we were pretending. I had forgotten about everything but us. That kiss was incredible, and now it felt tainted and dirty and *wrong*. I shoved him away, wanting to get as far away from him as I could. "That's great. Real great. Look, I have to get to class." I barely registered the surprised look on his face before striding away.

It didn't take him long to catch up to me. Damn my short legs. "What's wrong?"

"Nothing's wrong."

"Wait." He smacked his hand against his forehead and sighed. "I know what it is."

My heart stopped, and everything grew blurry. He couldn't have figured it out. I barely understood what was wrong. "You do?" I gnawed on my lower lip.

"Yeah, it's nothing to be embarrassed about. You should just admit it."

"What?"

"Admit that you were swept away by the kiss just now, like I said you would be." Seriously, his grin couldn't be any bigger than it was now.

My eyes lowered to the ground, and I laughed it off, knowing that it sounded pretty weak. Even to my ears. "Please." I started to walk faster, but he easily followed.

"Please kiss you again?" Evan laughed and wrapped his arms around my shoulders, pulling me into a half hug, half headlock. "Come on, just admit it. Come on. Come on."

"All right, all right!" I laughed and pulled away from him. "You were . . . satisfactory, I guess."

"I'll take that. Too bad you weren't."

I looked up at him, expecting to see a smile. To my surprise, he had a serious expression on his face. To make things worse, he caught my gaze and shook his head disappointingly. A bright blush climbed up my cheeks. "Well, it's not like I have your experience or anything, but—"

"That's definitely obvious. I mean, there was just *too* much tongue. Way too much."

The dimple in his right cheek popped up before he could turn his head away. I shoved him so he would be on the other side of the hall. "God, you're annoying."

"But you still like me." Evan ran his fingers through his hair, messing it up even more than I had, and adjusted the straps of his bag over his broad shoulders. "I was joking. You're a great kisser. Perfect even. And that kiss? Wow. I mean, it was just . . . sublime. Magical. I really think I saw stars for a moment, and that's not because of brain damage from your abuse."

"Shh!" I could see people turning around to stare at us as we walked by. I fumbled to cover his mouth. "Do you have to be so loud?"

"Why would I worry about a few people hearing about our *lurve*," Evan dragged out the last word as though he were singing. He ducked at the exact moment I reached out to smack him again. Instead, he grabbed my hand and pulled me closer to his side. "I'll be quiet if you walk me to civics."

I bit back the grin that crept up my face. "Fine."

His hand tightened around mine. "Well, come on. You don't want me to be late, right?"

Our arms swung between us, and I was surprised by how comfortable this was now. How nice it was to just laugh and not have to worry about who was watching. And to just do what we wanted.

Still...I couldn't help wondering if he was enjoying the moment as much as I was, or if it was just all in my head.

11

{Taylor}

Thanks for getting the snacks for me," I said over my shoulder to Brian. My eyes were glued to the computer screen as I finished typing up the checklist for Career Day to send to Mr. Peters. "I know I was supposed to prep for the meeting, but I have so much catching up to do for this event."

"It's fine. You know I don't mind helping."

"Yeah, I can always count on you. That's why I take advantage of you so much."

Brian chuckled and leaned against the edge of the table. "Gee, thanks for letting me know."

I gave him a cheeky grin. "No problem."

We were quiet for the next couple of minutes, but it was a comfortable silence as we both worked. Finally I clicked the Send button and swung around in my seat, stretching my hands over my head in triumph. "So, do you need me to do anything else?"

"Nah, I'm done." He checked his cell before shoving it back in his pocket. "And everyone should be here soon."

Nodding, I grabbed a small pretzel bag from the table and practically inhaled it within seconds. I was so excited today when Mr. Peters handed me back the reins for planning Career Day that I had barely eaten any lunch. I did have time to stop and smirk at Lin before leaving the cafeteria, though.

"So..." Brian cleared his throat a few times before continuing. "I've been meaning to ask you about Evan."

"Hmm?" With cheeks still puffed out, I swallowed and reached for another bag—Cheetos this time. "What about him?"

He shrugged. "It's just kind of strange. I mean, barely two weeks ago, you told me that there was nothing going on between you two. In this same room. And now you're dating?"

My eyes flicked down to the orange and blue bag in my hands. Did he suspect something? It sucked to lie to him, but I didn't have a choice. I couldn't tell Brian the truth. "I never *said* that there was nothing between us. I just said that nothing happened that night."

His eyebrows rose. "And now?"

"Uh..." Wait, was he asking me if Evan and I had had sex?

Suddenly realizing what he said, his cheeks flushed a dull pink—probably mirroring my own hot face. "No, I didn't—what I *meant* was that I'm just surprised you guys are dating. You guys don't look like you fit together. You're different."

Images of Evan and my conversations flashed in my head. "I thought so, too, but he's actually not that bad."

"Really? 'Cause he kind of seems like he doesn't care about school and college and stuff. You know, all the things that are important to you."

I got quiet at his words. Our relationship didn't make sense because *we* didn't make sense. Brian had me there. He saw things the same way I did. School and Columbia were my life. And even though I'd tried asking Evan about the college applications I had given him a few days ago, he never gave me a straight answer. No matter how many times I brought it up. I mean, he seemed interested at first, but I didn't know if he'd changed his mind at all.

But none of this mattered, since we weren't *actually* in a real relationship. It didn't matter if we didn't care about the same things or have anything in common. It didn't matter that our relationship experiences were on opposite ends of the spectrum. Or that his ex-friends-with-benefits friend was the image of raw sexuality, while I was a little choir girl. A choir girl who was studying to be a nun.

It didn't, because we weren't planning to ride into the sunset and live happily ever after. This was just for a contract. A deal.

The high of Career Day planning faded, and my appetite was gone. I crushed the remaining Cheetos in the bag into a fine powder. "We're just dating. It's nothing serious."

Nodding to himself, Brian scooted in and bent his head closer to me. He playfully nudged my elbow with his own. "Still, you have to admit, Evan isn't exactly the type of guy you bring home to your parents. Can you imagine the heart attack your mom might have?" His mock look of horror made me giggle.

At the thought of Evan hanging out with my parents, I couldn't help laughing even harder. "No, you're definitely right about that."

"Knock-knock."

We both looked up. Evan stood at the doorway. He had an easy smile plastered on his face, but it wasn't his normal smile. It was a little forced.

"Maybe I should have actually knocked." His hand rose and rapped against the heavy wooden door before he walked into the room.

How long had he been standing there? Did he hear us talking? Suddenly noticing how close Brian and I were, I awkwardly slid a few inches away from him. "Hey, what are you doing here?"

"I wanted to see if you needed a ride home. I could come back and pick you up."

Brian crossed his arms and straightened up, almost standing. "No, it's all right. I can drive her home later. It's on my way. Don't want to bother you or anything."

Evan's smile widened. "No, it's cool. Taylor could never bother me."

"But—"

"Uh, guys?" I waved my hands in both of their faces to get their attention. "I already made plans to go home with Carly. We're going to the mall later, so neither of you have to drive me."

"Oh." Brian sat back down.

"Okay, I just figured I'd ask." Evan flickered a sideways glance at Brian before coming forward and planting a quick kiss on my cheek. "I'll talk to you later, then."

"Okay." I echoed, feeling like I'd missed something. I wished Carly were here to explain what just happened, because I had no clue what was going on.

❧·❧

My physics homework was literally driving me crazy.

Biology was easy to understand, because it was something I could see—although I hated the guinea-pig dissections. I even understood chemistry to an extent. But physics? How was I supposed to see the relationship between the acceleration and mass of an object, much less calculate it?

It didn't help that I had a sucky teacher, either. Mr. Higgens was famous for two things. One: his pop quizzes. And two: his love for his son, Adrian, the famous doctor. All you had to do was ask about his son, and he'd talk the entire class period. Getting him to shut up was the problem.

I poked at my faded navy tights and watched my parents garden through the kitchen window. Mom played with the watering can and pretended to shower Dad. He shook himself like a dog, making her squeal with laughter. Oreo darted around and barked at their antics.

Despite being married for eight years, they were still lovey-dovey like a couple of teenagers. Although I was reaching the end of my teenage years, and I'd never acted like that.

My gaze turned to my reflection in the shiny window. I gathered my hair into a ponytail and turned my head from side to side. The simple hairstyle emphasized my face, and not in a good way. It made my face look longer and narrower. My lips seemed to swell in comparison. And my dark hair looked plain and lifeless as it hung straight down. Why couldn't my hair be a little curly or wavy, so it could have a natural bounce in it like—

Darn it. I was doing it again. I'd been subconsciously comparing myself to Lauren since Evan told me about their relationship. And the sinking pit in my stomach appeared every time I imagined them together.

"I'm not jealous. And I don't like Evan," I chanted out loud like a pledge. "This is just a business arrangement. No feelings or emotions are allowed. At all. It's in the contract."

Out of sight, out of mind. Today was my day off from the eyes and ears of everyone at school, and I was going to take advantage of this.

I chewed on the top of my pen and was deep in determining at what speed a 6-gram ball would hit the ground at a free fall off a 7-meter-high building, when a car door closed. My mind didn't absorb any information other than the fact that the noise was outside.

The next few minutes were quiet again, so I didn't think about it anymore. Until I saw my mom frantically waving for me to come outside while some guy talked next to her.

My eyes widened until they felt like they were going to fall out of my head. *What was he—why was he—*I shot out of my seat and was outside within seconds. I'd know those shoulders and spiky blond hair anywhere. But what the hell was Evan doing in my backyard, and why was he talking to my parents?

"Taylor, your friend Evan came by to visit. Isn't that sweet?" Mom exclaimed when I skidded to a stop in front of them.

"Yeah, sweet." I hoped my face wasn't as strained as it felt. My cheeks were stiff rubber bands that were still brand-new from the bag. I reached up to push my bangs out of my eyes, only to realize that the sleeves of my baggy gray sweatshirt flopped over my hands. I shoved both sleeves up my arms. "What are you doing here?"

His smile was wide and natural, as though there was nothing weird about him suddenly showing up at my house and chatting up my parents. Kimmy was plastered by his side, beaming up at him like he was her very own Prince Charming. I could practically see the bubble hearts shooting out of her eyes. "I was in the neighborhood and figured we could hang out. It's such a nice day that I assumed you'd be outside. Sorry if I'm intruding."

Mom linked arms with him. "No, that's fine. Taylor never has people over because she's always studying. To be honest, I didn't even know she had other friends besides Carly and Brian, although he never comes over. Even if Taylor wanted him to."

"MOM!"

Her blue eyes were wide and innocent when she looked over at me. "What, honey? It's true. There's nothing to be ashamed of."

Oh yeah? Then why did my cheeks feel like they were about to melt with humiliation? She was killing me, one embarrassing comment at a time.

Before I could answer, she turned back to Evan, flipping her hair over her shoulder like an infatuated teenager. *Flick. Swish.* Between her and Kimmy, it was like the start of the Evan McKinley Fan Club. "Why don't you and Taylor go inside? I think there's still some freshly squeezed lemonade in the fridge."

"Actually, I drank it all," I admitted before she shot me a disapproving look.

"Well, there's still some cola at least—"

"That's okay." Evan flashed his shiny smile that I knew cost Brandon a steep seven grand. His stepfather got the last laugh. Evan had told me the extractions hurt like hell, and he'd had to endure three years of braces. You wouldn't be able to tell if you looked at him now, though. At least I didn't. I just thought that he was one of those annoying naturally beautiful people.

"Actually, I wouldn't mind helping you weed." He shoved his hands in his pockets and tilted his head to the side. "If that's okay with you."

Okay, I had to be dreaming. Not only was Evan McKinley at my house, but he wanted to do yard work. *Offering* to be free manual labor.

Dad pounced on him. "Well, I'm sure as hell not going to say no to that." He wrapped an arm around Evan's shoulders. "You could finish up this patch right here. Want me to show you how it's done?"

"That'd be great."

Mom moved closer to me while they talked. "So how well do you two know each other?"

I pretended not to understand what she was asking. "Not that well. We've gone to school together for a while now but never had any classes together."

Just then Oreo trotted over to Evan and rolled over to lie against his side. Still listening to my dad, Evan squatted down and scratched Oreo's belly. His tail excitedly thumped against the grass.

She crossed her arms and gave me a knowing look. "Really? Because Oreo seems to disagree."

My face flushed, and I swept my hair up in a ponytail to give myself something to do. "That's great, Mom. You'd rather believe the dog than your own daughter."

"Well, Oreo doesn't know how to lie. And you do. You're a teenager, after all." She swept a couple of strands behind my ears. "At least I think you are. I'm not sure how old you are sometimes."

"Ha-ha."

Mom gave me a half smile. "Come on, Cole. I'm sure they can handle it. It's weeding, not rocket science."

"But it's very complicated—"

"How complicated could it be? You pull everything but the grass. I think even Taylor might be able to handle that," she teased, nudging my shoulder with her left elbow. "Come on, Kimmy."

Dad laughed. "You're right." They both moved a few feet away to the big teapot fountain they'd bought in Chinatown, dirt-smeared hand in dirt-smeared hand. Oreo raced over to join them. Kimmy gave us a sad look, but she followed Mom and Dad.

"What are you doing here?" I hissed through my thin smile.

Evan's grin brightened even more under the sun. "You got to meet my parents, so I thought it would only be fair that I meet yours."

"I met yours by *accident*."

"Technicality." He patted the patch of grass beside him. "Now, are you going to help me or not?"

I was tempted to, but I shoved that urge down. "I'm busy," I said, jerking my thumb over my shoulder at the house. "I still have to finish my physics homework."

"Aw, come on, you can finish that later. If you want, I could tutor you."

"You?"

Evan raised an eyebrow. "Yes, Ms. Know-It-All, me. I'll have you know that I have a knack for physics. The A I have in that class is the only thing that's saving me from my C in Spanish."

"You have a C in Spanish?"

"*Oui.* Hard to believe, huh?"

That's for sure. Stifling a laugh, I shuffled my weight from side to side before giving in. *Oh, what the hell.* I could use a break. The formulas weren't sinking in anyway. And it really was a nice day. Sunny, but still cloudy enough to give shade. There was even a light breeze that came by every few minutes. I sank down beside him and pulled at the weeds.

"So . . ." He scooted closer. "Brian never came over before?"

"No."

"Funny, he seems like the type of guy you'd want to bring home to your parents." The smugness in his voice was obvious.

His words rang in my head. I jerked around to look at him, and he had an amused, satisfied look on his face. "You over-heard our conversation yesterday?"

Evan rolled his eyes. "Well, it's not like you guys were whispering."

Not knowing what to say, I just ducked my head lower and pretended to be absorbed in digging out the roots.

"Don't get me wrong, Brian would be the better guy to bring home. He's perfect. Nauseatingly perfect." His voice grew softer. "Maybe you could start something up when we're done with 'our little thing.'"

This wasn't something that I hadn't thought of nearly a hundred times over the years. Brian hit every point on my list of the perfect guy. But I always figured that would happen later. "Yeah, maybe."

His eyes grew a little thoughtful at my answer. He stared at me for another minute or so before a huge grin crossed his face. "But you still won't work out in the end. You can't."

I didn't want to ask, but my curiosity got the better of me. "Why not?"

"Because you're both too smart. And I mean, *too* smart. Like any kid you have would be an evil genius who would end up taking over the world or something."

I snorted so loud that Mom and Dad looked over at us. I moved closer to Evan so they wouldn't hear. "I never thought of it that way."

"It's true. In fact, you're saving the world by being with me instead of him."

"Yeah, well, just call me Wonder Woman, I guess."

Now it was his turn to snort. "I wouldn't mind seeing you try on the costume." He looked me up and down in my oversize sweatshirt and tights and gave me a fake leer. "Definitely something to think about for next Halloween."

I sat back and pulled my knees up to cover my chest. "You'd just have to come up to New York to visit me at Columbia and see for yourself. Unless you'll be somewhere nearby anyway?"

"Yeah. Maybe."

Evan turned away and focused on the weeding, effectively ending the conversation like he always did when I brought up college.

I leaned my chin against my knee and rocked back and forth. Who would have thought that I, Taylor Simmons, would be weeding with Evan McKinley? Wasn't this what old married couples do?

Even though every girl at school lusted after him, I never did.

Okay, I did appreciate the great male specimen that he was, but he was too . . . burly. My eyes scanned his features. Although there's no denying that he looked good in his jeans and sweatshirt digging in the dirt.

He looked up and caught me midstare. *Crap.* I immediately dropped my eyes and attacked the weeds in front of me as though they were Lauren's hair. Or they had made me fail a class. He laughed under his breath, but he didn't say anything, Thank god. Still, I didn't dare look up again until my face stopped burning.

Having green thumbs clearly wasn't hereditary, since both Mom and Dad loved to garden, while Kimmy and I barely knew the difference between wet dirt and mud. But the weeding itself wasn't that bad. It distracted me. I just focused on the task at hand. See a weed and yank on it until the roots come loose. Mom was right. It really wasn't rocket science.

It wasn't long before Mom and Dad dusted off their hands and got up. "I think we should call it quits. It's starting to get dark," Dad said, already gathering the spades and shovels on the ground.

"I'll start dinner. You'll stay for dinner, won't you, Evan?"

"Sure, Mrs. Simmons."

When they left, Evan stood up and stretched. Despite my determination not to, my eyes couldn't help watching him roll his shoulders to get the kinks out. He stooped over, picked a dandelion from the trash pile, and tucked it in my hair. I never would have thought that gesture would be romantic, but my knees got a little weak. No one had ever given me flowers before. "Come on. Let's hang out for a bit."

"But my homework—"

"Will still be there in twenty minutes."

I stumbled to my feet and followed him to the hammock beneath the oak tree on the far end of the yard. He jumped on like it was a trampoline. It swung back and forth dangerously, but with his arms braced outward, he was able to keep his balance. When it finally slowed enough, Evan flopped backward. His right leg was propped up against the tree, pushing against it ever so slightly, while his other leg dangled inches above the ground.

At first I sat beside him, but the swaying kept knocking me over, and I ended up lying next to him, arms folded across my chest.

He let out a low chuckle, "You don't do this very often, do you?"

"What? Garden?"

"Let loose. Not be so uptight all the time."

"I'm not uptight."

"Oh yeah?"

Suddenly, Evan reached out and swept a dirt-smeared finger down my cheek. I froze. I knew he expected me to wipe it off. But I was more aware of his hand on my face than the dirt and dust that was filled with germs and the remains of various bugs and worms—okay, so maybe I was more than a little grossed out by it.

I rested my cheek against his shoulder, deliberately rubbing it against his sweatshirt. He chuckled but didn't move.

We rocked back and forth on the hammock. Side by side. Nothing touching other than our pinky fingers. Still keeping my eyes glued to the sky, I edged my hand even closer and nudged him. Out of the corner of my eyes, I could see him give me a sideways glance before hooking his pinky with mine, linking us together as though we were promising to keep a secret. Which in a way, we were.

⌒).~

After dinner, while Evan and my mom were getting chummy over the dishes, I sat at the counter and peered out the window. There was only a sliver of pinkish-orange hue on the horizon beyond the fence. The stars were already starting to peek out.

Evan sniffed at the air a few times. "Okay, I swear I was going crazy all through dinner, but I have to ask. Is there apple pie or something somewhere? I keep smelling it."

Mom laughed and handed him the dishes she had just washed so he could dry them. "No, I wish. I can't bake at all. I just love the smell of apples and cinnamon."

"Me, too. Although I wouldn't say no to apple pie, either," he said with a grin. "But dinner was awesome. Thanks, Mrs. Simmons."

She waved a soapy hand in the air. "I'm glad you liked it! Come over anytime you want."

Dad and Kimmy plopped down on either side of me with their bowls of ice cream. "Seriously, come every day if you want. We don't get to eat as well when you're not here," Dad said with a grin.

Mom shot him a dark look. "Are you saying I don't usually cook well?"

"No, just not *as* well." His grin widened. "I love you."

She rolled her eyes and turned back to the sink.

Kimmy fiddled with her curly brown hair. She had this weird dreamy look on her face. "Yeah, Mom, you made the potatoes all whipped and fancy, 'cause Evan said he likes mashed potatoes like that. I like picking out the lumps you usually have—"

Getting up from his seat, Dad rubbed the top of her head to interrupt her before Mom went nuts. "Well, lumps or no lumps, I thought it was delicious."

"I agree." Evan dropped the dish towel on the counter and strolled over to me. To my surprise, he took off his green-and-gray sweatshirt and wrapped it around my shoulders. "You looked kind of cold. So, ready for some physics fun?"

My mouth curled into a smile so wide that my cheeks hurt. "I've never heard the words *physics* and *fun* together in a sentence before."

"I thought we already established that you don't even know what the word *fun* means?" he quipped, dropping into Dad's seat next to me. He grabbed my notebook and textbook from me.

"Taylor?" On my other side, Kimmy tugged on my arm. Her big blue eyes blinked up at me, a startling shade of blue that was so different from my dull brown eyes. They sparkled with excitement. "Is he your boyfriend?"

I peeked over at Evan, but he was busy flipping through my physics book with a pencil in his hand. His forehead was kind of scrunched up as he read through the assignment. I looped my arm around her shoulders and leaned toward her.

"Yeah, he is," I finally whispered, not caring that she was probably going to tell Mom later. Or that Mom was going to go berserk on me.

Or even admitting to myself how nice that sounded.

12

-Evan-

Valentine's Day.

Usually a day I avoided like the plague. Not only because of the sickening couples making doe eyes at each other all day, but because single chicks would be on the prowl. Not always a bad thing, unless you hooked up with one of them on Valentine's Day. Then they'd think it was fate or some shit like that and get even clingier. Trust me.

But this year was different. This year I had a girlfriend—god, that still sounded weird to say—or whatever the hell Taylor and I were. We weren't exactly dating, but we were way past regular friends. She was fun to hang out with. And one hell of a kisser. I wasn't lying about that. That girl had the ability to get me hot within seconds. And I took extreme pleasure in making her kiss me in public whenever I could.

Not to mention, Brandon talked less shit about me when Taylor was around, and Mom seemed happier because of it.

Either way, I thought I'd surprise her with some flowers when I picked her up for school. Sort of as a thank-you for making my life bearable the past couple of weeks. Taylor was probably more of a pink-roses type of girl then red roses. Pink seemed sweeter.

When I grabbed my keys from the front table, I accidentally knocked over Mom's day planner. Little business cards and sticky notes spilled everywhere, littering the ground. Mom was a hoarder when it came to business cards.

"Damn it." I started stacking everything together when a letter caught my eye. A card with familiar handwriting on the front. *Dad's* handwriting. To Mom.

What the hell?

I stared at the creamy yellow envelope, but the jagged handwriting didn't change. My drawer was filled with loads of letters from him when he was in jail, or what Mom called his "work retreats." I knew exactly where he was but pretended not to. As long as the letters kept coming. Then Mom married Brandon, and everything stopped completely. I never heard from him again. So why was he writing to Mom? And why didn't she tell me?

Even if I was somehow mistaken about the handwriting, his name was right *there*. James McKinley, 5251 Alba Road, Destin, Florida.

Why did she say she *thought* he was "somewhere in Florida"? His address was right there. She *knew* exactly where he lived, and she never told me. Never mentioned a visit, despite the fact that she knew I missed him.

My mind raced with unanswered questions, but Mom

wasn't home to answer them. Brandon had taken her away for some fancy spa day. I didn't know if I wanted to know the answers, anyway. I just—I just needed to get out of here. To get away. I shoved the card back in her bag and stumbled to my feet.

My head was still in a daze, and my stomach clenched as though I'd been punched in the gut. Repeatedly. But somehow I miraculously made it out the door and into my car. But I didn't drive. Not yet. I cranked up my radio as loud as I could, not caring what song was on. I didn't even know what station it was. My breath came out in a steady stream, and all I could do was concentrate on breathing until the noise filled my head and I couldn't think anymore.

My ears were still ringing when I finally pulled up to Taylor's house. She was already sitting on the front steps, waiting. Her left hand tapped a rhythm against her thigh while she muttered something to herself. Probably cursing at me. A frown crossed her face when she spotted me. As ridiculous as it sounds, I was happy to see that frown. To me, that was the most beautiful sight in the world. At least I knew I couldn't obsess about my dad while she was lecturing me.

"You're late," she said as soon as she opened the door and slid into the passenger seat. Taylor heaved a heavy sigh before dropping her bag at her feet and clicking on her seat belt, all while still not looking at me. "And now so am I."

"Sorry."

That's all I said, but her head snapped up to look at me as though I had poured out all my problems in that one word. Her eyes searched my face for answers. Shit. Damn her and her intuition. I gave her a wide smile, but she still didn't look convinced.

"It's okay. It's not like anything important happens in homeroom, anyway." She carefully eyed me again before patting the dashboard. "Was Rudy giving you trouble or something?"

"No."

Our conversation died down, and though occasionally Taylor attempted to cheer me up, she couldn't erase my somber mood. At this point, I didn't think anything could.

There was always a tiny part of me that wondered if Dad hadn't fought for us because he didn't want us anymore. The fact that he was still in contact with Mom, yet never bothered to call or even write a postcard to me, made me wonder if I was the problem.

Shit. It was just so much easier to blame Brandon.

Taylor was concentrating so hard on figuring out what else to say that there were little frown lines on her forehead while she gnawed on her lower lip. Somehow, she managed to look like both a little kid and an old lady at the same time.

Despite my crappy mood, I couldn't help smiling at her. Something red poked out beneath her dark hair. What in the world . . . my fingers gently ruffled through her smooth hair and pulled out a single bright-red rose petal. "What's this?"

"What?" She reached behind her head and grasped my hand. The petal crumbled between our fingers. She squinted at it for a moment as though even *she* didn't know why it was there. "Oh, Dad asked me to help him with Mom's Valentine's Day surprise. We sprinkled rose petals around her while she was sleeping. Until Kimmy stepped on a thorn and started yelling." With a shake of her head, she laughed and dropped it in the ashtray between us.

Roses. The grocery store. I smacked my palm against my forehead. "Shit."

She stopped fiddling with the radio and glanced over her shoulder. "What's wrong?"

"I was going to get you some roses from the store." I shook my head. "I can't believe I forgot."

"It's fine. Don't worry about it."

But it wasn't fine. It only reminded me of *why* I had forgotten to get the flowers in the first place. My stomach tightened again as I gripped the steering wheel. My knuckles grew taut and pale, and I felt sick. Screw school. "Listen, I'm going to drop you off at the front steps, okay? So no one will see me."

"You're not going to class?"

I forced myself to loosen my grip and drummed a beat on the steering wheel with one hand instead. "No, I have some things to do. I'll be back later."

"Is it that drug-testing thing again?"

Although we'd only been "together" a little while, I had finally told her the truth, and she was pissed off on my behalf. Even though I didn't care anymore, it was nice to have someone on my side for once.

I could lie and say it was, but knowing Taylor, she'd probably weasel the truth out of me sooner or later. "No, it's not that. It's . . . complicated."

"Hmm . . . does it have something to do with your daddy issues?"

I nearly slammed on the brakes. "I don't have daddy issues."

"We both do. And yours are written all over your face." She gave me a teasing smile and shook her head. "Don't worry. I'm more screwed up than you are. My issues are all over the place." Her hand motioned up and down her body.

"Really? I'll have to check that out someday."

She poked a finger in my cheek and pushed my face forward. "The only place you'll see that is in your dreams. Now, keep your eyes on the traffic."

"Yes, ma'am." I pulled up in the front yard and parked right by the doors. "If you feel the need to make up an excuse for my absence, don't deny the urge. The more elaborate, the better."

"How about I tell people a dragon carried you off to its lair so you could be a nanny for its babies?"

"As long as it's a water dragon and not a fire-breathing one, then I'm good with that."

Her eyes narrowed, but she didn't nag me about going to class like I expected her to. She just leaned closer—her forehead was scrunched together with worry—and reached out to touch my arm. "Are you sure you're okay?"

As okay as I'll ever be. I froze for a moment, letting her soft touch calm me. When I felt semirelaxed, I let out a deep sigh and grasped her hand, holding it tightly to my body. "Yeah, I'm fine. Wait for me later. I'll bring something back for us for lunch."

"Okay." Taylor got out of the car, careful to close her door gently instead of slamming it like she usually did. "Text me later."

"I will."

As I drove away, I glanced down at the petal she left

behind in my ashtray. I half wished that I *had* asked her to go with me. Even though I was pretty sure she wouldn't, since she had a quiz in history later, she might have skipped if she'd known how much I needed it. How I didn't want to be alone right now.

But my pride kept me from turning around.

— • —

By the time lunch rolled around, I was back at school and almost back to normal. I didn't talk to Mom. She hadn't picked up any of my calls, and I sure as hell wasn't desperate enough to call Brandon.

And I was fine. There wasn't anything I could do, even if I wasn't. What was I supposed to do? Sit at home and pout and cry like a sissy until Mom came home?

Instead, I concentrated on my surprise for Taylor. Since I had already dropped the ball and forgot about her flowers this morning, I figured I could get lunch for her at least. And as usual, my brilliance stepped up. Along with Aaron. He even cut fourth period to help me set up the surprise. Although that was probably more because he wanted to avoid our Spanish test than out of best-friend duty.

I'd never done anything like this for a girl before, but it was kind of fun trying to figure out a way to surprise her.

As I leaned against the cafeteria doorway to wait for Taylor, a group of junior girls giggled when they passed me. I gave them a wink out of habit, and one of them blushed. It was nice to see that I still had it.

Finally, Taylor appeared with Carly and Brian. Their arms were all loaded down with art supplies and sketchpads. "'Bout time you showed up."

"'Bout time you got to school," she quipped in response. She looked relieved for a moment until an irritated expression crossed her face. Scowling, she nodded toward my fans, who scattered into the cafeteria at the sight of her. "Friends of yours?"

"You could say that. Jealous?"

"Ha! You wish."

Despite her snort, I could see the pink-stained cheeks that she tried to hide. I wrapped an arm around her shoulders and leaned in to whisper in her ear. "Don't worry, I still remember the rules of our agreement. No screwing around, remember?" I glanced over her shoulder at Brian, who was pretending not to watch us. "Or is it you who needs the reminder?"

Taylor rolled her eyes. "Whatever. Come on, I'm starving."

My arm shot out to stop her when she started to go in. "Actually, I was thinking we could eat outside." I shot a look at the other two. "Alone. Sorry, guys."

Brian opened his mouth, but Carly just pushed him aside and smiled brightly. "Of course. It *is* Valentine's Day." She juggled her stuff in the crook of one arm and took everything from Taylor. "You guys go ahead."

I cocked my head toward her. "I always knew I liked you, Carly."

"That's because I'm so understanding." She let out a dramatic sigh and flipped her dark hair over her shoulder. "It's both a blessing and a curse."

Brian rolled his eyes and scowled. "Whatever. Come on, I'm starving."

Taylor waited until they left before turning back to me. Her left brow arched up. "So why are we eating outside?"

I wrapped an arm around her shoulders and steered her down the hall. "Because it's nice."

"It's pouring."

"I didn't say the *weather* was nice. I just said eating outside was nice," I said, quickening my step. "Come on."

"That makes no sense." Taylor shook her head and hitched her backpack higher on her shoulders. "What is it with you and nature?"

"You'll see."

"Gee, you're being so mysterious and—oh!" Her jaw dropped, and she stopped in her tracks.

A long piece of clear tarp was draped from branch to branch of the trees outside. And beneath it, right in the center, was the long picnic table that Aaron and I had dragged over from the other end of the yard. It looked like a large tent in the middle of the yard. A large pizza box, along with paper plates and napkins, was right in the middle of the table, weighed down by a large rock I had found. Even the steady stream of rain falling from each corner of the tarp made the little shelter look more intimate and romantic.

I had to admit, I was pretty proud of myself. Yep, I couldn't do better if I tried.

Damn, I was good.

Ushering her forward, I used my hands to shield the top of her head from the rain. "Come on." I didn't know how long the tarp was going to hold, so we had to make it quick.

Taylor didn't say anything. She just followed me as though still in a daze. Her head whipped back and forth before she sat down. She didn't even seem to realize that the end of her ponytail was wet.

I opened the pizza box with a flourish and bowed like a waiter at a five-star restaurant. "Voilà! Made especially just for you, madam."

Her laughter practically filled the yard. She pulled the box toward her, and her eyes shone with tears as she stared inside at the large pizza, piled so high with mushrooms that you could barely see the tomato sauce and cheese. "Exactly how I like it."

"This is the first-ever mushroom pizza where there's more mushrooms than bread." I handed her a plate. "Everyone gave me a weird look when I ordered this. They made me re-peat myself three times to make sure I wasn't joking. One guy even took a picture of it when they were done."

"But this is totally worth it." Taylor bit into her slice, and bits of mushrooms fell on her plate. She picked up each of them and popped them in her mouth. A look of ecstasy crossed her face. "Yum! It's like I've died and gone to heaven."

"You have a pretty weird idea of what heaven is like."

"It's whatever you want it to be." She shoved another bite in her mouth. "So for you, it'd be a beach filled with girls and Rudy right in the middle."

I grinned. She acted like she knew me so well. Although the idea she painted *did* sound pretty good. "You forgot video games."

"Right, the zombies and aliens."

For the next few minutes, she was so absorbed in her

pizza, it was like she forgot I was even there. I didn't mind. I just kept watching her as I dug in. And I couldn't help comparing her to the other girls I'd dated. A lot of them were used to doing what they wanted and played games with me. Like it was a challenge to keep me interested. Which it was. But Taylor . . . she could be happy with a dandelion or even a few extra pieces of mushrooms. And I never grew bored with her.

Even though I bought a large pizza, Taylor was able to eat almost as much as I did, despite the fact that she was a third of my weight.

She let out a satisfied groan and wiped her mouth with a napkin. "I'm dying, and I still want more."

"There's still one slice left."

"Jeez, don't tempt me. I'm this close to having you carry me to class." She held her thumb and her index finger an inch apart.

"We could still do that. I mean, now that our relationship's old news, we have to do something to spice it up again." I flexed my arms and grinned. "Even with the pizza, I think I can still handle you."

Taylor laughed and closed the pizza box. "I thought the point of us being together was to make the gossip die down?"

Was it? Sometimes I forgot why we were pretending in the first place. Being with her was so natural. It was easy and fun. I almost didn't miss the lack of bed action these days. Almost.

"I have something else for you. Sort of," I said, changing the subject as I pulled the packet of papers from my book bag and waved them in front of her face.

"More?" She took the papers from me with a confused look. "But these are the applications that I gave to you . . ."

"Except now they're filled out."

Her brown eyes widened with shock, and she fumbled through them. "Wait, what?"

I couldn't help but grin with pride at her surprise. It was Aaron's idea. Sort of. I was going to get flowers with the pizza, but he told me to do something that was important to her. And the college applications just popped in my head. Still, I tried to play it off with a shrug. "I had nothing better to do earlier, so I figured why not?"

Her eyes shone with excitement. "This is way better than roses. Even better than jewelry!"

I rolled my eyes and laughed. "You're really weird, you know that?"

"I prefer the word *special*." Taylor gave me back the applications with a huge smile. "So you're going to mail these out, right? Like today? Right after school?"

"Yeah, but that's it. No promises after that." I still didn't know if I wanted to go to college. Hell, maybe Taylor was right and it was already too late. But if it wasn't . . . it was kind of nice to have the option. Keep the door open, at least.

She lifted her legs on the bench and leaned back on her palms. "I can't believe you did all of this for me."

I shrugged and mimicked her stance on the other bench. "It's not a big deal. It wasn't that much trouble."

Her voice grew so soft that it was hard to hear her over the rain. "No, it is a big deal. It's a *huge* deal. I—" She broke off and looked away.

"What?"

"Nothing. I just wanted to say thanks."

There was more that she wasn't saying, but I wasn't going

to force it out of her. I doubted that I could. Not only because she was a girl, but because sometimes she could be one of the most stubborn girls I'd ever met.

"No problem." I glanced at my watch and frowned. Damn it. It was already almost time to go. How did the hour pass so quickly? "We should get back. Don't want to be late for class."

"Nope, don't want that." She laughed to herself.

"What's wrong?"

"Nothing. I just think it's weird to see you worried about class, that's all."

It *was* weird. But I wasn't worried for myself. I was worried for her. I snorted at the irony and tucked the box beneath my arm. "Well, stranger things have happened."

"You mean, like us getting together?"

"Just about." We stood on the edge of the shaded tarp and peered out at the rain. "Maybe we should wait for the rain to die down."

In response, a streak of lighting tore across the sky, and the rain pounded down even harder than before.

She chewed on her lower lip. "We'll be here forever."

"Is that so bad?" Without waiting for her answer, I grabbed Taylor's hand, and we raced across the grass. Our shoes made wet suction noises with each step. Even though we ran as fast as we could, we were both drenched when we got to the door. Taylor didn't seem to mind, judging by her laughter, which grew louder when I shook my head. Droplets flew at her.

"Evan?"

"Yeah?" My breath got caught in my throat. Her hair

glistened with raindrops. Dark strands were plastered to her face. And her cheeks were pale from the cold. I don't know how I ever thought she was plain. She'd never looked more gorgeous to me.

Taylor grasped the top of my arms, and I froze. I could only watch wordlessly as she lifted on her toes to gently kiss my lips, even though there wasn't anyone around to watch. "Happy Valentine's Day."

13

-Evan-

There was a surprise waiting for me onshore after my morning surf that Saturday. Lauren was lounging on a huge beach blanket with a carton of fresh strawberries and a brand-new jar of Nutella. Her long-sleeved cream dress barely skimmed her thighs and was so sheer that I could see her blue bikini underneath. Small, stringy, and fitting in all the right places. And definitely not leaving much to the imagination. She lay on her stomach with her feet kicked up in the air behind her. "Hey, stranger."

"Hey." Propping my board on its side, I dropped down beside her with a surprised grin. "Why are you here so early, bearing gifts?"

"I just thought we could hang out and have breakfast." She bit into a strawberry and licked at the juice that ran down her fingers. "Maybe sweeten you up a bit so you won't say no."

I grabbed a strawberry and used the tip to scoop up a huge chunk of the chocolate spread. "Say no about what?"

"About going on a date tonight." She reached out and swiped a little bit of chocolate off my strawberry with a grin. "I have some concert tickets at the new club downtown. I figured we could have a couple of drinks before heading over there. And then, who knows what happens next."

It sounded tempting. Really temping. Especially because I knew that Lauren's idea of "what happens next" would probably have us in bed somewhere. Or in the back of a car.

I whistled low under my breath and turned away, avoiding her gaze. Her offer was so tempting, and god knows it had been so long since I'd had sex that I had practically forgotten how to do it. But I couldn't do that to Taylor. Fake relationship or not.

I had thought that having a steady, routine relationship would be the most boring thing in the world, and I'd rather jump off a cliff than be in one. Regular dates. Hand-holding. Seeing the same person every damn day. Kissing the same lips all the time. *God, kill me now.*

But it was . . . nice. And more fun than I expected it to be. I was even looking forward to the next time I would have dinner with Taylor's family. It was nice to sit through a family dinner. Mom tried to get Brandon and me to eat together all the time, but just seeing his face gave me indigestion.

At my hesitation, Lauren pursed her lips together in annoyance. "Let me guess, you're busy tonight?"

I took a bite of the strawberry before answering. "Yeah, I actually am. I have a date with Taylor."

She rolled her eyes. "Figures. What's wrong with you?"

"What do you mean?"

"I mean you're always busy these days." Her blue eyes narrowed, and she sat up. Her arms crossed across her chest. "Everybody knows about that picnic you two had at school. I thought you had a sacred rule about not doing anything on Valentine's Day?"

I popped the rest of the strawberry in my mouth and tried to hide my goofy grin as I thought about our picnic. And the sweet kiss Taylor gave me afterward. No need to get Lauren even more pissed than she already was.

All my rules were breaking for Taylor these days. Like today. I was supposed to come over and help her babysit Kimmy so she could focus on some Student Council thing. Or a presentation. She was always doing so many things that it was hard for me to keep track of everything. But I didn't mind. Much. I never would admit it to anyone, but I wanted to hang out with Taylor. Even if it was just to be her minion for the night. Plus, she had a way of taking my mind off missing dads, lying moms, and shit like that.

"I thought I told you before that Taylor's not like the other girls?"

That was definitely the wrong thing to say. Lauren's face grew even colder. "So you're saying that *she's* different, but I'm just like one of the other girls."

"No, 'course not. You're my friend—" Her right eyebrow rose even higher. Crap, nothing I said would make this better. Man, she was touchy today. Probably best to just retreat while I still could. I hopped to my feet and grabbed my board. "You know, I think I'm going to surf a bit more before heading home."

The water was icy cold and the waves were rough, but I'd rather face those crazy conditions than the pissed-off girl onshore. Lying on the board, I paddled my way farther into the ocean. I knew I couldn't stay out there forever, but I could still try.

Maybe Aaron's cowardice was contagious.

— • —

My head slumped down into my arms, and I sighed. Again. Which Taylor ignored. Again. "Has anyone ever told you that you're a slave driver? Dude, you're like a work Nazi. Don't you ever take a break?"

"I'll take a break when the work is done." Her eyes were still glued to the laptop she balanced on her lap. Without looking up, she shoved a pile of papers on the coffee table toward me with her foot. "Which, by the way, is never going to get done if you keep taking a bathroom break every two seconds. Are you sure you don't have diabetes or a prostate problem or something?"

"I don't have diabetes, and my prostate is perfectly healthy." I leaned toward her and raised a suggestive eyebrow. "You want to check to make sure?"

"No, thank you. I have my hands full as it is."

Even though Taylor denied it, I knew I was definitely rubbing off on her. A few weeks ago, she had blushed bright red at the mention of her underwear, and now here she was, sitting all prim and proper in the living room, talking about my junk with barely a tint of pink in her cheeks. I'm pretty sure I deserved an award for that. Instead, I was stuck working on the senior-class budget because, according to Taylor, our class treasurer was "a flake." I had to take her word for it, because I didn't know who the hell our treasurer was.

I didn't even know we had a class budget.

Still, I kind of thought she was kidding. Rule number one about Taylor: The girl never kids when it comes to schoolwork.

So here I was at her house babysitting Kimmy while her parents were partying like normal people. Actually, they had gone to an office dinner, so probably not quite the partying I was used to, but they were still out.

Don't get me wrong, I'd babysat with girls before, but I usually got some action in return when the kid fell asleep. And I definitely didn't spend the entire night punching numbers into a calculator.

I thought about Lauren a couple of times. Kind of hard not to. She kept texting me every ten minutes to see what I was doing and if I had changed my mind about meeting her.

My phone buzzed again, and Taylor peered over at me with a frown, as if she were a teacher and my phone was interrupting her class. "Lauren again?"

"Uh, yeah." Her frown deepened until finally I turned off the phone and tossed it on the coffee table. "So if I didn't tell you already, your idea of a Saturday night is awesome. Way to be wild."

Her gaze stayed on the laptop screen, but a smile tugged at her lips. "Thank you. And I do know how to be wild. Just in a responsible way. I'm doing this work now so I can be free to go to a play with Carly and Brian tomorrow."

My hands rose up in mock surrender. "Whoa, wild and responsible. Maybe I should call the police." I waited a minute for her to finish laughing. "So a play, huh? With Carly *and* Brian?"

"Yeah, one of Carly's theater friends is in it, and she was hoping to meet the director. Maybe act in a couple of his other plays this summer. We're just going to give her some moral support."

I nodded. "Thanks for the invite, by the way. I like plays, too, you know."

She looked up at me in surprise. Even I had to cringe at the jealousy in my voice. "I figured you'd be busy. You told me you had some epic boys' night planned with Aaron tomorrow, right?"

Shit, she was right. I was supposed to be his wingman. I'd been so busy with Taylor these days that Aaron had pulled the best-friend card to get me to help him with some chick he was crushing on. Although *epic* wasn't the word to describe what he had planned. The girl Aaron liked only worked at the bowling alley on Family Sunday Funday, so we'd be spending the night with parents and their kids. I didn't want to go, but he blackmailed me with embarrassing stories about my first time. Let's just say I was nervous and shaking so much that the girl asked if I was having a seizure.

Still, the thought of Brian and Taylor together in a dark theater made my stomach clench. Who cares about bro code and stories that could ruin my reputation?

Taylor was still staring at me, so I flipped through the pages she handed me before changing the subject. "You know, I should just ditch you. You'd never be able to catch me with your short legs. And by the time you walked to my house to yell at me, I could have at least twenty minutes of game time. Even longer, if my mom doesn't let you in."

Taylor's grin was wide and beaming over the top of the screen. "But you know that she will. She loves me. And don't even think about locking your bedroom door, either, because I know how to pick locks."

"Whatever."

"It's true. Kimmy used to accidentally lock herself in her room all the time when she was small, so I learned how to pick the lock. I could do it with a credit card or a bobby pin. Heck, I could even do it with a fork."

My eyebrows rose. "Really? A fork?"

"Seriously." She lifted her arms and made a popping motion with her hands. Her lips even smacked together to make the popping noise to emphasize it. "A few seconds, and you'd have nowhere to hide."

I laughed and shook my head. "And just when I thought you couldn't surprise me anymore, I find out about your burgling talent. I guess that's something you could fall back on if the lawyering thing doesn't work out."

Her lips pursed together, and she shook her head. "Yeah, that's not going to happen. There's no falling back on anything."

Jeez, we couldn't even joke about her failing. Even though Taylor wasn't a stuck-up, stick-in-the-mud Ice Queen like everyone said she was—and believe me, this was the *nicest* thing they said—she never joked about her aspirations to be a lawyer. Her determination was annoying, but admirable at the same time. Like Taylor herself.

Although some days, she was more annoying than others.

My toes poked Oreo in his side as he lay beside the coffee table, gnawing on a chew toy. At first he didn't move, but after a couple of jabs, he growled, grabbed his toy in case I was going to steal it, and scooted back a few feet until he was out of reach.

Taylor rolled her eyes and laughed. "Yeah, you're working *really* hard."

"Well, harder than I've ever worked on a Saturday."

"That's not saying much."

Her sarcastic tone made my mouth jerk into a half grin. "That's true, but that's because I'm usually *enjoying* myself on Saturday."

She snuggled deeper in her seat. Her feet were crossed on the table between us. "Yeah, I can imagine exactly how you enjoyed yourself with other girls. But doesn't that get boring after a while?"

"Not if you're doing it right." Taylor didn't say anything and went back to typing on her laptop. "And I did plenty of stuff with them." *And on them,* I silently added. "Lauren was a pro. Maybe you should ask her for some tips."

Her hands froze. Finally, that got a reaction out of her. She sat up straighter and glared at me. "Like what?"

I wasn't sure why this irritated her so much, but I couldn't resist pushing her even more toward the edge. "Anything, really. She really was something else. I mean, you're great and all, but it's not like you have me eating out of the palm of your hand."

She cocked her head to one side and crossed her arms. "Oh really?"

Another push. "You could *try,* but I doubt you could pull it off."

And over the edge she went. Her dark eyes flashed and narrowed until they were small slits. Taylor snapped the laptop shut with one hand. "There's one more thing you need to learn about me."

"And what's that?"

"I don't like to be challenged."

She got up and, in one fluid motion, flopped on the cushion beside me. Intrigued, I folded my arms and sat back, waiting to see what she would do next. Not wanting to scare her off or make her change her mind, I didn't move. My eyes watched her every movement. Every deep breath that she took. Every inch she slid closer.

I had lied. Sort of. Taylor did have me in the palm of her hand. She just didn't realize it. Not like the other girls. They used their bodies to get what they wanted from me. Cheesy as it was, Taylor used her heart. I did whatever she wanted just to make her happy. Hell, that was the reason we were in this relationship to begin with.

Like I said, *Taylor* wasn't like any of the other girls. She was sweet. Fun. And it was easy to be with her. No games. I didn't feel like I had to impress her like the other girls. With them, I had a reputation to uphold. With Taylor, I thought she'd rather forget I had a reputation at all. Hell, even her inexperience made things fun.

She wasn't acting inexperienced now, though. I didn't know who this girl was and what had come over her, but I couldn't be happier. This was the first time that she had ever taken charge. God, it was hot.

And she was taking her sweet time. Every inch that she got closer felt like an hour. I didn't think it was possible, but the waiting made things even hotter. We weren't even touching yet, and my nerves were already going haywire.

Finally, she laid her hand on my shoulder and leaned toward me. Her fingertips played with the sleeve of my T-shirt, sliding beneath it to stroke my arm. My skin. I could smell her breath—feel it—minty and warm on my cheek. My heart started pumping overtime. My hands fell to my side and clenched tightly, fighting the urge to grab her.

Right before her lips touched mine, they quirked into a smirk, as though she knew exactly how affected I was, even though I tried to hide my eagerness. Another thing I didn't know about Taylor. She was a tease. A major one.

Even though I was dying to deepen the kiss, I held back, determined to let her set the pace. It took all my willpower to stick to that when her hand slid even farther and stroked my chest. Her touch was light and brief, but each spot she touched was burning and made me ache for more. *Don't grab her. Don't push her against the cushions. Don't—*

Damn it, why didn't I wear a baggier shirt today?

With her lips still on mine, she snuggled even closer until she was almost straddling my left leg. And she didn't do it very gracefully, either. Her knee jabbed my thigh. I grunted and shifted my position so she wouldn't accidentally hit me in the wrong area and ruin the night. Hell, if she hit me *there*, it would probably ruin my entire week.

When the danger was gone and everything was

protected, my hand ran through her hair, letting the soft strands wrap around my fingers as I held her as close as I could. The hell with letting her call the shots. This was the closest I'd been to a girl in ages, and I was a starving man at a buffet. Taylor in a field of mushrooms.

Taylor didn't seem to mind. Her arms wrapped around my neck and pulled me upward until our bodies were plastered to each other. My hands slid down her back, hesitating for a few seconds when I felt the warm, soft skin between the hem of her t-shirt and the top of her shorts. She stiffened and stopped the kiss, but she didn't push me away. Instead, she rested her forehead against my neck as though she were enjoying my caress. I ran my finger along the edge and wondered if I could get away with reaching in and—

A small voice spoke up. "Taylor?"

Taylor jerked upright and jumped off my lap within a blink of an eye, shoving me away from her side. Her cheeks grew blotchy and red as she tried to fix her hair. "Hey, Kimmy. Did you—did you just wake up?"

Kimmy rubbed her eyes and let out a yawn so wide, I could see a silver filling on the bottom right side. "Yeah, I wasn't sleepy."

"Talk about bad timing," I muttered, grunting when Taylor smacked my shoulder. "*Urgh*, I mean, that sucks. Are you *sure* you're not sleepy? Maybe some milk or NyQuil to help? It's yummy." Taylor smacked me even harder.

Kimmy didn't take the hint. Instead, she planted herself on the floor right between us. Her face was propped on the couch cushion and her eyes were wide as she stared at us.

The fact that I was still turned on made things more than just a little awkward.

Taylor let out a sigh. "Fine, you can stay up a little longer, but after that, you have to go straight to bed." Her eyes flickered to my hopeful face. "When Evan goes home."

Damn, she couldn't get any more blunt than that. Playtime was over, and another cold shower was waiting for me when I got home. I stifled another groan and slumped down on the cushions.

Kimmy's eyes lit up, and she crawled up on the couch beside us. "Do you want to play date night with us, Evan?"

Taylor coughed and frantically waved her hands. "No, no, I don't think he wants to play."

Her panicked tone piqued my interest. "Why not? What's the date-night game?"

"It's when I get Taylor ready for her date," Kimmy said brightly, while Taylor buried her face in a blue tasseled pillow behind her sister's back.

"Real date?"

"No, Taylor never goes on real dates." She let out a squeal when Taylor clasped her hand on her mouth.

"I *do* go on dates!"

"Of course you do," I replied in a calming tone to placate her. It didn't work, though. When she turned her irritated face to glare at me, I saved Kimmy from her grasp. "Why don't you get me ready for a date, Kimmy?"

Taylor shook her head. "Oh no, I don't think you want to—"

" 'Course I do. Kimmy and I are tight like that." I wrapped an arm around Kimmy's tiny shoulders. "Besides, it sounds like fun."

When Kimmy gleefully ran out of the living room to get her "stuff," Taylor sent me a look that told me I'd regret my offer.

I did.

Minutes later, my face felt tight and heavy with cream and powder. Even though I told Kimmy I wanted a nice and natural look for my date, she aimed for all the bright primary colors in Taylor's brand-new makeup set. My cheeks were swollen from being stabbed by the makeup brushes' bristles, and my eyes ached from the eyelash curler. I didn't know why girls put up with doing this every day.

But it was all worth it as Taylor lay on the floor beside us, weak from her peals of laughter. She would clench her stomach and try to sit up, but one look at me and she'd collapse again.

Her cheeks were wet with tears. She beamed up at me so wide that I could barely see her eyes.

Yeah, it was definitely worth it.

14

{Taylor}

The night wind rustled through my hair as I leaned out the passenger window of Brian's car and pointed a finger at Carly. "Are you sure you don't want us to stay? We could go to the party with you. We don't mind."

"Positive. How am I supposed to start my schmoozing if you guys are hanging around?" She slung her purse over her shoulder and winked at us. Her flowy green skirt swirled around her legs. "No offense."

"None taken," I said drily. I still wasn't sure about leaving Carly behind, but she wanted to join this theater group after graduation, and this party could be her way in. Besides, if there was anyone who could take care of herself, it was Carly.

"Speak for yourself. I'm very offended." Brian jabbed at the button to roll up the window. "Let's go, Taylor, before she changes her mind."

I laughed as Carly jumped back and stuck out her tongue at

us before heading back into the theater. Brian pulled the car out of the parking lot and slowed down next to her. "Good luck. You'll knock them dead."

"I know. How could anyone resist me?"

Brian snorted and drove off once she got back inside. "Nice to see that she doesn't need any help in the confidence department."

"Yeah, but I like to think that she still needed us for moral support." Without waiting for his answer, I scooted a little closer and held my thumb and index finger an inch apart. "Just a tad. No harm in taking a little bit of the credit."

"Hell, she's not here. We could take *all* the credit."

I grinned and patted his shoulder. "You're right. It was all because of us. We're awesome!"

The car swerved the teeniest bit as Brian snickered into his left fist. "As long as you don't let it get to your head."

"Too late. I do regret one thing." I let out a sigh and patted my stomach. "I shouldn't have skipped dinner."

Switching hands on the steering wheel, Brian opened the compartment between our seats and fumbled through the neatly wrapped wires for his cell charger and iPod. "Well, I don't have anything to feed you, but maybe this would help." He handed me a pack of spearmint gum.

I accepted the gum with a grin. "Thanks. Do you want one?"

"No, I have my own." He patted the chest pocket of his green-checkered button-down shirt. "I don't like spearmint."

"Oh, right." I forgot that he liked fruity bubble gum. I hated those with a passion. They were so sweet that I'd always end up swallowing them when I was younger. My mom told me that since gum doesn't digest, sooner or later it would just build up and fill my entire stomach. Great thing to tell your daughter right before Halloween.

I popped two pieces in my mouth. "Why do you have this spearmint gum if you don't like it?"

"It's for you." He gave me a small grin. The streetlight flickered in his dark eyes. "I always buy some to have around in case you want it."

I blinked dumbly at him. "Me?"

His grin faded a little, and he looked away. "Well, you and anybody else that wants it. You know what I mean."

"Oh." For a split second, I thought he meant specifically me. Which made no sense. Why would he buy something just in case I would want it someday? It was crazy of me to even *think* that.

Still, something in the air was a little weird. I leaned forward to mess with his CDs in the compartment beneath the stereo. My fingers ran along the plastic covers. They were already perfectly lined up—according to specific genres—and facing the same direction.

In fact, everything in Brian's car was immaculate. No dust or dirt on the carpet or dashboard. Windows were so squeaky clean that a bird could probably fly right into them. And it still had a new-car smell, even though he had driven this car since he moved to Wilmington. This was exactly how I imagined my car would look if I had one.

Suddenly, I thought of Rudy with her rust and grime and was immediately filled with guilt. Like I was cheating on her for admiring another car.

Maybe I needed to sleep more. I think I was starting to get a little delusional.

"So, did you decide on which college you're going to yet?" I asked to kill the quiet.

A small smile played on his lips, but his gaze remained straight ahead. "Would you kill me if I said Columbia?"

"Ha-ha, if you're going to Columbia, then you better stop the car now so I can beat you up."

He let out a low whistle under his breath. "Can we wait until we get home first? I don't really want to have other witnesses around when you're whooping my ass."

"Well, it's no fun to do it in private."

Brian chuckled, but he didn't say anything else. And he refused to look at me. I narrowed my eyes at him, and fluttery waves of panic washed over me. "Wait, you're joking, right?"

"Sort of." He let out a snort and finally turned to look at me when we reached a red light. His eyes laughed down at me, and his dimple was like a crater in his cheek. "I decided on NYU for journalism. So at least I'll be nearby."

"Oh." Of course he wouldn't fight me for Columbia. He knew how much it meant to me. "So premed's definitely out of the picture?"

"Yeah, it would be interesting, and Tulane's definitely where my parents want me to go, but I doubt I'd be happy."

This was something that had been troubling him all year, so I was glad that he finally had it figured out. And it was the exact decision that I thought he should make. "That great, Brian. It really is." I laid my hand on his arm and gave him a reassuring squeeze. "What made you change your mind?"

His eyes glanced down at my hand. "Actually . . . it's because of you."

"Me? How?"

"You know exactly what you want to do. And you worked your ass off to get there. Your passion and determination . . ." He shook his head. "I guess I just want that, too. To be in love with my job. Even if it means I'll probably have to spend my life eating canned beans and noodle soup while you're dining in five-star restaurants with judges and senators."

Touched that he thought so highly of me, I gave his arm another light squeeze. "Don't worry. I'll bring you as my date to one or two of the dinners. For old times' sake."

Brian snickered. "Thanks in advance for the free food."

"No problem." I pulled away and looked out the window as he turned onto my street. "So I guess we'll be seeing a lot of each other, then. If I ever get my acceptance letter."

"You will. They'd be stupid not to take you, and Columbia isn't for stupid people." His confident tone reassured me. "Are you glad I'll be close by?"

"Of course." At least now that I knew he wasn't out to take my spot. He let out a snort and I hit his arm. "Seriously, I am. It'd be nice to have someone there with me. That way I won't be too lonely. You know, when school starts and everyone hates me."

"Nobody hates you," Brian cut in with a frown.

"They do when it comes to school stuff. Don't lie."

The car grew quiet again as he pulled up in front of my house. Finally, he cut the engine and nodded. "All right, maybe they do sometimes, but not me."

"I know you don't. That's why we're friends even though you're the valedictorian and I'm not." I was only half kidding. A part of me was still burning over not being able to give the speech. It was something I dreamed of doing when I was little. When I first learned what the word *valedictorian* even meant.

"If you want, I could screw up in my classes for the rest of the year and you could take the spot."

"Whatever."

He unbuckled his seat belt and turned in his seat to lean toward me with a little grin. "Seriously, you just say the word."

Even though I knew he was just kidding, his offer cheered me up. I leaned toward him, mirroring his stance. "The old me may have considered it for a second, but the victory would feel too hollow. Besides, there's still a chance that I might get it on my own. Fair and square." Slim, but the chance was still there.

"All right, I won't make it easy for you, then."

"I wouldn't want you to." With a grin, I leaned back in my seat and reached for my seat belt.

"Have you ever thought about what it would be like if we ever started dating?" Brian suddenly asked. His dark eyes were bright and intense as he gazed at me.

I was too surprised by his question to respond at first. My hand just froze on the belt buckle, like it had forgotten how to unlatch it. Time stood still as Brian's question ran over and over in my head like an annoying Energizer Bunny.

It was a simple yes-or-no question. And one that I knew the answer to. Yet why couldn't I just say it? This was a perfect opportunity to find out about his feelings toward me.

Because I wasn't ready for the answer. Not yet. This wasn't part of the plan. "What do you mean?"

He ran his hand through his hair, messing it up. "We just seem so compatible. Perfect, even."

"Well, yeah, but maybe we're also too perfect together," I said echoing Evan's words. "Like evil-scientist kind of perfection."

Brian laughed. "I don't really know about that. Can things ever be *too* perfect? Sometimes perfect just means . . . perfect. Because that's how it's supposed to be. Because that's how you know it would last."

Goose bumps ran up and down my arms as he spoke. I shook my head. "Why does it feel like you're getting all philosophical on me?"

"It's just something I've been wondering about for a while now."

Before I could respond, he leaned even closer to me, until his face was inches from mine. My breath got caught in my throat, and all I could do was stare at him. With a small grin, he suddenly pressed on the belt buckle to release it and tugged the strap away from my body so it would spring back into place. He didn't move away, though. He just continued gazing at me.

There are certain moments that you've dreamed of and planned for your entire life.

I wouldn't be lying if I said I'd thought hundreds of times of the moment Brian and I would share our first kiss. When we were in college hanging out. Him doing his journalism while I studied for law school. Hours would pass, and we'd suddenly get quiet and look at each other and just know.

This moment was eerily close to all of them. And with Brian living in New York with me, it seemed like something that was destined to happen.

I don't know whether he moved or I did, but next thing

I knew, the inches between us shrank down until they were barely one. I was unable to look at him anymore without getting cross-eyed, and my eyelids fluttered closed, despite my uncomfortable, churning stomach.

Tap. Tap. Tap. We both jumped apart when someone rapped on the passenger window.

It was Evan.

My heart slammed in my chest as I leaped out of the car. I stumbled on the grass but managed to catch myself in time. Or rather Evan did. He immediately let go of my arms and shoved his hands in his pockets. His expression was blank as he gazed down at me. The churning in my stomach multiplied, and I had to look away.

"Uh, hi, Evan." The greeting came out as a high-pitched squeak. I cleared my throat and tried again. "Hi." Great, now I sounded like a forty-year-old trucker who smoked. Was my throat always this dry?

Brian also got out of the car and slowly came around until he stood on my other side.

Evan glanced over at Brian for a second, and his forehead scrunched up like he was deep in thought. I felt like I should say something, but I didn't know what.

Suddenly, within a blink of an eye, his face softened and a bright smile crossed his face. Even though it was so wide, it didn't reach his eyes. They were still dark and stormy. "Fancy meeting you guys here."

Brian shrugged. "Not really, since this is Taylor's house. Have you been waiting long?"

"A bit."

If I didn't know any better, I would have thought Evan was

jealous, but there was no logical reason for him to be. That would be crazy. Brian and I hadn't done anything. And it wasn't like Evan and I were in a *real* relationship. He even joked about Brian and me getting together a bunch of times.

Then why did I feel so guilty?

After what seemed like hours—although it was barely a minute—Evan took another few steps toward me until I was within arms' distance. He didn't touch me, though. "It was nice of you to drive her home, Brian."

Brian took a few steps closer to me, too. "Of course I would. Taylor knows that she can count on me for anything. I'm always here when she needs me."

"Yeah, you are the *good* guy." Evan's tone was so mocking that he made the word *good* sound like an insult.

"Well, someone's gotta be."

Evan's eyes narrowed, but his smile never wavered. It was kind of creepy and amazing at the same time. "It's great that Taylor has such a good friend like you around."

My head whipped back and forth as they talked. "It really is. Why don't we—"

"Yeah, you know what they say. Friends last a lifetime." Brian cut in like I hadn't even said anything. "And I'm going to be around for a while."

"I'll bet."

They were both staring each other down over my head. In fact, I don't even think they realized I was still between them anymore. It was like some sort of power struggle that I didn't understand. And one that I had absolutely no desire to be a part of.

Thank god we were interrupted by loud barking. Oreo was a

blur of black and white that shot toward us before skidding to a stop a few feet away. His pink tongue hung out of the side of his mouth, and his tail wagged back and forth like a windshield wiper.

Having already met my dog a few times whenever I brought him to the park, Brian squatted down and stretched out his hand toward Oreo. "Come here, boy."

At the same time, Evan smacked his hand against the side of his jeans. "Come over here."

Oreo's head whipped back and forth between the two guys before he let out a whimper and just flopped on the grass. He curled up into a little ball, and his head turned to the side. And he refused to look at any of us anymore.

I kind of wanted to do the same.

Don't get me wrong. I loved confrontation as much as the next lawyer—or would-be lawyer—but only when I got to be on one of the arguing sides. I used to be the captain of the debate team before everyone quit and the club was cut. (Despite what the majority of the student body thought, it was *not* my fault. If anything, it was everyone else's fault for not coming to the daily meetings like I asked.)

But that didn't mean I wanted to take sides between Evan and Brian.

Deciding to put Oreo and me out of our misery, I swooped down and scooped him up in my arms. He let out a sharp yelp at the sudden movement, but I just held him close to my chest and backed away from the two surprised guys. "Uh, I still have to study for that . . . test I have tomorrow. Don't want to be un-prepared or anything. I'll—I'll see you two tomorrow."

Before either of them could respond, I raced back into the house without a second glance. Slamming the door behind me, I rose onto my tiptoes and peeked out of the long window-pane at the top of the door. Brian and Evan had both turned away from the house and were walking back to their cars. And within minutes, they were gone. Each drove off in the opposite direction.

Oreo let out a loud bark to get my attention. And I swear, I could see pointed accusation in his eyes.

"What? I'm not being a chicken. I just—well, you didn't pick, either." He cocked his head to the left and just kept staring at me. Great, now I was arguing with a dog. "Oh, shut up."

My brows wrinkled together in frustration, and I slid down the door. Oreo wiggled closer until his head was tucked beneath my arm so he could snuggle against my body.

15

-Evan-

With a towel wrapped around my neck, I grabbed my keys and got ready for the beach. I hadn't planned to go today. The rumbling clouds outside should have been enough for me to get back into bed. But I needed to do something. Anything to get my mind off Taylor and that stupid-ass idiot.

Okay, so Brian wasn't *actually* an idiot. If anything, he was too damn smart. And he could be nice. Sometimes. But that didn't make him any less of a stupid ass. I mean, what kind of guy goes after another person's girlfriend? Or sort-of girlfriend. Or—

Screw it. I needed to surf. I needed to get out on the water and forget everything and everyone. Even if it was just for a few hours. After I texted Taylor that I couldn't drive her today, I grabbed my board and headed downstairs to grab a bite.

Too bad Brandon was sitting in the kitchen eating breakfast when I came downstairs. Already, this day had gone from crappy to worse. "Skipping school again. That's no surprise. I actually didn't think you knew how to wake up before noon."

I grabbed a couple of blueberry muffins that Mom had baked the day before from the plate on the counter. Without reacting to his jab, I turned around to face him and stuffed half of one into my mouth, knowing that he hated when I talked with my mouth full. One of the few hundred things he hated about me. "And I didn't think that you knew how to be a douche bag 24/7, but somehow you managed that," I finally commented without swallowing.

He glared at me over his plate. "I don't understand how that Simmons girl could stand being around you. She should be smart enough to know that she deserves better than that."

"Yeah, well, you would know all about smart women staying with jerks, wouldn't you?"

Brandon slammed his hands on the table and glowered at me. "If there's anyone who was a jerk to your mom, then it was your deadbeat dad. She should have left that bastard before he even ended up in jail. Thank god she finally realized it in the end. Just like your little girlfriend will soon realize that you're going nowhere. She's about to get out of this town and make something of herself. Do you really think she needs someone like you weighing her down?"

In a burst of fury, I grabbed his shirt collar and yanked him toward me. His fists punched at my arms and shoulders, but I didn't care. I didn't feel any of it. "Shut the hell up before I beat your ass so hard you—"

"Brandon! Evan! You let him go this instant!"

I loosened my grip, but I still didn't let go. "Great timing, Mom."

She dropped the groceries at her feet and pulled at my arms. "I said let him go!"

Scowling, I finally released him, and Brandon stumbled backward. His face was purplish red. He massaged his shoulders and neck with both hands and glowered at me. "That's it! I don't care if he's your son, Eva. I won't take this anymore. I meant what I said before. Once he graduates, I'm kicking him out of this house."

I took a step toward him. "Why don't I save us both the trouble and just leave right now?"

"You said it. Now, pack your bags and get the hell out of here before I call the police on you. You ungrateful piece of—"

"THAT'S ENOUGH!" Mom suddenly burst out. "Both of you!"

Brandon and I were so surprised that we both stopped yelling and stared at her. In the four years that Brandon and Mom had been together, she had never yelled at him before. Hell, I never even heard her talk to him in a loud voice, much less her "You better listen to me before I get even more pissed off" voice. Even I rarely got that voice. Only once, when I got in a fight with Brandon's nephew at their wedding. (I won. Although it didn't feel like much a win after Mom was through with me.)

She let out a shaky, deep breath and shook her head. "Brandon, don't you have a surgery this morning? You don't want to be late, do you?"

Brandon looked like he wanted to argue, but for once, he was smart and decided to keep his mouth shut. He just nodded and left the kitchen.

Mom closed her eyes and massaged her forehead with one hand before bending down to gather the dropped groceries. "Great, you made me break the carton of eggs I just bought. How am I supposed to make treats for you and Taylor now?"

"Sorry, Mom." I stooped down to help her. "I'll pick up another carton later."

"Yeah, you better."

Not wanting to piss her off even more, I grabbed a towel from the oven handle and handed it to Mom so she could wipe up the battered eggs. I continued to pick up the rest of the stuff without another word. I even crawled beneath the kitchen table to retrieve some bruised peaches.

Finally, when there was nothing left to do, I shifted my weight side to side and cleared my throat to get her attention. "I'm sorry for . . . you know, before. I shouldn't have grabbed him like that." Or at least next time, I'd make sure I didn't have an audience. Especially if he ever mentioned Taylor and Dad again.

"I don't blame you. I heard what he said." She arranged the canned foods in the pantry beside the stove. "He shouldn't have talked about your dad like that."

I blinked at her. Wow, another first. Mom was actually admitting that her saintly husband did something wrong. In defense of Dad. Sort of.

This was the first time she had ever brought Dad up in a conversation. I wanted to continue being pissed at her, but I couldn't. I think a small part of me always realized that she knew where he was. After all, she knew everything else.

"He talks like that all the time," I said with a shrug. "Why are you finally seeing how much of a jerk he is now?"

"He's very good to me, Evan. To both of us," she said with a sigh, as if that should absolve him of all his flaws. Maybe to her, it did.

"He's good to you. He's tolerable toward me."

"Well, can you blame him? You push him every time you're around each other."

I scowled but didn't say anything. It was true. I guess I did deliberately piss him off every chance I got. But it wasn't like I was the only one. He did, too.

"I know you think that he's the reason why I kept your dad away from you, but it was my decision." She ran her hands up and down her legs as though the friction would give her more courage. "I love Brandon, Evan."

"Okay . . ." I didn't see where she was going with this.

Mom let out a deep breath. "But I also love your dad. Even now. And Brandon knows it. But he loves me so much that he doesn't care as long as I stay with him. I wish he felt the same way about you, but you just remind him of your dad and that I don't love him in the same way that he loves me."

I gripped the countertop in both hands and leaned against it. There was no denying that Brandon was good to Mom. Really good. That was the only redeeming quality he had. And the only reason I couldn't completely hate him. But now—after Mom's explanation—I kind of felt sorry for the guy. "But how could you stay with him if you're in love with Dad? Why didn't you just stay with Dad?"

She lifted her eyes to stare at the ceiling. "You have to

understand. Love is wonderful, but it's not everything. And it's not enough. Life with your dad was hard. I never knew where he was, what he was doing, or when he'd come home. And I was *so* tired of taking care of everything. Especially after my double shifts at the hospital." Mom finally lowered her head to look at me. "I couldn't take it anymore."

Shit. I knew life had been hard for Mom, but I didn't think it was that bad. "Sorry, Mom. I didn't know."

"But things are better now. Which is why I usually turn a blind eye whenever you two argue," she continued. "But Brandon was wrong to talk about Taylor like that. Is that why you're so pissed?"

"Don't worry, I rarely listen to him," I said, evading her comment about Taylor. Not wanting to even admit the truth to myself.

I thought I was immune to any stupid crap that Brandon said, but I couldn't help snapping when he talked about Taylor. Especially when his words brought back images of Taylor and Brian together in his car. I knew that Brian had a thing for Taylor. It was impossible not to notice him glaring at us whenever we were together. Or how he was always by Taylor's side, helping her, studying with her, talking to her. The only person who didn't see it was Taylor.

So yeah, I knew. But I didn't *know* how it would feel when she was actually in his arms. When it looked like she was going to leave me and go to him. I wasn't ready for the anger and the wave of frustration that hit me at the sight of them. It was like nothing I had felt before. And it sucked ass.

Mom interrupted my thoughts. A bright smile crossed her

face, like she hadn't just been pouring out her heart to me seconds ago. "Taylor's with you, though, isn't she? She chose you. If she cared about all that other stuff, then she would have gone out with Brian Long instead of you."

For a split second, I thought I had been talking out loud, and that's how she knew about Brian and Taylor. "How do you know about Brian?" I realized by the way that she was avoiding my eyes that she may know more than she was saying. "Mom?"

She fidgeted with the wooden spoons hanging beside the stove. "I just heard . . . some things . . ."

This wasn't leading anywhere good. "Mom . . ."

"Okay, okay. I . . . may have asked the other parents and teachers at your school. Got to know some people who are friends with his family. And . . . done some Internet stalking on the boy. Did you know that he won Ohio's Scholastic Award for three years straight before he moved here? And that he already has college credits for English, calculus, and chemistry because of his AP classes?" She waved her hand in the air like it was no big deal, but I could tell that she was impressed. Who wouldn't be, with those kind of stats?

"No, I didn't." Man, Mom really knew how to kick me when I was already feeling like crap. She didn't mean to, but all this just reminded me even more that even if I was starting to like Taylor—and I'm not saying that I was—I didn't deserve her. She should be with someone like Brian, the Golden Boy. Not the town's slacker.

I don't know if the expression on my face changed or she suddenly realized what she'd said, but Mom leaned across the counter and patted my arm. "But other than that, he's not very impressive. And none of that matters, right? Like I said, she chose you. You're the one that she likes."

"Yeah. Right."

She was wrong. Taylor didn't have a choice. Not then and not now. But maybe it was time that I gave her the chance to make things right again. To give her back her choice.

16

{Taylor}

Throughout the rest of the week, I couldn't shake the feeling that something was wrong with Evan. He skipped school more, and I could have sworn he was avoiding me. When we did see each other, he was still his laughing, joking self, but I just *knew* that something was wrong. And I was determined to help. Somehow.

But first I had to find him. And since Evan wasn't in school again, I had to settle for the next best thing.

Aaron's eyes widened when he saw me waiting by his locker, and his steps faltered. Despite being a huge football player, he always looked like a deer stuck in headlights when I talked to him. I was always nice to him, but I don't think he forgot that one time I was pissed at Evan after our one-night stand. (There was no other way to refer to that night.) Not exactly my best moment.

"Hi, Aaron. How was class?"

He sneaked glances at me as he twirled the combination on his locker. "It was all right, I guess. What's up?"

"I was just wondering . . . do you know where Evan is? He's not picking up his phone." I fiddled with the coin necklace that Evan had given me while I waited for his answer.

Aaron shook his head. "No. I thought if anyone knew where he was, it'd be you."

"I don't. Do you know if he has any plans later tonight, then?"

With a small frown, he leaned against the locker next to his and chewed on his thumbnail. "There's a party at Wrightsville Beach tonight. I'm pretty sure Evan's going to be there. In fact, now that I think about it, he's probably there now. He cuts school sometimes to go there during the day. That's his favorite place to surf."

"It is?"

"Yeah." He gave me a funny look, and I almost smacked my forehead for slipping. That was probably something that a good girlfriend should know. "Do you know where it is?"

"I think so. I passed it before when I went to Carolina Beach with Brian." Another funny look. *Darn it.* A good girlfriend probably didn't talk about their dates with other guys so casually. Even though it wasn't really a *date.* "Carly was with us, too."

Aaron shoved a couple of books into his locker and slammed it closed. He turned to face me again, tugging on his left earlobe with his hand. "I can drive you to the party if you want a ride," he offered to the locker over my head.

I struggled not to laugh. Even though he still looked a little skittish, I wanted to give him a huge hug. He could barely talk to me for a few minutes, yet he was offering to drive me to a party. The ride would be too torturous for us both. "No, that's all right. Thanks, though."

"No problem." He turned to leave, but tilted his head around to nod at me. "See you at the party."

"Bye." A smile crossed my face when he disappeared from sight. Aaron really was a sweetheart. He was too awesome not to have a girlfriend. I would hook him up with Carly, but I'm pretty sure she'd eat him alive.

Speaking of the man-eater. I dug my phone out of my pocket and speed-dialed Carly's number. "Hey, Carly, do you mind if I borrow your car tonight?"

❧•❧

I realized too late that I could have just waited for him at his house. It wasn't like he was never going to come home. And it was probably a bad idea to come to the beach party. Especially with all the laughing drunk people roaming around the large bonfire. I wished Carly were here with me, but she was being dragged to some career seminar with her mom.

Five minutes later, I was sure it was a bad idea. Stupid, stupid idea. I wove my way through the crowd, trying to avoid getting stepped on or having a drink tossed in my face, when someone pulled me back from behind.

"Taylor! You're here!"

"Er, hi." I saw a glimpse of Aaron's face before he swept me into a tight bear hug, like we hadn't seen each other for years instead of just a few hours. My feet dangled over the sand for a few moments as I struggled to breathe. I patted his shoulder to get his attention. "Where's Evan?"

"Evan? He's drinking somewhere over there." His hand waved around the entire party.

Great. That was really helpful. "Somewhere over there" covered about a hundred or so teenagers drinking and shimmying down each other's bodies to the music. Even though I was their age—younger, since I'd skipped a grade—I felt as out of place as a hippo at a Sunday tea party.

I tried to slip away, but Aaron was too fast and tugged me right back. He pulled me into a tight embrace as though we were dancing. My head was smooshed against his neck, and the alcoholic fumes hit me in the face when I tried to pull away. *Urgh.* He was stinking, fall-on-your-back, stick-your-head-in-the-toilet drunk. As further proof, his red-rimmed eyes squinted down at me. "Let's go find him, Tay!"

He maneuvered us around and half tangoed, half skipped into the center of the party.

We had barely taken ten steps when three other large guys decided to join us in the "fun." They whooped and hollered around me, and we all danced—well, they danced, I stumbled—toward the fire.

I never imagined I would ever be in a center of a guy pile and be this miserable. This was as close to an orgy as I'd ever get. And I was beginning to think it was severely overrated.

"Let her go!"

Even though that was the same thing I had been telling them to do for several minutes, they listened to the commanding female voice and fell away from me. I straightened up with a sigh and a grateful smile for my savior, which instantly faded when I realized whom it was.

"Well, look who we have here. Little Ms. Perfect's finally off her throne for the weekend."

Lauren. Lauren and her curvy body clad in tight jeans and a white tank top, on display in all its glory. The bright-red bikini top shone through the thin fabric. How the heck was she *not* freezing? My shirt had sleeves and goose bumps were still popping up all over my arms. Maybe her snarkiness kept her warm. Like an internal mean girl heater.

Her auburn, curly hair was loosely braided to hang midway down her back. She managed to look innocent, sensual, ethereal, wild, and reserved all at the same time. I didn't know how she managed to look like she could take over the world with one hand yet wouldn't mind the occasional shoulder to lean on once in a while. But I could see why Evan used to date her. Any guy would jump to do her bidding. Guys were such idiots.

God, I hated her.

My head whipped back and forth as I searched for someone to save me. Anyone. Given the choice, I'd rather go back to the orgy. "Um, yeah. Great party."

"You don't belong here," she said, hands on either side of her hips.

"Tell me about it." I rolled my eyes before realizing I'd said it out loud. Lauren stared at me as though I were a water slug slithering up the shore to join the party. No, scratch that. The slug would have been more welcome than I was. "Uh, do you know where Evan is?"

The hardened expression on her face showed that she *did*

know where he was, but that didn't mean she was going to tell me. Not by the tight line her red lips formed.

Was this hostility because she didn't think I belonged here or because she didn't think I belonged with Evan? If you asked me, *she* never deserved him. She was clearly an A-rated bitch, while Evan was . . . well, Evan.

Either way, it didn't look like I was going get past the bodyguard anytime soon. "You know what? Never mind, I'm gonna go."

I had barely taken a few steps when her voice reached me. "Yeah, you better go back to your precious books. Best to leave Evan with people who really understand him."

"What makes you think I don't understand him?"

Lauren looked me up and down and sneered. Yes, *sneered.* Her left hand spread wide on her hip. "Do you really need to ask?"

That was it. I'd had enough of her smug ass. I crossed my arms and stood my ground. "On second thought, I think I'll stay. I *am* Evan's girlfriend. Why shouldn't I hang out with his friends?"

Ouch. I knew I had hit a sore spot when her mouth fell open. She recovered pretty quickly and looked around at the people watching us as if we were a reality show. Like that would ever happen. I'd need another two cup sizes before a show about my life would ever have a *chance* of getting picked up.

A devilish look entered her piercing blue eyes, and my stomach sank in response. *Oh no. I think I poked the bear. Stirred the hornets' nest. Unleashed hell.* "Fine, stay here. Come have fun with the rest of us." Lauren reached into her pocket and pulled out a small white tube. She held it out to me. "Go on. Take it."

It was a joint.

She had called my bluff. And now I didn't know what to do. *Crap. Crap. CRAP.*

I rolled it around in my fingertips. It was so small and harmless looking. But I'd attended enough D.A.R.E. meetings to know how dangerous it could be. I still wore the antidrug T-shirts to bed. I still helped out at the yearly fundraisers. Heck, I even won the award for best essay in my district division just a few years ago. I knew *all* about the consequences.

But now all that seemed to fade into the background with everyone staring at me. All the arguments, all the facts. *Poof!* Gone.

"Taylor?"

We both whirled around, and there was Evan. His mussed hair stuck up in all directions. He was in a threadbare black T-shirt and khaki shorts that were covered with dark, wet splotches.

I'd never been so happy to see anyone in my life.

His gaze jumped back and forth and finally landed on the joint in my hand. With a fierce scowl, Evan snatched it from me. "You know what? I don't even want to know. Come on. Let's go," he muttered, sticking it in his back pocket.

We had only taken a few steps when Lauren grabbed his arm and pulled him back, inadvertently knocking me off balance, since his other arm was wrapped around my shoulders. "You're just going to leave? Just like that?"

The simple question had a thousand other questions attached it.

He scanned the party for a long moment before he finally released me. Time froze and I stepped back, feeling dejected. He was going to go with her. Probably deciding this ruse had played through long enough. A wave of disappointment washed over me. Not because I liked him or anything. No, because I thought we had become friends.

NOT because I liked him.

The smugness on Lauren's face grew as she came to the same conclusion I did.

To everyone's surprise, Evan just pried her hand off ever so lightly—finger by finger—until she was no longer touching him, and he dropped her hand. He backed up a few steps until he was at my side again. With both hands raised as though he were surrendering, Evan nodded. "Yeah, I am. Just. Like. That."

17

{Taylor}

I don't know if Evan understood what he had just done. I barely understood. Even if he was naive—and I knew he wasn't—there was no mistaking the pissed-off look in Lauren's eyes before we left. It was weird to see her eyes so icy when her hair and ruby lips looked like they were on fire. You could practically feel the waves of hatred radiating off her body.

Even now I could feel her eyes piercing through my back. I didn't know if Evan felt it, too, but he tightened his grip. And he never looked back. Not even when Aaron let out a loud "Whoop!"

We didn't head for the parking lot. Instead, we strolled along the water's edge, hand in hand, but not looking at each other. Not saying anything. I was glad. I didn't know what I was supposed to say. My mind was still reeling.

He chose me. Me over Lauren in all her red-bikini glory. In front of everyone. His hand was warm and steady in my hand.

It was both comforting and made me tingle from head to toe. And it was getting kind of hard to catch my breath.

Finally, when the party was way behind us, he let go and sank down into the sand barely a few feet from the shore. He watched the waves crash against each other in the distance. White foam glowed against the black sea. A couple of gray-and-white seagulls pecked at the sand around us, cooing at each other every other minute or so.

"So, that was kind of crazy," Evan commented after a while.

"Yeah, a bit." Sitting down next to him, I tried to sound confident. "I could have handled it, though."

"I'm sure you would have." He waved his hand in front of my face. His index finger and thumb were half an inch apart. "I helped a little bit, though."

"Maybe." I batted his hand away. "Or maybe I let you play the knight in shining armor to boost your ego. Big as it already is."

"I think we both know that my ego is already at its max," he said with a lopsided grin that made my stomach flop.

"You said it, not me."

With a laugh, Evan shifted to the side and dug the joint out of his pocket. "Better get rid of this now before I forget. Mom and Brandon would freak if I accidentally brought it home." He wound his arm back and pitched it into the ocean. Dusting off his hands, he turned to look at me. "So why are you here?"

I wrapped my arms around my knees and rocked back and forth. "What do you mean? This is my scene every Friday night. Before Lauren showed up, I was the life of the party out there."

A wide grin came across his face. "Something makes me really doubt that, since you consider homework fun." His hair flopped around as he shook his head. It wasn't spiked up at all tonight, and parts of his hair were still damp. He must have been surfing before the party. "Are you sure there's no other reason?"

Was I such a bad liar? It was like he saw right through me. "I was worried about you. You seem different. Like you're mad at me or something. Especially after the other night with Brian—" I broke off when his jaw visibly tightened. Uh, maybe this wasn't the best time to bring up Brian. "Do you regret this?"

He stared out at the water. "Depends what you mean by *this*."

What the hell. There was no turning back now. I let out a deep breath. "The contract. Us pretending to be together. Do you regret it?"

Even though I had asked the question, I wasn't sure if I really wanted to know his answer. Because I was afraid of what it would be. Just because he chose me over Lauren once didn't mean anything. Maybe he was being nice.

He finally looked down at me, and his face softened a bit. His gray eyes searched my face like he wanted to find the right answer there. His hand brushed my hair out of my eyes, and I fought the urge to lean against his hand. "No, I don't."

A shiver ran down my spine at his words. "Thanks. Even if you're lying, it's still nice to hear you say that," I joked to cover up my nervousness.

Evan didn't deny or admit that he was lying. He didn't say anything. He just flashed me a small grin and pulled away from me. He found a small blue plastic shovel someone had forgotten on the beach and dug an oval hole. Soon a small crater was between us.

Using my feet, I pushed sand into the hole he was making, ruining his efforts. "So we're good?"

"Yeah, perfect." With a flick of his wrist, he threw a glop of wet sand on my legs. "Oops, sorry. Slip of the hand."

Oh, we'll see about that. With my eyes narrowed, I dug my toes into the sand to get more ammunition before launching it at him. It landed directly on his crotch. Perfect. "Sorry, I was stretching."

"No problem. As long as it wasn't on purpose," he said with a shrug before smashing a handful of wet sand on the top of my head. "'Cause that definitely was."

I let out a shriek and jumped to my feet. My hands ran through my hair to shake the sand out as Evan rolled on the ground laughing. This was war now. Before he could react, I straddled his lap and used both hands to dig up as much sand as I could to bury him.

My plan immediately backfired. He clasped my arms together and rolled over until I was pinned beneath his body. "Now, this is much better . . ."

I rolled my eyes and shoved him, but I couldn't hide the glimmer of a smile on my face. My heart hammered in my chest, and I was half scared he would feel it. "Get off. You weigh a ton."

"Hey, there's no reason to get nasty. I've been working out, you know."

"I hadn't noticed."

He laughed and stood up. Granules of sand were still stuck to his arms and shoulders. Taking my hands, he pulled me to my feet and hugged me. His heartbeat thumped against my cheek.

Leaning back slowly, he bent his head until our faces were inches apart. My eyes automatically fluttered closed.

Suddenly, my feet were off the ground as Evan lifted me up in his arms, carrying me like a bride over the threshold. My eyes flew open in shock. "What are you doing?"

"Getting payback." He took a couple of steps forward. I could feel the cold water hitting the back of my thighs with each wave. It soaked through my shorts and underwear.

Crap, that was cold! My arms flew around his neck, and I tried to pull myself up, practically choking with laughter now. "You wouldn't dare!"

"Guess what? I don't like to be challenged, either." And with that statement, he dove us both right into the water.

I let out a shriek as the cold water surrounded us. My hands gripped his shoulders so I wouldn't get swept away, but I didn't need to worry. Evan had a tight grip around me. He bounced me up and down in the water. Not so low that my head would go underwater, but low enough that everything else was drenched. My loose shirt billowed out like a balloon as the water got underneath it, and I just thanked god that I wasn't wearing white tonight.

Suddenly aware that the water was also pulling the wide neckline down, showing off my plain gray bra, I shoved against Evan. "Let me down."

He gently set me down, and I immediately moved away from him, turning so he couldn't see me. The water only reached my boobs, but it still made my shirt flop open, no matter how many ways I held it down. With my head bent, I tied a knot into my neckline to make it smaller.

"Taylor, are you okay?" His concerned voice was a few feet away. "Did the saltwater get in your eyes or something?"

I froze. "Yeah, I think so. It's stinging like crazy right now."

"Shit, I didn't mean to hurt you. Let me see." Once he touched my arm, I whirled around and used my hands to splash a bunch of water at him. His dripping, shocked face turned to laughter. "Now that's the girl I know and love."

My heart skipped a beat when he said the word *love,* but by the goofy look on his face, he didn't even realize what he'd said.

He flopped backward and floated in the water like a piece of driftwood. Hunky driftwood. The waves didn't bother him at all as he bobbed up and down in sync with them. So at ease that it looked like he did this every night. He must have been part merman in his past life.

The water was still kind of cold, but I was getting used to it. It was crystal clear and beautiful, but I couldn't really see much in the moonlight. I could see my hands and arms floating, but my feet faded into blackness. Usually this would freak me out. I mean, who knew what was in the water? I could step on a jellyfish. Or there could be sharks and barracudas swimming around me right now, and I wouldn't even know.

But now all those fears seemed to fade away. Maybe because this felt like a dream. Or maybe it was because I knew Evan would never let anything happen to me. He'd probably fight a shark if he had to, partly so he could brag to people that he'd done it. But I'd like to think saving me would be the main point.

If I thought it was weird to garden with Evan, that was a walk in the park. I had never imagined I would be swimming with

Evan at night. Another *Dear Diary* moment, I guess. Funny how many of them I'd had since Evan.

After I almost drowned last summer, I made myself learn how to swim. But I never really figured out how to float. I guess I just skipped that step. So I just waded in the water a bit as Evan drifted around me.

I don't know how long we stayed out there. Could be two minutes, could be twenty, but everything was so quiet and peaceful that I didn't want to leave. I was genuinely disappointed when Evan suggested getting back to shore.

I wrung the water out of my stringy hair as Evan shook his head like a wet dog. His hair sprang out in a bunch of directions, and I couldn't help laughing. He looked like a porcupine. My laughter faded when he pulled off his wet shirt. I'd barely had time to register this when his hands drifted down to his pants. "What are you doing?"

"Just getting out of my wet clothes," he said with a shrug, like it was no big deal to strip in front of me.

"But, but . . ." My hands flew up to cover my blistering-red face, and I stumbled over my own feet in my rush to turn away. "Seriously, dude!"

He laughed. "What are *you* doing?"

"What am I doing? What are *you* doing? You can't just strip down wherever you want to! There might not be anyone else around, but we're still in public! You could get arrested! Oh god, you're going to get us arrested for public nudity. It's going to be on my record forever."

"Will you just turn around?"

"No!"

"Come on, Taylor. I dare you."

Cursing at him under my breath, I cautiously turned back, but my eyes stayed glued to the starry sky over our heads. Even when I heard him come closer. Finally, Evan took my hand and put it on his hip—on smooth fabric. My head snapped down, and I stared at the blue shorts he was wearing. Not shorts, but—

"Swim trunks," I said blankly. "You're wearing swim trunks." At least I think they were swim trunks. They were dark navy and thin and very, very snug. Like tights or something, but shorts. I mean, technically he was covered up, but I could still see the lines of his thighs and stuff . . .

. . . and I was staring. My eyes snapped back up to his laughing face.

"Of course, I'm wearing swim trunks. You don't know the Boy Scouts motto? Always be prepared."

"Yeah, I don't think *this* is what they had in mind." I felt stupid and a teensy bit disappointed. But mainly stupid. "And I have a hard time believing that you were ever a Boy Scout."

"That makes two of us. I try to block those two years out of my life." A ghost of a grin appeared on his face. "It's nice that you were thinking of me naked, though. You're kind of a perv, aren't you?"

My cheeks burned, and I tried to pull my hand away. "Shut up."

His grip was tight around mine, and he led me to where he laid out his T-shirt and khaki shorts like a small picnic blanket. They were still pretty wet, but at least it prevented the sand from sticking to our butts. After we sat down, he finally let go of my hand, but only to wrap his arm around my shoulders. His bare skin was both cool and warm at the same time.

I peered up at him, and he just gave me a half smile before watching the water again. I couldn't help wondering what Evan thought of me. Sure, we got along pretty well, and I could tell he liked hanging out with me. But did he ever feel more than that?

Not knowing the confusing thoughts running through my head, Evan wrapped an arm around my shoulders, pushed my head down, and rested his chin against the top of my head.

I laid my head on his chest and listened to the rapid beating of his heart. *Thump. Thump. Thump.* Hmm . . . it was so comfortable here. Nice and warm. His heart was like a drum, mingling with the crash of the waves to play a song just for me. My fingers fiddled with the chain around my neck. His hand touched the coin at the same time I did. His hand was nice and warm, too. Hot, even.

Maybe it didn't matter how he felt. This was enough.

For now.

18

-Evan-

I should have been asleep. Hell, I should have been at home instead of lurking in front of Taylor's house. And throwing sticks at her window like a creepy lunatic.

I dropped Taylor off and went home for a while. But as I was lying in bed, I realized I didn't want to be *there*. I wanted to see Taylor. I wanted to talk to her. Be *with* her.

Luckily, her head popped out just as I ran out of sticks and was searching for a rock that wouldn't smash her window.

"Evan? What the heck—what are you doing here?"

The rock fell to my feet with a clatter, and I grinned, not sure if I was happy because of the sight of her or because her hair was smashed to one side like a horn. "Come out here for a minute."

"What? No."

"Come on!"

She threw out her hand to shut me up and nervously looked behind her. I didn't realize till then that I had been yelling. I winced and mouthed "Sorry." Taylor gripped the window-sill with her other hand and looked down. I could practically see the wheels in her head working overdrive before she gave me a tiny nod and disappeared.

I met her at the back door. She wore a baggy white hooded jacket that looked like she had just thrown it on over her T-shirt. The hem ended halfway down her thighs and barely covered the plaid shorts she had on. No, wait, were those . . .

"Boxers?"

Taylor followed my gaze and quickly tugged the hem down. "I wear them to sleep, okay?"

"Hey, I'm not judging. I'm actually wearing the same kind now." I grinned when her eyes jerked down to my sweatpants. "Want to see?"

"Uh, no thanks." Even though it was dark, I could see her flaming cheeks. She ducked her head even lower and cleared her throat. "What do you want, Evan?"

"To talk."

"Talk? Now?"

"Yeah, why else would I come to your house in the middle of the night?" I laughed and shook my head. "Never mind, don't answer that. That was too easy."

Even her ears were red, but at least she laughed with me. Taylor wrapped her arms around herself and nodded toward the hammock in the corner. "Fine. Come on."

As I followed, I couldn't help admiring her from the back. Over the past couple of weeks, Taylor got prettier every time I saw her. Those boxers were damn sexy. Thank god it was warm tonight. I wasn't lying when I said I had a pair just like them. I couldn't help imagining that the pair of boxers she had on *were* mine and *why* she would be wearing them in the first place.

I shoved my hands in my pockets and subtly adjusted the fabric around my crotch.

Taylor sat on the hammock, and my eyes drifted from the alluring plaid fabric to her white legs that obviously didn't see the sun very much down to her small feet. I could feel heat climbing up my face.

I sat down beside her and awkwardly shifted back and forth, torn between wanting to get closer and not wanting to get too close, because I didn't know if I could hold myself back. She leaned away from me and gave me a funny look.

"What?"

A half smile appeared on her face. "I didn't know you wear glasses. It makes you look cute. Smart."

My brows rose in surprise. Did Taylor Simmons just call me cute *and* smart? I made a big show of adjusting the wire-rimmed glasses on my nose. "Yeah, well, blame it on computers and video games at a young age."

"Ah, now that I can believe. So what do you want to talk about?"

"I wanted to see if you were okay?" I asked lamely. Damn, why couldn't I think of a better excuse?

"Um, yeah, I'm fine." She folded one leg beneath her. The other foot pushed at the ground, and she swung us back and forth. "Are you? Honestly?"

My arms crossed beneath my head. "Honestly, no, not really."

I had perfected lying over the years, so I always thought I was a pretty good actor. But Taylor noticed something was wrong. And she came to a party where she clearly didn't want to be just to make sure I was all right. She made me want to talk to her. To tell her everything that was bothering me.

But I couldn't tell her about how jealous I was of her and Brian. And how I had picked a fight with Brandon because of it. I still had my pride.

Instead, I told her about Mom and the card I found in her purse.

"So did you end up talking to her?"

"Yeah." I stared up at the stars peeking out between the branches and leaves. A lot of good that had done. I had tried to talk to Mom again a few more times, but she still refused to let me talk to Dad. I should have just swiped the card when I had the chance. "She said he's tried to contact me for a while, but she didn't tell me because it was for my own good." I let out a humorless laugh. "Brandon said it was better that way. So I could make a new life. Be happier. Thinking that my dad abandoned me."

Taylor wrinkled her nose. "Well, it's easy to see why Brandon chose to be an anesthesiologist rather than a psychiatrist. He doesn't know what the hell he's talking about."

This time I laughed for real. "That's for sure."

It got quiet for a moment, and I couldn't help imagining that we were back at the beach. Alone and quiet. It was almost completely dark in this corner except for a flickering streetlamp over the far gate.

"So what are you going to do now?" Taylor said.

"What do you mean?"

She turned on her side to face me. "Are you going to find him?"

I shrugged. "I don't know. I haven't thought about it."

Taylor poked my shoulder. Hard. "Lies."

"Ouch, you've got one bony finger." In response, she raised both index fingers and reached toward me again. "Fine, fine, I'll admit that the thought has crossed my mind once or twice."

"And?"

"And ... I haven't decided, all right?" I pushed myself upright, making the hammock sway under the sudden shift.

Taylor waited until the rocking slowed before sitting up, too. She edged closer until we were almost pressed against each other. "What are you afraid of? From what you told me, he's great."

A million answers came to mind, but I gave her the one that I didn't even want to admit to myself. "What if he's not? I built him up to be this Perfect Dad. What if I find out that he's not at all what I remembered? That's he's exactly the type of person Brandon always said he was—that I would become someday?"

"That's true. He could turn out to be a douche like my dad." She shook her head. "Nah, that wouldn't be possible. There couldn't be two of them in this world. God's not that mean."

I laughed and wrapped an arm around her back. She didn't pull away. In fact, she leaned a fraction closer until our sides, our hips, were touching. "You know, chances are your dad probably *won't* live up to your expectations. Things usually don't. But that doesn't mean it's a bad thing. And you won't know until you try. It's your choice." She grimaced. "Sorry, you came here to talk, not get a lecture. I'll shut up now."

"It's all right. I've gotten used to your bossy self." I pulled her in for a tight hug. My cheek rested on the top of her head. "And you're right. You didn't live up to my expectations, and *that* wasn't a bad thing at all."

"Oh, and what were your expectations with me?"

"You don't want to know."

She laughed. "You're right, I probably don't. It's getting late. You should go home before you're too sleepy to drive."

Taylor untangled herself from my arms and moved away. Or at least tried to. I tightened my grip around her waist, not wanting the moment to end yet. "Could you stay here with me a little bit longer?" I asked.

"Um, sure."

As we lay back and looked up at the stars, I felt calm for the first time that week. More in control. She was right. It might not be my choice to be apart from my dad for so long, but now it was my choice whether I wanted it to stay that way. I closed my eyes and sucked in a deep breath. I'd figure that out later. Right now I just wanted to stay here as long as I could.

Before I faded off, Taylor took hold of my hand. Although I was too tired to open my eyes, my lips curved into a smile.

I don't know how long I would have stayed asleep if it weren't for the damn sunlight shining straight in my face. I sure as hell wasn't ready to wake up yet. I couldn't even open my eyes, much less get up. Taylor tossed and turned beside me, and I knew she had the same problem.

"It's sunny," I muttered.

She moaned and turned her head back and forth. "Gee, Sherlock, I hadn't even noticed."

I threw up an arm to cover my face, but it didn't help. "Can't you do something about it?"

Taylor sighed and snuggled even deeper into my side, hiding her face. "Sure, let me turn back time so it can be night again."

"Your sarcasm is not appreciated so early in the morning." Suddenly, a shadow fell across my face as I yawned. I let out a sigh of relief. "That's better. Thanks."

"I didn't do anything."

We both sprang upward at the exact time and nearly toppled out of the hammock. Probably would have, if Mr. Simmons hadn't reached out to steady the rope.

Shit.

19

{Taylor}

Grounded. That was my life sentence. Or at least until Dad was old enough to have memory loss. Could have been worse, though. Dad looked like he was ready to kill Evan, and probably would have if Mom hadn't stopped him. He just sent Evan home and lectured me every minute since then. During dinner, to school, from school. He even lectured me on the way to the bathroom. And refused to let anyone say Evan's name in front of his face.

Mom was a lot easier. She gave me the safe-sex talk (after which I wanted to die), but after that, she was fine.

Thank god I was still allowed to have visitors, as long as they weren't Evan.

"Okay, what's up with you guys?" Carly dropped her bag on the floor and jumped on my bed. I bounced with her a few times until she settled down next to me.

"Hi to you, too." I grabbed a blue throw pillow to play with. "Are you going on the Art Club field trip next Friday?"

"Let's see, I get to skip trig *and* visit the Bechtler Museum for a discount. You can bet your pretty little ass I'm going," she said with a wide grin and linked her arm through mine. "You're going, right?"

"I haven't decided. I might have to do something with the newspaper. If I don't, can you take some pictures for me? I want to write a report on the Joan Miró collection for extra credit."

"Of course. We wouldn't want your average to slide below an A+ now, would we?" Carly yawned so wide, I could practically see her tonsils. Not a pretty sight. "You know, sometimes it really sucks being friends with you."

I grinned and laid a hand on my chest. "Thanks. I really feel the love."

She bumped her shoulder against mine. "Whatever, loser. Now, back to my first question. What's up with you guys? Did you finally have sex?"

My eyes burned from the instant blush that shot up my face. "Carly!"

"Come on, you had to be doing *something* to get grounded. Your parents never ground you. Am I supposed to believe that you two actually just *talked* all night?"

But we did. And it was one of the best nights I'd ever had. "We talked and slept. And *only* slept, so get your mind out of the gutter," I said, tapping her forehead with my index finger a bit harder than necessary, to get the point across.

"Ouch! Fine, if you say so." She yanked the pillow from my lap and tossed it into the air. "But it sucks that you guys can't see each other much anymore. I mean, even I think your parents driving you to and from school is overdoing it a little."

"Yeah, well, I wasn't exactly in the position to argue."

"Okay, I'll concede on the sex thing, but I still think some-thing is up with you two. You're *different*."

I shot her a curious look. "Good different or bad different?"

"Good. More relaxed. Like you're a real couple now." She shook her head and lay back against my pillows. Her fingers toyed with the fringe on the end of my lace pillow. "I mean, even though I know the truth about you two, sometimes I can't help forgetting. You're both so cute. And you fit together."

"Are you kidding me? We're nothing alike."

Carly rolled her eyes. "You don't need to be alike to be per-fect for each other. Look at Monica and Chandler. Ross and Rachel. Beauty and the Beast. Jack and Rose."

My eyebrows rose. "Beauty and the Beast?"

"You know what I mean. Stop pretending to date and just go for the real thing."

I tugged on my comforter, smoothing it on my bed. I had joked with Evan before that he would never make my list of re-quirements for a boyfriend, but it was sadly true. In more ways than one. He had way too much experience for me. And I hated that. Heck, just the thought of him being with Lauren made me sick to my stomach, and she was only *one* girl. I didn't want to keep meeting new people and wondering if Evan had ever been with them.

Not to mention, he'd never had a long-term girlfriend before. (Our fake relationship was probably his longest.) I'd never had a boyfriend, either, but I knew I wanted a steady, stable relationship like my parents had. I didn't even know what Evan wanted. He didn't seem to care much for his future. Or about anything.

He was also kind. And funny. And sweet. Though we didn't

care about the same things, he always made an effort about things that were important to him. And he had a vulnerable side to him that made me want to protect him.

My hand reached up to grasp the necklace, playing with the coin. "I don't know. I still don't know how I feel about him. I mean, who says I even like him?"

Carly gawked at me like I was stupid. "Uh, you think about him constantly. You talk about him all the time. You miss him when he's not around. And you make out with him enough to make *me* blush." She smacked me on the head with the pillow. "Guess what? That means you like him, you dummy! I thought you were supposed to be smart?"

I blocked the pillow with my forearm before she gave me a concussion. "Okay, okay! Maybe I do *kind of* like him. But it takes two to actually start dating. What if he doesn't feel the same way? Or worse, he calls off this whole thing because he's afraid of leading me on? What if actually trying to advance our relationship *ruins* our relationship? Then what?"

Carly blinked at me. "You think way too much. Just take it one step at a time. You don't need to have all the answers now."

"But I do." I gnawed on my lower lip. That was who I'd always been. I planned things. I prepared for them. I made sure everything I did worked toward my goal. Whether it was going to Columbia or just a summer vacation to SeaWorld. Everything needed to go according to plan. Everything needed to be logical and make sense. And Evan... wasn't part of the plan. At all.

But that was the best thing about Evan. He didn't fit into any of my neat slots. He never did what I expected him to. Every time I learned something new, something surprising, about him, it only made me want to know more. And be closer to him. But did that mean I loved *him*?

Dad knocked, interrupting us, before opening the door. "Taylor, I have a letter for you."

"Thanks, Dad." I wondered how much of our conversation he had heard. Probably not much, since he didn't look very mad today. That was an improvement.

He shifted his weight from side to side. The same way I did whenever I was nervous about something. "So, I couldn't help noticing that you've been getting some letters from other colleges."

I glanced down at the letter he handed me. My thumb scratched at the return label on the envelope. "Yeah, the counselor made me fill out the applications, even though I told her I was going to Columbia. Kind of a waste of time, but it was good practice filling out applications." I tossed it on the desk with the others.

Carly grabbed the letters. "Let me see this." She scanned each one, and her eyes grew bigger and bigger until I thought they were going to pop out of her skull. "Cornell. Yale? Seriously? These are your backup schools? God, my mom would die to have you be her daughter." She held each letter up to the light and squinted. "This one from Loyola is pretty thick, too. I'm pretty sure you got in."

My jaw tightened, and I looked down at my hands on my lap. "They're not backup schools, because I don't need backups. I'm going to Columbia."

Out of the corner of my eye, I saw Carly and Dad shoot each other a look. "Of course you are," Carly said. "And, uh, have you heard anything back from them yet?"

"No, but I know they'll reconsider after the Career Day program. I've been working on an introduction speech that will knock the socks off the guest speaker." My voice barely trembled.

I wished I were as confident as I sounded. The truth was that I was terrified. I was terrified that I was going to mess up the presentation. That I wasn't going to get accepted and that I would have to go somewhere else. The counselor didn't push me to fill out these applications—I did. Just in case I failed.

Dad took a couple of steps into my room and patted my head. His big hand was heavy but comforting on top of my hair. "I'm sure you can go wherever you want. Whether it's Columbia, Yale, or a clown college. You'll be a star, no matter what."

I gave him a small smile. "Thanks, Dad."

"No problem." He cleared his throat and reached into his pocket for two twenties. "Why don't you two go out? Watch a movie or something? Relax a bit."

"I thought I was grounded?"

"Today can be an exception. You can be grounded again tomorrow."

Carly swiped the cash and waved it at Dad. "Thanks, Mr. Simmons. I'll make sure Taylor gets back home in time for dinner."

He nodded and after giving my head another pat, he left.

Carly laid the two bills on the bed between us. "So do you actually want to go to the movies, or do you want to see Evan? I don't mind covering for you if you want to hang out with him tonight."

It was a simple question, but I knew what she was really asking. My normal life or Evan? Plans or risks?

She sat there and watched me. I knew Carly was dying to tell me exactly what to do, but she didn't. Even though she told me not to think, she knew I needed to think and rationalize everything out anyway. And that's why she was my best friend. She gave me tough love and told me what she thought, but she left me to make my own decisions.

My fingertips tapped on the twenties. I kind of wished this were one of the times when she would tell me what to do. "Let's just go to the movies for now."

Disappointment was etched across her face, but Carly just nodded. "All right, let's go."

I knew she thought I was making a mistake, but I wasn't. I wasn't choosing my life without Evan. I was choosing to have time to imagine my life without him. And whether the *chance* of being with him was worth the risk of my heartbreak if he didn't feel the same way.

20

-Evan-

I searched up and down the hall for Taylor, but she was nowhere in sight. Even though it was only sixth period and
we had just seen each other at lunch, I missed her. We'd gone
from seeing each other every single day to barely seeing
each other at all. Now I felt like something was always missing. I didn't know how I'd gone through my life without Taylor
before.

I couldn't even call her whenever I wanted to, in case her
dad was around. He was pretty pissed. I felt bad for Taylor,
since I got to escape and she was stuck. After all, I was the one
who came over. I had asked her to stay with me a little longer
before we fell asleep. It was my fault that she was in trouble in
the first place. It was *always* my fault.

After I got my history book from my locker, an arm curved
around my torso and someone leaned into my back. Taylor. An
automatic grin crossed my face, but I tried to play it cool. Like

I hadn't spent all day thinking about her. "I know you missed me, but this is a surprise. I thought you didn't care for PDA? Not that I mind."

The arms tightened. "You know I could never keep my hands off you, whether we're in public or private."

I spun around just as Lauren moved in closer. "What are you doing?"

Her pink lips pouted. "I would have thought that you'd know exactly what I'm doing."

I was surprised to see her. She had called me a few times since the beach party, but I didn't pick up. Partly because I didn't want to hear her bitch at me, but also because I was a little pissed about the way she had treated Taylor. I understood how Lauren could be, but Taylor didn't deserve that.

But I knew I couldn't avoid Lauren forever. *We were friends.* Are *friends.*

She leaned against the locker beside mine and looked down at the ground, only lifting her blue eyes to look up at me. "I broke up with Paul last week."

"That's . . . great."

A flicker of confusion crossed her face, but she quickly recovered. She edged closer and slid her hand lightly down my arm. "I was expecting a more enthusiastic response than that, but I'll take it. My parents are out of town at the moment. You could come over to my house."

I held my hand over hers to make her stop. "Look, I'd love to, but—"

She pouted. "Not even for old times' sake?"

Before I could even answer, a high-pitched voice interrupted us. "Not even for the winning lotto numbers."

♥ 216 ♥

We both looked up, and Taylor stared at us. Her teeth gnawed on her lower lip, but she raised her chin and glared at Lauren. I couldn't help feeling a tinge of pride.

Lauren moved back but still didn't release my arm. "Maybe we'll play next time, when you get rid of your babysitter." Catching me off guard, she jerked my wrist until I tilted to the side and gave me a loud kiss on the cheek. She gave Taylor a smirk and strolled off.

Damn it. I stayed frozen in the hunched position. My eyes squeezed shut. I honestly didn't know what to do or say. Technically I didn't *do* anything wrong, so I didn't know why I felt so guilty. Like I was in a shitload of trouble, and I didn't even know why.

Like a kid who'd just gotten caught with his hand in the cookie jar, I slowly peeked up and grimaced. Taylor's face was burning red, and her jaw was clenched so tight that her lips were practically invisible.

My first instinct was to bolt. Get as far away as I could before she went possessed-Carrie psycho on me. But I couldn't just leave Taylor when she was mad. Didn't want to.

Craaap. My life was so much easier when I didn't care. "Taylor, I can explain—"

"Forget it." She turned away and walked so quickly that I had to practically jog to keep up with her. Her sandals smacked on the tile floor with each stomp. I could barely hear her muttering over them. "I should have known that you'd jump back to her. One flutter of her fake lashes and you'd come running. God, what an idiot. Stupid. Obnoxious, two-faced—"

"Hold up. Are you talking about me?" Without waiting for her answer, I caught her elbow and forced her to stop. She continued staring down instead of at me, as if I were a bug on the ground. Probably one she'd squash in a heartbeat. "In case you didn't notice, I was blowing her off when you showed up, so why am *I* an idiot? And believe me, there was much more than just fluttering lashes that was being offered here."

Her blazing eyes flickered up, and I automatically backed up a step. I probably could have left that part out. Crap, I think I preferred her to not look at me. "Oh, I heard enough about how you'd love to meet her, but you're stuck with your boring girlfriend who's as appealing as a dentist appointment, right? So why don't you go tell her that you changed your mind? Your babysitter's busy tonight." Her rant came out in a stuttered rush.

"Damn it, I never said any of that!" My exasperated breath came out through my clenched teeth like a hiss. Why was she tripping out? Was it her time of the month or something? "You know I don't think that about you." I reached for Taylor's arm. Or at least tried to.

She jerked away from my touch so fast that she bumped into some kids by their lockers. "I just—I don't know what to think anymore." Taylor glanced around the crowded hall and ducked her head down again. "Let's talk about this later. When we're *alone*."

Right, because of her precious reputation. Wasn't that the reason we were in this crap to begin with?

For some reason, this only fueled my anger. I shoved my hand in my hair in frustration. I'm not a stranger to angry women—heck, I was a pro at defusing them—but only if it was my fault. Which it usually was. But not this time. Why was she playing the martyr in the situation? Why did I feel like crap as I defended myself? What did I even *do* wrong?

If anyone was mad around here, it should be me. I was the one turning down sex while Taylor was off going to plays and almost kissing guys in cars. For once, I was the good guy here. I didn't even call her out on it. I'd been a freaking saint ever since I signed that stupid contract.

I leaned down to mutter in her ear. "Fine, we'll continue this later." She stiffened at my closeness but didn't pull away this time. "But I don't know why you're so worked up about this like a jealous girlfriend. We're not *really* dating, remember?"

Shit, that was definitely the wrong thing to say. I wanted to take the words back, but it was like I couldn't stop myself. "You said that this was just a business arrangement, or are you just full of crap now?"

21

{Taylor}

Evan's accusations were like gunshots. Not because they were loud, but because of the intensity of his words. How dare he? As though it had a mind of its own, my hand rose to slap him. He didn't flinch at all. In fact, I could have sworn he leaned down a bit so it would be easier to hit him.

I stopped and lowered my hand back to my side. "Never mind. You're right."

His face looked pained. "Wait, I didn't mean it like that," Evan began, his hand stretching out to grab my arm.

For the first time, I barely paid any attention to his touch. Nothing registered in my mind. Not the fact that we were in the middle of the hallway. Not the audience who was straining to hear us. Nothing. I just wanted to get away from him.

"We both knew what we were getting into. And we knew the limits of this *relationship*. I was the one that got things mixed up. Stupid of me." My voice turned sweet and calm. And indifferent. Like I was ordering a tuna sandwich for lunch. Hold the pickles.

"No, you're not—"

I shrugged away from him. "But everything's ended up pretty well. People stopped gossiping about us a long time ago. Maybe we should just end it. I've been waiting ages for things to go back to normal."

"You have?" Now it was his turn to look shocked.

"Of course. I'll even take you out to dinner to celebrate our breakup. Somewhere nice. But until then, remember our deal. No cheating on each other," I joked halfheartedly. The lump in my throat grew until I could barely talk anymore. I had to get out of there. I cleared my throat and smiled at him, a wide, beaming smile that hopefully hid the way I was feeling. "I have to go to class, but I'll see you after school."

His mouth opened as though he wanted to argue with me. My heart soared when his grip on my arm tightened, only to crash to the ground when he let go. "See you later."

༄•༅

I didn't know *why* I was so pissed at Evan. So Lauren was putting the moves on Evan. Big whoop. Like he said, we weren't anything to each other. A few kisses didn't mean that we were dating. Nothing had changed.

Except me. Why was I so stupid to think that we could—that he might—

Stupid. STUPID. Stupid.

I needed something to do. Something to distract me. And

I knew the perfect solution. With the deadline for the new issue of *New Voices* just days away, Brian would be holed in the media room so he could go over each article and piece himself to make sure it was perfect. Each issue was his baby.

I stared at the wooden media-room door and willed myself to just forget about Evan. At least for a few hours.

With an unsteady hand, I pushed the door open. Brian's lanky body hunched over pieces of paper that were spread out on the table. The skinny tie that he wore with his white button-down shirt was loosened until it was nearly untied. His shirttail poked out of his dark-wash jeans.

The first thing that I noticed—besides how tired he looked—was that he needed a haircut. Badly. His black hair repeatedly fell into his eyes, and he absentmindedly batted it out of the way. He alternated between chewing on his thumb and his lower lip as he moved the pieces around. His dark eyes squinted as he tried to visualize the order they should go in.

I shut the door with a bang. He looked up and smiled, the familiar smile that had tugged at my heart since the first time I met him. "You're late. Did Higgens keep your class back talking about his wonderful son again?"

Brian didn't take physics. He had lucked out and was placed in the honors microbiology class upon his parents' request. But he'd heard me complain about Mr. Higgens a thousand times. "No, I just had stuff to do."

"Don't worry. I don't blame you for ducking out on me. Every month I ask myself why I put myself through this torture." He scratched at his neck and shook his head. "But now that you're here, do you mind looking over this article? I don't know if it should go before or after the pep-rally recap."

"Yeah, sure." I sat on a desk a few feet away. My feet tapped against the metal rungs.

Brian handed me the articles, but he didn't let go when I grabbed them. Instead, he gave me a funny look. "What's wrong with you?"

"Nothing."

Still scrutinizing me, Brian leaned back against the table, not even caring that several pieces of paper were sliding off the edge. He crossed his arms. "Come on, tell me what's wrong."

I squirmed under his intense gaze. "I just have something on my mind, that's all."

"Something or someone?"

Trust Brian to always know exactly what I was thinking, unlike a certain surfer. "Someone." It was kind of weird to talk about this with Brian. Not only because we'd never talked about relationships before—or my lack of relationships—but also because the other night in his car, when we had almost kissed, was still fresh in my mind.

Or at least I thought we almost had. It certainly felt like we were about to, but the next day, Brian had acted like nothing was wrong. He was so normal that I almost thought that I had imagined that entire evening.

"I guess Evan's giving you some trouble, huh? What happened?"

My foot kicked the desk a bit as I stared at the ground. "We just had a fight. He said some things. I said some things. Maybe it was my fault. I was kind of harsh."

Brian laughed. "That's just who you are, though. Blunt, hard-core, heart-crushingly honest."

"Gee, thanks a lot. You make me sound like some type of wrecking ball."

"The good kind." He kicked his long legs against the metal rungs of my desk, letting the low, hollow ringing vibrate through the room for a minute or two. "So, do you think you'll work it out?"

"I don't know." An image of Lauren snuggled against Evan flashed through my mind, and I let out an involuntary sigh. I slid off the desk and knelt down to pick up the papers scattered on the ground. "I have a feeling we won't be together much longer."

"Good." To my surprise, he reached down for my hand and pulled me upright. "Because I've been meaning to talk to you about something. About us . . ." His voice trailed off, and it was his turn to stare at the floor.

"Us?"

Brian let out a deep breath and massaged the back of his neck with his other hand. "You know that I've always admired you despite how crazy you are. And I don't know why it's taken me so long to say this, but . . . I like you." He shook his head. His eyes were bright as he tightened his grip on me. "Like really like you. I always have."

"Huh? You have?" I cringed at myself. Oh god, that had to be the worst response to a confession ever. EVER. "I—when?"

"Since my first day of school, when you came up to me to find out my IQ score. Even after you snapped at me when you found out my score was five points higher than yours." There were crinkles in the corners of his eyes as he laughed. His hand rested in the nook between his neck and shoulders. "I never had a chance."

The papers in my hand crumpled. "Brian...I..." I didn't know what to say. What could I say?

If this were a romance novel, this would be the scene when I could declare my love, too, and fall into his arms to live happily ever after. I mean, this was Brian. *Brian.* The guy who brought over my homework assignments when I was out with the flu for nearly a week. The one who stayed up late helping me cram for my physics exam even though he didn't take physics. And he was *still* good at it. The one who fit into all of my plans *perfectly.* The logical choice. Maybe the right choice.

I couldn't have found someone better if I spent the next hundred years trying. *He was a great guy.* Is *a great guy.* We made sense.

So why did I feel like running for the nearest exit?

My head spun with all my questions until I was dizzy.

His hand tightened on my arm as though he were trying to bring me back to reality. "It's all right if you don't feel the same way. We could just forget this ever happened. Like I didn't open my big mouth."

The resigned expression on his face ate away at me. Especially since I was the reason. "No, it's not that. It's just...so sudden. I don't really know how I—I never really thought about it." That was a lie. I'd thought about us being together before. But that was all before Evan.

Brian's eyes softened with hope, and his hand drifted up to cup the back of my neck. "Why don't you think about it, then?" And just like that, without another word, he came closer and closer. He paused for a few seconds right before the kiss, in case I wanted to pull away.

I didn't.

It shouldn't have surprised me that Brian's kiss would be perfect, like him. It was sweet. Gentle and soft. Like the kiss that the prince would give the princess at the end of the story, right before they rode off into the sunset toward their happily ever after.

Being with Brian was so effortless. He knew who I was and loved me. We had the same goals. The same views on life and our future. Hopefully we'd both be in New York next year. Maybe this was how things were supposed to be. Maybe things were starting to fall into place again. Like he said, things fit for a reason.

His other hand slid up my shoulder and accidentally tugged at my necklace beneath my shirt. Evan's necklace. Evan's face flashed in my head, and I jerked away from Brian like he had electrocuted me.

My hand flew to my mouth. "I—I can't do this. I'm sorry, but Evan—"

A flicker of realization flashed across Brian's face. "Do you love him?"

"No, of course I don't." I shook my head. "I mean, I don't... know."

His face displayed all the hurt and confusion that was in his voice, making it crack. "He'll hurt you in the end. You know that. We all know what he's like. He's a player who's never serious about anyone. He's only out to get as many girls as he can."

A flicker of anger hit me, searing through my confused thoughts. "You're wrong. You don't know him at all."

"Taylor..." His hand stretched out to grab hold of me, but I darted out of reach. "I'm sorry. That was stupid. I don't know why I—"

I held up my hand, and he immediately froze. "No. Just stop talking." I grabbed my bag from the floor and turned away from him. I stopped at the door, but I couldn't bring myself to turn around and look at him. "I'm sorry."

22

-Evan-

Aaron came over just as I was in the middle of pounding my head against my locker. "So I heard about your little fight."

Smack. "Why am I so stupid?" *Smack.* "I screwed everything up." *Smack.* "It's over. She's never going to forgive me."

His hand shot out and blocked my head before I could make a dent in the lockers. "Dude, chill out. Just go apologize. Everything will be fine."

I sighed. "You don't understand. I really screwed up. Big time." The hurt and shocked look on Taylor's face swam in my head, tormenting me. Why did I have to say all those things to her? Why didn't I keep my mouth shut?

"Oh, I know. To be honest, I've been waiting for you to screw things up with Taylor for ages now."

"What?"

He leaned back against the lockers with crossed arms and

rolled his eyes. "Look, you may be an expert when it comes to hooking up with girls, but you suck at actually having a real girlfriend and keeping one. I mean, you may be Zeus, but when was the last time that dude had a real relationship?"

Aaron didn't know that Taylor and my relationship wasn't a real one, either. But sometimes it felt real. There was no denying that she meant more to me than any of those other girls. And Aaron had a point. He was better at this stuff than I was. He'd had a couple of girlfriends here and there. I may have dated tons of girls, but Lauren was the closest I'd ever been to a real relationship before Taylor. Two incomplete, warped relationships.

And his words gave me hope. "So what do I do to fix it?"

He leaned in real close, like he was about to give me the secrets of the universe. "It's going to sound really stupid and crazy, but just talk to her. One fight could break up a fling, but not a real relationship. You just have to work it out."

I gave him a skeptical look. "Seriously? Your big advice is just to talk to her?"

"Well, it's better than your stupid plan of banging your head through the locker. Besides, that's what you have to do in a real relationship. You talk about your feelings. It's annoying and frustrating. You may have to try a couple of times if she doesn't feel like talking yet, or you might even talk for hours. And you'll probably want to grab a drink afterward, but that's the point. You have to try. Because if you don't bother trying, then what's the point in being in a relationship?"

He made sense. I never bothered trying with the other girls. Never wanted to go through the effort. What was the point when there were other girls to date? But there wasn't another Taylor. "But just talking seems a little too *easy.*"

"Trust me, sometimes the easiest way is the best way." Aaron stroked his chin with one hand and patted me on my head with the other. "Listen to me, you shall, Obi-Wan. All right, things will be. Wax on, wax off."

I laughed and shook off his hand before giving him a short jab in the shoulder. "You're mixing up your masters."

"No, I'm not. I'm combining them because I'm just *that* awesome." He grinned and shoved me off. "Now go find her."

It took a while to find Taylor. She didn't pick up my call, and Carly told me that Taylor's parents hadn't picked her up yet. But she didn't know where she was, either. For the next half hour, I searched the entire school. I even poked my head into the girls' locker room to check. Nobody was there except Coach Jill checking some of the lockers. I bolted before she caught sight of me.

Where could Taylor be?

Somehow I found myself standing beneath the tree where we had our Valentine's Day picnic, remembering how excited I was to bring Taylor here. Her ecstatic face when she saw my surprise. Things were so much easier then.

And it was the exact place to find Taylor. I had almost missed her at first. She was half hidden behind the oak tree, facing toward the football field. She must have heard me coming, but she didn't move. Not even when I came up behind her.

"So you decided to stand me up to watch the jocks practice?" I leaned against the tree. My shadow fell over her small, curled-up form. "A little heads-up would have been nice."

"Sorry." Her face was squished in her arms.

I squatted down next to her, but she turned her head and just snuggled deeper in her sleeve. I let out a deep breath and remembered Aaron's words. *Just talk.* "Are you still mad about the Lauren thing? I wasn't going to meet her. I swear."

"I know you weren't."

"Then what's the matter?" When she didn't answer, I poked at her shoulder until she finally looked up at me.

There was a small smile on her face like she was trying to look happy and normal. But I could tell that something was wrong. Her eyes were red and a bit swollen. And even now, her lashes were slightly damp with tears.

I sucked in a deep breath and my fists clenched together. "What's wrong? Did something happen? Did someone say anything or—"

Taylor grabbed my arm before I could jump up and beat up everyone in sight. "No, it's just . . . it's nothing."

"Doesn't look like nothing." I wiped away a remaining tear clinging to her cheek. "So, do you want to talk about it?"

"No."

There goes Aaron and his stupid plan. *Try. Just keep trying.* I sank down next to her, but she avoided my gaze. Her fingers just plucked at the blades of grass next to us and placed them in a neat pile, crisscrossed in a pattern.

"Can I ask you something?"

She let out a sigh. "I thought you understood that I didn't want to talk?"

"Just one question, I swear." I coughed into my fist a few times. "You're not crying because of me, right?

Her hand knocked against the grass pile, knocking it over.

"Don't flatter yourself. I'm not crying. My allergies are just going crazy right now."

"Okay, allergies." I didn't believe her lie for a second, but if she didn't want to tell me, then I wasn't going to push her. And if she was going to blame it on her allergies, then I was going to let her. I climbed to my feet and nudged her elbow with the tip of my toe. "I'll take you home."

"I don't really want to go home right now."

"But what about your dad?"

Taylor gnawed on her lower lip and looked down. "They're not expecting me home anytime soon. I'm supposed to be helping Brian with some newspaper stuff. But he—he doesn't need me today."

There was something weird about her voice. But I was just glad that we could spend more time together. I reached out and took her hand, lacing my fingers through hers. "I know the perfect place to go where your allergies won't bother you anymore."

— • —

"So where's this mysterious place you're taking me?" Taylor asked after we got our hot dogs. She trailed a few steps behind me as we crossed the street, still licking the chili off her fingers.

"God, are you *still* hungry? I should have let you eat mine, too."

"Like I would have had a chance to. You inhaled yours before I even put on the mustard. Did you even chew it?"

"Nah, I have a pretty big mouth." I walked backward so I could watch her, hands shoved in my pockets.

"I noticed."

"Are you done? Can I hold your hand now?"

She pulled a small bottle of antibacterial gel out of her purse and squirted a glop on her hands. "Why? No one's here."

I waited until she finished before grabbing her. "Call it a habit. Besides, I don't want you to get lost."

"Well, I wouldn't get lost if you would only tell me where we're—oh!" Taylor skidded to a stop by my side. "We're going to the aquarium?"

A feeling of contentment filled me as I looked up at the large white-and-blue building. This place was like home to me. When I was little, I wanted to move into the janitor's utility closet. Even tried to pay him rent. "Yep. Come on."

We walked through the various rooms, and she cooed over the otters—especially Rachel, Shayda, Elana, and Lily, the four show-offs in front—and skidded away from the eels. She leaned in so close over the petting tank to touch the stingrays that I had to hold onto the back of her shirt to make sure she didn't fall in.

I'd always loved being there, but it was a different experience with Taylor. She hadn't been here in years, so she had the enthusiasm of an eight-year-old.

Finally we reached my favorite room of all. The Seas Room. It was a large room with benches on descending stairs like at a theater, and the stage was the largest exhibit in the aquarium. The entire wall was a glass tank that measured twenty-five-feet deep and held 600,000 gallons of water. And it was filled with various colorful schools of fish, sharks, sea turtles, and sting-rays just swimming back and forth.

Since it was nearly dinnertime, the room was empty, except for one couple and their little kid walking back and forth. They were more entertained by their kid than by the amazing ocean life in front of them. The little girl was pretty cute, though. Her red hair bounced on her shoulders as she danced in circles to her mom's singing.

Taylor's eyes widened, and she stepped right up to the tank. Her hands reached out to touch the glass. "It's beautiful here. And those turtles are huge!"

"There used to be an even bigger one. Nearly twice as big as these babies, but poor Rudy died two years ago."

She turned to me with a little smirk. "Rudy, huh? I guess I know who your car's named after now."

"Yeah, well . . ." I didn't continue. She was right, but I couldn't help feeling a little stupid. I mean, who names their car after a dead sea turtle? Instead, I turned and headed for the center seats, plopping down on the bench. My feet kicked my book bag beneath the seat. "My dad brought me here for the first time on my eleventh birthday. I loved it so much that he bought us a frequent pass, and we'd come back here every few weeks after that. You know, when he wasn't in jail."

"You know, you say that so casually," Taylor said, sitting next to me. "It doesn't bother you that he goes—that he's in there a lot?"

"No. Not as much as it should." I stretched out my legs on the seat in front of me. "It annoys me whenever Brandon mentions it, but that's because he's always trying to prove that he's superior to us."

"But he's not."

"Hell, no."

She gazed at me for a long moment before changing the subject. "It's strange how they could be so peaceful together in there. They're all swimming with the sharks." Her hands waved around to emphasize her point. "If I were the sea turtles, I'd be scared out of my mind in there."

"Well, they get fed regularly, so there's no danger of the sharks eating them." I leaned an arm around her shoulders. "Hey, if we could get along, then why can't they?"

"That's true. Here I am, alone with you, and I'm not scared at all."

"Don't flatter yourself. You're more like the shark than any other animal in that tank," I teased.

Taylor laughed. "Whatever. You're more dangerous than anyone I know."

"Oh yeah? And what are you in danger of?"

She stared at me for a moment before raising an eyebrow and turning back to the tank. "Nah, you're right. I am the shark."

"Told ya."

I watched for any indication that she was bored so we could leave, but she didn't seem to mind being here. In fact, she slipped off her shoes, sat cross-legged, and leaned back on her hands, looking like she didn't mind staying here forever. I know I didn't.

Letting out a deep breath, I tried again. "So are you ever going to tell me what's wrong?"

Her lips pursed together into a tight line, and Taylor shook her head. "It's just ... college stuff that's stressing me out. I don't want to talk about it."

Not sure if she was telling me the truth, I leaned back against her side and nodded, just glad that she wasn't mad at me anymore. And she *had* been stressing about being wait-listed for a while. Maybe someone else had gotten in or something. The people at Columbia were idiots for not accepting her in the first place. Taylor was amazing.

"Do you ever wonder if we'd be friends if it weren't for that stupid party?" I didn't know why that question popped out, or why the answer was important to me, but it was.

"Probably not." She looked at me out of the corner of her eye and smiled. "You're kind of an ass."

"Yeah, I am, aren't I?"

"That's okay. I'm kind of a shrew."

"Kind of?" I threw up my hands when her eyes narrowed. "All right, *kind of* is right, I guess."

Her lips curved in the first genuinely happy smile I'd seen from her all day, the kind that was so wide it practically covered her small face, and suddenly the world seemed brighter. Though it was probably because of the sun setting right through the window by the front entrance.

"Do you remember that night? I don't remember much of it."

Not much, but some bits and pieces had come back to me every once in a while. Awesome bits and pieces. "Yeah, you say a lot of weird stuff when you're drunk."

"I did?" Taylor groaned and her arms swung up to cover her face. "God, I know I'm going to regret asking this, but what did we—what did we talk about?"

If I were a nice guy, I would have lied and spared her the details. I wasn't going to, though. It was too hilarious to forget.

"Nothing much. You told me about your love for blue cotton candy and how you're rotten and mean on the inside. Oh, and you told me that you have dirty thoughts all the time, and then you hit me."

Her head slowly lifted, eyes wide with shock and horror. "What?" She sounded hoarse and strangled.

"You did. Right here." I solemnly nodded and pointed to my right cheek. "I'm surprised you didn't see the red mark."

"And what about . . . the other stuff?"

"Oh, you mean the dirty stuff?" I smirked. "Well, it was pretty cold, so I couldn't take off my clothes like you wanted me to, but I did let you feel me up above the waist. I drew the line at the pants, though. I'm not *that* kind of guy. You have to take me out to dinner first."

Her hand moved so fast that I almost didn't see it. Almost. I shielded my head with my arms, but she was still able to smack me right by my left ear. The other couple and some workers were starting to stare at us. "Ouch! I'm sorry! Next time I *will* take off the pants!"

Smack! This time it was even harder than before. I ducked, but she was prepared. "Stop." *Smack.* "Saying." *Smack.* "That! It's not funny!"

Finally I had to grab her arms to make her stop. "Settle down. We're in a public place, you know."

Suddenly my words sank in, and Taylor backed off. Her face was beet red, but she stared at the tank again until every-one stopped looking at us. Her shoulders still silently shook with laughter.

I don't know how long we sat there in silence watching the

fish, but when it got dark, I knew it was time to go. I didn't want Taylor to be late for dinner and get in even more trouble because of me. I grabbed a bag from my backpack. "Here."

"What's this?" Without waiting for me to answer, Taylor pulled out a stuffed otter I had bought from the gift shop. She wordlessly blinked at me.

"Just something to say sorry. For your allergies." Brian popped into my head at that exact moment. "If you ever need to talk, just call me. I could be here for you, too."

Taylor blinked at me again as though absorbing everything I'd just said. Finally, with a little squeal, she hugged me. "Thanks."

"No problem." I pulled away and beamed down at her, glad that she was happy again. "That's what friends are for, right?" Within a few seconds, her delighted smile faded as she hugged the toy to her chest. "What's wrong?"

"Nothing."

I narrowed my eyes at her, but she went back to watching the sea turtles. Her cheek pressed against the top of the otter, cushioning her frown. It's strange how a single word could sound so heavy and be, well, *not* nothing at all.

God, girls were confusing.

23

{Taylor}

Leos were known for their bravery in desperate times."

Ha! This proved that horoscopes were a bunch of crap. I wasn't brave. I was a coward. A cowardly lion. Bring on the Wizard of Oz.

Hiding wouldn't solve anything. I knew that. Heck, it probably made things worse, but I couldn't go to school. Not when Brian's kiss was still fresh in my brain. And Evan's aquarium date.

Since Evan and I weren't dating, I wasn't *necessarily* a cheater. But I still felt guilty. And it did violate the contract. Never in a million years would I have imagined that I'd be the one to break that clause. Thank god I didn't add a penalty fine like I had planned.

Mom came into the kitchen just as I fished a fat pickle out of the jar. With pursed lips, she watched me chop it into even, microscopic pieces. She finally spoke up when I reached for another one. "Are you feeling better now?"

"Yeah, I just had a headache this morning, but I'm okay now."

"Good, now you can tell me what's wrong."

I wiped my juice-covered hands on a white dishtowel, staining it light green. "What do you mean?"

"I mean, you skipped school today, and now instead of studying or working on something, you're chopping up enough stuff to feed an army." She crossed her arms on the countertop across from me and leaned forward. "What's bothering you?"

Jeez, what was with the third degree? I let out a sigh and scooped the pickles into the mixing bowl. "Can't a girl make some tuna in peace?"

"A normal girl, yes. You? No." Mom cocked her head to the left and smiled. "After you got your wait-list letter, we had enough tuna to feed an army of neighborhood cats for months. Then there was the time after your physics exam that you swore you failed. And before that—"

"All right, I get the point." I hadn't realized that I always made tuna when I was stressed, but I guess I did. We had one of those swift-chopping blenders that cut everything up for us, but I liked chopping out the ingredients. There was something calming about meticulously cutting everything myself. It took more time, but I always felt better afterward.

Just then Dad walked into the kitchen and stopped in his tracks at the sight of us. "What's with the nightly meeting?"

"Taylor's making tuna."

His eyes widened. "Oh. Umm, I'm going back into the living room, then. Let me know when it's safe to come back for my ice cream."

I watched him rush out of the kitchen and turned to Mom,

who was trying to hide her grin. "Does everybody know about this tuna thing?"

"Basically." She picked up one of the hard-boiled eggs and knocked it against the countertop. "So what's wrong?"

My eyes shifted down to my cutting board, suddenly embarrassed to be confiding in Mom. "I'm having some trouble with ... guys."

She let out a little squeal and clasped her hands together. "You don't know how long I've waited for you to say that. For us to finally have a mother-daughter talk. Is it Evan? What did he do? Is he pressuring you about sex?"

"Oh god. No, Mom!" I smacked my hand against my forehead. Maybe asking her was a mistake. I should have finished my tuna in peace. "Just forget about it."

"Nooo!" She grabbed my arm and tugged on it like Kimmy did whenever she wanted me to buy her candy from the store. "I'm sorry, just tell me what's wrong."

"It's just ..." I swallowed the lump in my throat as I tried to figure out how to ask her opinion without revealing too much. "Why do you like Evan so much?"

"What do you mean? He's sweet. Fun. And you have to admit, he's pretty easy on the eyes."

My brow wrinkled. "Yeah, but ... we don't have anything in common. At all. I'm just surprised that you're so supportive of us dating, that's all."

"I suppose he is one of those boys I should be warning you about. Or hiring a chaperone to follow you two everywhere." Mom pursed her lips together in thought as she continued peeling the rest of the eggs. "I guess I'm just glad that you're finally acting like a normal teenager. Dating and having fun. I was fully prepared for all the angst and fighting that comes with a teenage daughter, but you were never like that. You got terrific grades. You're driven, and you know exactly what you want to do with your life. And nothing gets in the way of that. You barely go out, so you don't break your curfew. And you always help out around the house and do what you are supposed to do."

"I'm . . . sorry?"

She laughed. "I'm not complaining. It's just . . . you became an adult by the time you were eleven, and sometimes I wonder if that's because of your dad. The real one. And our fighting all the time. You never got to be a kid like Kimmy."

I traced the flower designs on the countertop. "Some people are just different."

"Yeah." Mom let out a sigh and walked over to the sink to wash her hands. "I just don't want you to miss out on anything because of me."

Guilt swept over me. Mom was always so happy and cheerful—even flaky at times. Now I felt bad for being annoyed whenever she would try to get me to go shopping or get manicures. I'd never understood why she seemed so obsessed with that sort of stuff.

"I'm making tuna because of Brian," I finally said, throwing her a bone. "And Evan."

Her eyes got so bright and round that I wouldn't have been surprised if she started jumping up and down with joy. Her straighter-than-a-ruler daughter finally acting like a real teenager with boy problems and faking sick to skip school? Not to mention, two boys were vying for the hand of that uptight, driven daughter? Cue the newspapers. This was a dream come true.

Luckily, she tried to play cool about it. "So they both like you? That's interesting. But not surprising, of course," she quickly added.

"Well, Brian told me he does. For a while now. But Evan . . . I don't think we'll last much longer." I chewed on my lower lip. "Especially since there's this other girl that likes him, and they have a *history.*" Mom didn't need to know the specifics of Lauren and Evan's history. I definitely didn't want to think about it.

"Oh. Well, Brian is quite nice, too."

"He's great. He's perfect for me. Like Dad is for you. And it makes sense for us to be together. I always figured we'd end up together, anyway." I shrugged. "But I don't know why I'm hesitating now."

She reached out and swept my bangs out of my face before tilting up my chin with her index finger. "Usually, that means you don't actually want it. No matter how much you thought you did. For once, go with your heart and not your head. Even if it's crazy."

"But that's really hard."

"Life is hard. Give yourself some time to figure things out, then. And if someone bothers you about that, you can tell them to go to hell."

I rolled my eyes and laughed. "Thanks, Mom. That's great advice."

"That's what I'm here for." A wide smile crossed her face. "Do you want to go shopping after school tomorrow?"

I shuddered inside, but I nodded. "Sure, that'd be fun."

Mom *did* say I needed to take some time for myself, so I took that as having parental permission to stay home the next day. Hopefully, an extra day would help me figure out things.

I didn't count on Brian coming to visit.

"You look pretty healthy for someone who's supposed to be on her sickbed. And to think I cut first period to come all this way to check up on you."

My head popped up from the pillow I had propped against the wall. I was in my usual spot in the living room, curled in the armchair by the bay window with a romance novel in my hand. Evan's otter plush was on my yellow-and-white-striped lap. "Brian! How—how did you get in?"

His thumb jabbed over his shoulder. "Your mom let me in before she left for work."

Ah, that traitor in Vera Wang pumps and Ralph Lauren Romance perfume.

He handed me a large pink daisy. "Here. I remembered you liked daisies."

I think I had only mentioned that once, but of course, Brian would remember. "Thanks." I touched the soft petals for a few seconds before putting it on the tiny table next to me. Damn, this was hard.

"So are you ever coming back to school, or are you planning to hide out at home until the end of the year?" Brian leaned against the white doorframe. His ankles crossed in the opposite corner. He was so tall that his lanky frame seemed to fill up the entire doorway, making any thoughts of escape impossible. "Even though you're smart, I doubt the school will let you graduate from home. And it'll be a shame to be a high school dropout just because some idiot confessed his feelings for you."

My heart wrenched at his forced-playful tone. He told me he liked me, and how did I respond? By running away and hiding until he had to come look for me himself. When had I turned into a six-year-old kid again? And most importantly, why couldn't I be sick for real? Dante's hell was too good for me. "I'm sorry, Brian. I just didn't—"

"You don't have to say it. I did kind of spring it on you. I had all these scenarios of how I would tell you, and blurting it out like that wasn't one of them. And you holing up at home is a pretty clear indication of how you feel." He swallowed loudly. "Right?"

I hesitated for a second and gave him a small nod. I didn't want to hurt him, but it wasn't right to lead him on anymore. Even if we did try to give it a shot, it would never work out. No matter how many chips were in our favor. I couldn't make the feelings suddenly appear. Mom was right. I had to go where my heart wanted me to be. Even if it meant it could get broken. Even if Evan only considered me a friend.

Brian gave me a half smile and tapped his temple with his index finger. His left dimple appeared. "I figured. I'm not the smartest person in school for nothing, you know."

Feeling awful, I pushed my green ottoman toward him. "So are you going to sit down or what?"

"Well, with an invitation like that, how can I refuse?" Instead of sitting, though, he straddled it. His feet kicked at the carpet while his finger poked at the torn hole in his faded jeans.

Twiddling my thumbs, I said the first thing that came to mind. "I've never seen you in old jeans before."

He looked down as though he had forgotten what he was wearing. "Yeah, it's been a while. I forgot how comfortable they were."

"Why didn't you ever wear them before?" Were we seriously discussing his clothes choices? Out of everything else we could have talked about, why did I—

"Because of you."

"What?"

Brian shrugged. A light blush was on his high cheekbones. "Carly told me before that you liked guys who dressed up so . . . you know." He gestured toward his jeans.

I blinked at him. That was the one answer I wasn't expecting, but it was the sweetest, most perfect answer. There really was no other way to describe him. "Oh . . . sorry."

"Don't worry about it. It was kind of a stupid plan." He shifted from side to side and ran his fingers through his dark hair. "Although can you do me a favor?"

"Anything."

His blue-striped feet knocked against the bottom of the ottoman. "Could we forget about the other day and just go back to being friends?"

My heart wrenched. Again. But I couldn't help the relief that swept through me. I wasn't going to lose him as a friend after all.

Unable to help myself, I got up and wrapped my arms around him for a tight hug. His arms instantly came down around me. It was warm and comforting, like a bowl of soup when you're sick. Or your thickest favorite sweatshirt when it's cold outside. He squeezed tightly once before pushing me away.

Brian cleared his throat and shook his head. His black bangs fell into his face, covering his eyes. He still needed a haircut. "I stopped by your physics class to pick up your missed classwork, and it turns out you didn't miss a single thing. It was his son's birthday, so he had a party in his class. All day." He laughed loudly. "I was a fool not to take that class."

Taking the hint, I smiled and sat back on the sofa. "But you needed that biology class to get into the premed program at Tulane. You could still change your mind about that, you know."

"I think we both know that Tulane and med school afterward are NOT going to happen. Poring over books all night long and cutting into cadavers the first year? No, thank you."

"I didn't think so."

We continued talking about our classes as if the past two days hadn't happened, then he had to leave for a biology quiz. It was nice to have my friend back. Even if it was only for just a little bit.

24

-Evan-

My mind was still stuck on Taylor when I pulled into the garage that afternoon. Her face. The way she hadn't even looked at me when she mumbled goodbye and ran into her house after the aquarium. And then she didn't come to school for the next two days. Something else was wrong. Something more than just Columbia. It killed me that I didn't know what it was. That she didn't trust me enough to tell me. And that I couldn't fix it for her.

I grabbed a Coke from the fridge and headed toward the stairs when something in the corner of the dark living room moved. The hairs on my neck stood up. I was always the first person home. Every day.

I grabbed the closest thing at hand—Mom's blue-and-yellow flowered umbrella—and I crept into the room. Then I used my elbow to flick on the light and leapt forward. My right hand waved the umbrella in the air like a sword or a lightsaber.

Mom shrank back on the couch. Her wide eyes stared at me while both hands clutched at her chest. "What are you doing?"

"Oh, hi." I dropped my arm and coughed with embarrassment. "Sorry, I didn't know you were there. I'll just—let me put this back." I shoved the umbrella back in its wooden stand. "Why are you sitting in the dark?"

Her hands fell to the cushions on either side of her. She looked around the room as though she didn't know herself. "I was just thinking about stuff while I waited for you."

"For me?"

I waited for her to continue, but she didn't. Instead, she reached out to organize the magazines and glass coasters on the table. They were the kind that you could put a picture in. There were some with Mom and me and some with Mom and Brandon. None of us all together. There was no point in forcing the *family* label on us when we weren't one.

"I want you to understand how glad I was that Brandon came into our lives. He's not perfect, but life with him is. He's reliable, and he takes care of us. And he puts me first. He makes my life easy. And the only way I can repay him is to make him happy. Even if that means cutting your dad out of our lives." Mom smoothed the wrinkles in her pants before standing up and pulling a piece of paper from her pocket. "But that wasn't my decision to make. It should have been yours. So here."

The yellow sheet was barely three inches wide and had a long, ragged tear on one side. Some numbers were scribbled on it, squished together. A bank account? "What's this?"

"That's your dad's phone number."

Bam! And just like that, I slumped down on the arm of the seat across from her. It slid back a few inches on the hardwood floor. I clenched the paper so hard, it crumpled in my hand. "I thought you didn't want me to contact him."

"I didn't. I still don't." Mom crossed her arms and looked away. She chewed on the inside of her cheek. "I just don't want you to hate me for it later on. And you're right. It's your choice whether you want to see him or not."

Her sad tone nearly killed me. Judging by the circles under her eyes, this had been bothering her for a while. And the slight indention in the couch cushion that refused to go away showed that she had been waiting for me for a *pretty* long time.

I was a shitty example of a son. The worst ever.

"Mom." I stood up when she headed toward the kitchen. She stopped, and her shoulders stiffened. I swallowed and shook my head, even though she couldn't see me. "If you never gave me his number, I wouldn't blame you. Yeah, I was a little pissed for a while, but I wouldn't hate you. I can't."

Mom finally turned around. Her eyes shone with unshed tears, but I wasn't too worried. She cried over everything. Once she cried because the neighbor's dog died. And she hated that thing, said it barked at her every time she came home. That didn't stop her from crying for an hour when it got run over, though.

Besides, the broad smile on her face as she walked toward me was a big indication that everything was better now.

She had to tiptoe to kiss my cheek, something she hadn't done in years. I hadn't noticed how small she was now. Or how much taller than her I was. "Just go do what you have to do. I'll call you down when dinner's ready."

I nodded. Now that the crisis was averted, I barely even noticed when she left the room. My eyes were glued to the numbers in my hand. Ten digits. Something small and simple that kindergarteners were learning. Yet now it seemed like the most important thing in the world to me.

My footsteps thundered up the stairs as I raced to my room. I dropped my bag and paced. Back and forth. Should I call now? Maybe I should wait. Florida was in the same time zone as North Carolina (or at least close enough), so he was probably getting ready to eat dinner, too. Now might not be the most convenient time to call.

But when *was* a good time to call and say, "Hey, Dad. Remember me? Your son that you haven't talked to in years? It wasn't either of our choices, though. So what's up?"

What was I going to say to him?

As I stared at the little piece of paper, I could hear Taylor's voice in my head. And not in a very good way. Okay, she was yelling at me to stop being a wuss and just dial the damn number. And she was right.

Still, my hands shook as I punched in the numbers. I could feel myself getting sick from the clenching and twisting of my stomach. That feeling grew with each ring.

"Hello?"

There it was. The voice I hadn't heard in over four years.

And just like that, my nervousness disappeared. Like nothing had ever happened. I was eleven again, waiting for him to come home from work so we could go to the aquarium.

"Hi, Dad."

25

-Evan-

As I drove to Taylor's house, I replayed my conversation with Dad over and over in my head. And his offer to move in with him after graduation. He had a spare bedroom at his rental, and Troy University was nearby. It even had a good marine-biology program, one that I actually got into because of Taylor. To be honest, I had just filled out the paperwork to get her off my back. I didn't really expect to get in. But now . . . now everything was falling into place. It was perfect.

Even though I was dying to get away from Brandon, I still didn't know how I could be away from Mom. She didn't want me to go, but I had to do this for her. She wouldn't have to be between Brandon and me anymore. She could finally be happy.

While Mom updated Brandon on the situation—I'll bet he was breaking out the good wine to celebrate—I raced over to Taylor's house. I wanted to tell her about Dad. I wanted to tell her about the university acceptance. I needed to tell her everything.

In my excitement, I didn't remember about Mr. Simmons until I had already rung the doorbell. *Shit.* I wondered if there was still enough time to hide.

The door opened just as I was about to dive behind the rosebushes. Thank god Taylor was the one who opened it. "Evan? What are you doing here?"

She looked beautiful. I had to physically stop myself from hugging her. "I wanted to talk to you about something. Is the coast clear?"

"Uh, yeah, Dad's out with some friends. And Mom's on the phone with my grandma in the kitchen." She looked around for a few seconds before stepping back. "Do you want to come in?"

I still didn't move. "Are you sure your mom won't mind?"

"Doesn't matter. She'd probably let you in herself, anyway," Taylor muttered under her breath.

"What?"

"Nothing. It's fine." She took my arm and pulled me inside. "I actually wanted to talk to you about something, too. Let me just tell Mom that you're here first."

"Okay." I went into the living room to wait for her. Oreo was already lying on the rug, and he let out an excited bark when he spotted me. He didn't get up, but he did roll over so I could scratch him. I stood and rubbed his belly with my foot.

As I waited for Taylor to come back, I picked up a pink daisy that was sitting on the coffee table. It was lying on top of a couple of calculus worksheets with today's date on them.

That seemed weird. Taylor hadn't gone to school today—how did she get the assignment already?

Taylor came into the room just as I picked up one of the sheets. "Did Carly drop these off for you?"

"Uh, no, not really." My eyes took in every detail of her. She looked tired but still beautiful, with her dark hair pulled back from her face. She sat down next to me. Not as close as I would have liked, but it was probably better this way. I didn't want to get another ass kicking from her dad. "So, what did you want to tell me?"

My leg bounced up and down, already anticipating the excitement my announcement would get from Taylor. Oreo flopped back and forth at the frantic movement. "Why don't you go first? My news is really important, and I'm pretty sure it's going to blow yours out of the water."

She gave me a half smile. "I don't know about that. I have some big news, too."

"Is it good news?"

Her smile faded a tiny bit, and her eyes flickered to the flower in my hand. "Not *all* of it."

I looked from the pink daisy to the calculus work on the coffee table. Something clicked in my mind, and I could feel my good mood fading. Damn. Dad and college blended to the background as I stared at her, hoping I was wrong. "Who brought you this homework?"

Taylor swallowed loudly before answering. "Brian. He came over this morning."

"And the flower?"

This time she didn't answer. She just nodded.

Brian was here. She didn't call me or text me, but he came

over. Here, alone. So much for me being the only guy to visit this house. Although he probably got a real invitation from her. Which meant . . .

I dropped the flower on the coffee table. My hands clenched together as I leaned back onto the couch, moving away from Taylor now. Already distancing myself from what I knew was coming. "Does your news have something to do with him?"

"Yes." She sucked in a deep breath before continuing. Her fingers gripped the pillow on the sofa between us. The words poured out of her like a waterfall. "The other day, before you took me to the aquarium, Brian told me he liked me, and then we kissed. I'm sorry. It was totally unexpected and I didn't know what to do. I never thought he felt that way—"

I barely heard the rest of her story. Only a few words stuck in my mind. *Other day. Brian liked her. And then they kissed.*

That wasn't really a surprise. I'd watched them hang out together. Each time she smiled at him. Every time he looked at her. Brian was Mr. Perfect. Just like Taylor was Ms. Perfect. Literally. Those were the class titles they had won, along with Most Likely to Succeed. They belonged together. All I'd won was the Class Troublemaker title. And Most Attractive. Brian probably couldn't wait to march over and introduce himself to Mr. Simmons as the new boyfriend. The ass.

Even though I had been expecting it, the pain still hit me like a crashing wave. You can see it coming. You can even prepare yourself for the impact, but it can still flip you over on your board. The shock of the cold and the sting of the salt in your sinuses. Over and over again. The thought of Taylor and Brian officially *being* together made me sick. "You know what? I have to go."

Taylor grabbed my hand. "No, Evan, you have to understand! Kissing Brian made me realize my true feelings. I finally know now—"

I pushed her away before she could finish her sentence. I didn't want to hear it. I didn't want to hear anything about it. All I wanted to do was get out of here. "I get it. You're sorry. Apology accepted." It only took a couple of strides to get out of the house.

"But—"

As quickly as I'd driven to Taylor's house earlier, I must have beat the record by half just getting out of there. I could hear Taylor calling my name, asking me to listen, but I didn't turn back. I just jumped into my car and sped off.

Images of Taylor and Brian kissing and laughing kept running through my head like a damn video on repeat. Of them holding hands and going to college together and living happily ever after like the freaking perfect couple that they were.

On an impulse, I yanked my phone from my pocket and dialed. "Hey, Lauren, are you free right now?"

— • —

She slid into the front seat with a grin. "It's about time I got you all to myself." Lauren threw her purse in the backseat and curled her legs beneath her before turning to face me. "I even considered pretending to be a damsel in distress to get your attention. I know how you can't resist a girl in need."

Annoyed as I was with Taylor, I couldn't help snorting. "You're no damsel, and you'd beat up anyone who caused you any distress."

"Well, you're right about the first part, but not the second. The cause of my distress is looking fine and healthy right in front of me."

I didn't take her bait. "So, where do you want to go?"

"Anywhere." Lauren leaned even closer until her chin was on my shoulder. "You're the one who called me, remember?"

My jaw clenched. I grabbed my sunglasses from the compartment beneath my radio and slipped them on before jerking the shift stick into drive. My abrupt movement dislodged Lauren from my shoulder. "I didn't really have anywhere in mind. I just wanted to get away."

She nodded. "Then how about the lake?"

The lake wasn't really a lake, more like a giant puddle that was a mile off the freeway. The cool thing about it was that no matter how hot it got—even if it hadn't rained in weeks—or how much it poured, the puddle was always the same size. It never evaporated or anything. It was also the first place where Lauren and I had hooked up when we started dating the first time.

My fingers drummed on the leather steering wheel at a red light. I snuck a glance at her out of the corner of my eyes. She was sprawled out on the passenger seat. Her red curls swept back as she leaned out of the open window.

There were barely any cars on the highway when I pulled onto the deserted road. I parked the car beneath a tree by the lake's edge and rolled down the windows, breathing in the musty air. Dark clouds rumbled in the distance. It was going to rain soon. This was probably a bad idea.

I turned my head to suggest that we go to the mall or something instead, when Lauren pounced.

As she pressed her pouty lips against mine and ran her

tongue along the thin line of my mouth, dozens of images washed over me. Our first time at this very lake in this very car. Hanging out in the park. Snuggling together in the back of the worst movie showing so we'd be sure we'd be alone.

Suddenly, a picture of Taylor and Brian alone in the library flashed in my mind. Arms touching. A harmless hug. A light kiss. Something more. A lot more. And that was it. Something inside me snapped. I wanted to prove to myself that I didn't need to be with Taylor. My lips opened against hers, barely parting a centimeter.

But a centimeter was all the invitation that she needed. Lauren climbed onto my lap with the grace of a cat, never stopping the kiss as though she couldn't even if she tried. Her right hand ran through my hair while the other took my hand and laid it on her waist beneath her shirt. I rubbed against her silky smooth skin and pressed my hand against the small of her back. Her body fit against mine perfectly.

She let out a sigh and leaned her head back so my lips could trail down her throat.

We moved together with ease like we'd done this a thousand times—which we had. I breathed in the familiar scent of the perfume on her neck. Flowery, like lavender or something. Lauren always wore the same perfume. The smell alone used to turn me on, but now it was just that. A smell. And no longer one that I liked. If only it was a little sweeter, like vanilla or cinnamon. Or maybe the fresh smell of apples.

Like Taylor.

With a sigh, I gently pushed Lauren off my lap. I shouldn't do it. I couldn't. Not when my head was filled with thoughts of Taylor.

"What's wrong?"

Yes, what was wrong? I glanced over at Lauren's indignant face—shirt crumpled and still raised enough that I could see her tanned, flat stomach—and groaned. Damn, she was sexy. *Shit.* I closed my eyes and rubbed my temples, mentally cursing myself out for being an idiot. "Nothing, I just don't think this is a good idea anymore."

"Is it because of Taylor? Have you seriously fallen for her?" I don't know what she saw on my face, but something convinced her that she was right. "Look, I was fine with you messing around with the little virgin, because I thought you were just having fun. But she's different from us. She'll never understand you."

She was right. About everything. But that didn't make my feelings for Taylor change. If anything, it made me like her even more. And in some ways, Taylor actually understood me better than I understood myself. "I don't know what you want me to say."

"I want you to tell me that there's nothing going on between you two."

"I can't." I winced at the way my voice cracked, and I shook my head. "Why does it even matter to you how I feel about her?"

"Because of the way you looked at me at the beach party! Like I didn't matter!" Lauren lashed out. Her hands were like claws as she dug at her jean-clad thighs. "Because no matter how many girls you dated or who you had sex with, you always came back to me. Because you cared about me."

My hand flattened hers until she stopped. "I *do* care about you."

"And I care about you, too." She let out a deep, rattling breath. Her hand tightened on mine. "We belong together, Evan. You and me."

I was stunned. Lauren never spoke about her feelings, so I never even imagined that she felt *this* way about me. Especially because I never felt *that* way about her. I couldn't help feeling like a complete ass when I pulled my hand from hers. "Lauren..."

"Is it because I won't commit? Because I can. We could go to prom together or get a billboard to tell the world we're exclusive if you want. And then after graduation, we could—"

"After graduation, I'm going to college." Even though I'd just made this decision, it was still weird to say out loud. It made it more real.

"Yeah, right, and I'm going to Yale." When I didn't answer, her laughter faded until there was just silence. Raindrops were just starting to come down, splattering the windshield. "Wait, you're serious? Where are you going?"

"Troy University." I finally looked up at her stunned face.

"And that's..."

"In Florida. Fort Walton, actually."

"So you're just going to move there after graduation. Just like that. Because of her?"

I let out a deep breath. "This isn't for her. This is for me. My dad lives there. Well, Destin. And I'm going to live with him for a few years while I go to school."

"Your dad?" She stared at me as though I had suddenly sprouted horns and was doing a hula dance in the front seat. "Isn't he in jail or something? I don't understand why you would want to live with him. You've got it good here."

It's so weird that we were friends, but I'd never bothered telling her about my dad. Or anything important. The only one I had ever opened up to was Taylor. That should have been my first clue about my feelings. "You're right. Taylor is different, but she makes me different, too. She makes me want to have a future. Do something with my life. And I like the person she's made me into."

"Well, I don't. It's like I don't know you anymore." Lauren ran her fingers through her hair until it was a tangled mess around her shoulders. "You already planned out your future? Without me? Did you even consider me, think of me, at all?"

I didn't. I had deliberated over every little detail of my decision, but Lauren never came up. At all. "We'll still be friends."

She scoffed. "Friends? Really? Is that what we are?" She closed her eyes and swallowed a few times before angling her body straight forward. Her arms crossed tightly against her chest. "You know what? I think you should take me home. Anything is better than sitting here and listening to you gush over Little Miss Sunshine."

"Lauren . . ."

I reached out to touch her arm, but she jerked away like I had hit her. Her eyes flew open and were glued to the water in front of us. "Just take me home. Now."

I let out a sigh and turned the engine on. First I had lost Taylor as a girlfriend, and now I'd lost Lauren as a friend. What started off as an awesome day was quickly turning into hell.

26

{Taylor}

Evan wasn't home, and he wasn't picking up any of my phone calls. But he couldn't avoid me forever. I'd camp out on his lawn if I had to.

My eyes glanced over at the empty driveway, and I chewed on my lower lip. I almost regretted telling him about the kiss, but I had to tell him the truth. I had to explain that I was *glad* that Brian kissed me, because it made me face my heart and realize that I wanted to be with Evan.

The door flew open, and Mrs. Willard almost ran over me on her way out. Her purse knocked against the back of my head. "Sorry, Taylor, I didn't see you. What are you doing here?"

Rubbing my throbbing head, I hopped to my feet. "I'm waiting for Evan."

Her eyebrows furrowed together. "You're not with him? I could have sworn he went over to your house to tell you the good news..."

"He did, but I—" My face flushed, and I didn't know how to continue. "We didn't really get a chance to talk."

Pursing her lips together, she silently scrutinized me. "Do you want to come in and wait for him? He might be home soon."

"No, I can just wait outside if you're about to leave."

"It can wait." Mrs. Willard reached out and placed her hand around my arm. She tugged me toward the door. "Come in. Do you want something to eat?"

"Thanks, but I'm okay." I followed her into the living room and sat on the couch facing the TV. I clasped my hands tightly on my lap. I glanced around the room and tried to take my mind off how I had messed up everything with Evan. "You said something earlier about Evan having good news?"

She laughed a little bit to herself and leaned her hip against the arm of the couch. "Well, it's good and sad. At least for me. I don't really want him to leave, but it's his choice. I can't protect him anymore."

I got a little light-headed, and my vision blurred. I still didn't understand what the heck she was talking about, but I didn't like the direction this was going. "I don't—wait, Evan's leaving?"

Her grin slowly faded. "He didn't tell you anything?" She grimaced and chewed on her thumbnail. "Oh boy. This feels kind of awkward now. Maybe you should wait for Evan."

Like there was any way I could wait for this. I reached out and grabbed her arm. "No, tell me." I tried to give her the best puppy eyes I could, channeling Oreo on steak night. "Please?"

It only took another minute or so, but she caved. "He called his dad."

I blinked at her in surprise. "That's awesome!" This was huge news! So he finally called him. No wonder Evan looked so excited earlier. Or at least he did before he found out about Brian and me. "Is he going to visit him?"

Mrs. Willard looked down at her feet. "Actually, his dad asked Evan to live with him in Destin next year while he goes to college. And he said yes."

Bam! The world crashed at my feet. I sank back into the couch and stared at her. Destin? But—but that was so far. How could he—where was he—and college? When did he even get accepted? It was like I had missed out on everything.

"Honestly, I'm actually proud that he made this decision. Don't tell him I said that, though." Mrs. Willard pretended to zip her lips. "I'm still counting on guilt-tripping him into coming back here to visit as often as he can."

"Okay . . ."

"It was actually because of you that all of this even happened," she continued with a grateful smile as she grasped my hand. "To be honest, I was worried about Evan. I didn't know what he was going to do with his life. But he told me that you helped him find schools to apply for, and one of them just happened to be Troy University in Florida. Isn't that a coincidence?"

It was a coincidence. I remembered looking at the Troy University brochure and thinking how pretty the campus looked. Of course, it was Florida, so it was sunny with colorful flowers everywhere. That was actually one of the few I helped Evan with. Even as we filled it out, I didn't think much of it because of his nonchalant attitude. I didn't realize how far it was and what would actually happen if Evan got in. I didn't think it through. At all. "When is he leaving?"

"Right after graduation. His dad already got him a job at the fisherman's wharf on the weekends for some extra cash. His first day is a week after graduation."

"Oh." It looked like everything was already planned. But where did that leave me? Evan had his life all set, while I still didn't know what I was doing. How's that for irony?

Just then, the house phone rang, interrupting my daze. Mrs. Willard moved backward toward the kitchen. "Let me get that. It might be Brandon calling about dinner."

As soon as she left, I fumbled with my phone and pulled up various airline websites. Maybe it would still be possible to visit each other and be together. Maybe it wouldn't be that bad.

Maybe.

Twenty minutes later, my phone dropped to my lap. It wasn't bad. It was *really* bad. Plane tickets from Florida to New York were about $300 round-trip. Maybe $200 if I booked it a few months in advance and didn't mind two stops on the way. I didn't, if it meant I could see Evan.

Assuming that Evan did want to give our relationship a shot, how would this work? I was already saving everything I had for rent and stuff in New York. I didn't have extra money to visit Evan. And I couldn't imagine Brandon giving him any money to see me. Evan would probably have to work overtime.

And would it even be enough? Relationships were hard enough as it was without being a thousand miles apart. Literally. Columbia was 1,215 miles away from Troy University. I looked it up.

Even if we could somehow work it out, he still had to use some money to visit his mom as much as he could. I couldn't take that away from her. I didn't want to distract him and have him worry about me, too. Be his burden. He had enough on his plate already. School. A new job. His family. His new relationship with his dad. This was his chance to reconnect with him. He'd waited so long for this, and he couldn't screw any of it up.

My fist clenched around the coin necklace around my throat. *I won't let him.*

Slipping my phone back into my pocket, I sighed. The thought of not seeing Evan every day was painful. I was already missing him. But if there were this many obstacles, this many problems now, what would it be like later? It was better to end it now, here, before I—we—did something stupid. It was the best thing for everybody. Our futures were already set. Our dreams were on the right course. It's just too bad that they were in opposite directions.

Making up my mind, I took off his necklace—the first time I'd taken it off since he put it on for me.

Mrs. Willard came back into the living room just as I got up. "Are you leaving already? I thought you were going to talk to Evan?"

"No, I have to go home." My fingers ran through my hair, tugging it forward a bit to hide the fact that I was lying. And the tears that I was fighting back. I held out the necklace to her. "Could you just give this back to him for me?"

She took it from me with a confused look on her face. "But—"

I backed up out of her reach. "I—I really have to go. Thanks for everything, Mrs. Willard."

Before she could say my name or try to call me back, I ran out of the house. I jumped into Mom's car and drove home, all the while trying my hardest to keep the tears from pouring out. Because I knew once I let them go, they wouldn't stop.

When I got home, Dad was waiting for me on the front porch with a huge grin on his face. In his hands was a large yellow envelope with a Columbia return-address label. It was thick and bulky. Way too bulky to just be a rejection letter.

Which meant that they accepted me. Finally, everything I had worked for, suffered for, and given up was all worth it. I got what I always wanted. My dream of going to Columbia and living in New York was finally coming true. I should have been elated. Ecstatic.

So why did I feel so empty? Like I could practically see the thousand miles between New York and Florida paved out in front of me.

Dad waved the packet around. "I wanted to wait for you to come home to celebrate, but I couldn't—wait, those aren't happy tears. Taylor, what's wrong?"

Without answering him, I ran right into his arms and burrowed my face into his shoulder. All I could do was hold him tighter as the tears poured out.

27

-Evan-

After I dropped Lauren off, I sat on the beach for hours to clear my head, but it didn't work. For once in my life, not even the water could make me forget my problems. I was still pissed at Taylor, but I wanted to see her. To talk to her. My fingers ached—literally ached—to feel hers. Time dragged on until each second was like an hour, each hour was like a day, and—well, you get the point. And all because I missed Taylor. Really missed her. Like I was seconds away from writing sonnets about her. Yeah, I don't know what the hell she did to me. God, I should have been annoyed at her for screwing up my life if I didn't love her so much.

It was way after dinnertime when I finally got home. Mom attacked me as soon as I came through the door. Her hands were covered with flour. "Where have you been? I've been trying to call you for ages."

"Sorry, I had it turned off." So I wouldn't be tempted to call

Taylor. I grabbed an oatmeal cookie from the counter. "What's wrong?"

"Taylor was here."

The cookie crumbled in my fist as I stared at her. "Why? When?"

"She was looking for you earlier. Said she needed to talk to you about something." With a sigh, she nodded at something on the counter. "And she wanted to give you back your necklace."

"My neck—" On top of a pile of magazines, I spotted the silver chain nestled around the twisted coin. No. I grabbed it from the counter, not wanting to believe that this was really my necklace. That she actually gave it back to me. That it was all really over. "Shit. I screwed everything up with her."

My fist hit the granite countertop in frustration. Maybe if I had just let her talk. Maybe I could have been able to change her mind. I bet stupid Brian would have listened to her. Stupid, tall Brian who's always there for her.

God, I hated that dude.

Mom's hand curved around my arm, leaving a dusty flour print on my forearm. "Then fix it with her. Go tell her you're sorry for whatever you did."

I shook my head. "It doesn't matter. She picked Brian. She's going to be with him now."

"Are you sure? Because she looked really sad when I told her that you were moving in with your dad."

My head snapped up to look at her. "You told her what?"

Her fingers laced together and white dust fell onto the tile floor. "Yeah . . . it was an accident. I thought you already told her about it yourself!"

I meant to. I was going to tell Taylor all about Dad and my plans and the fact that I actually *had* plans because of her. And that my plans for the future now included her. But when she told me about kissing Brian, everything just disappeared. I didn't know what to do.

I was kind of hurt that she didn't stay to talk to me. To tell me she was proud of me. To break up with me in person. But what did I expect? She tried, but I was the one who left first.

Maybe I shouldn't have run away. I should have just stayed to talk to her. That would have been the responsible thing to do. At least then she could have given me back the necklace, and we could have said goodbye properly. And I could have hugged her one more time.

Or I could have gone to Brian's house and kicked his ass. Yeah, that's what I should have done.

Still not too late.

— • —

Later that night as I laid on my bed, I stared at the stars on my ceiling. My hand clenched the necklace so tightly that the edge of the coin cut into my palm. I didn't care about the pain in my hand. I didn't even care when Brandon came into my room earlier to gleefully drop off a calendar marking off the days until graduation, when I would move out.

There was another knock, and Mom poked her head in for the tenth time in the past hour. "You have company."

I shot upright but scowled at the sight of Aaron instead of Taylor at the door. "Oh, hi."

Instead of leaving, Mom just lingered at the doorway while Aaron sat down on the desk chair. It squeaked a little under his weight. "Your mom told me everything. Look, we're all used to you making an ass of yourself, because that's not really anything new. Usually, it's kind of fun to watch. But this moping is just sad."

Mom cleared her throat. "Honey, what Aaron is trying to say is that we're just worried about you."

"Yeah, worried."

"Well, I'm fine. And I'm not moping. I just don't feel like doing anything." I flopped on my back and went back to counting the stars.

He rolled his eyes. "Dude, you're the mayor of Mopetown. And for no reason. Taylor's not with Brian."

"How would you know?"

The chair squeaked even more. "Carly told me. I called her to ask."

I rolled on my side to stare at him. "What else did she say?"

"Carly? She just told me that Taylor is definitely not with Brian and uh . . ." He coughed and glanced at Mom. "Basically, she told me to tell you to man up and get Taylor back before it's too late. Or at least that's the PG version of what she said."

A spark of energy hit me, and I sat up. So . . . she wasn't with Brian. Yet. "Before it's too late. Does Carly mean before she starts dating Brian?"

"Actually I don't think she intends to date him. Ever," Mom spoke up from the doorway.

"What do you mean?"

Her wide gray eyes were the picture of innocence. Fake

innocence. "I'm not sure, but I think I heard that Brian turned down that scholarship to NYU. Now, I'm not positive, but wouldn't it make sense for him to *go* to NYU if they were going to date later on?"

"Where did you hear that from?"

"Just . . . around."

"But . . ." I stared down at the necklace in my hands. I didn't doubt Mom's sources—whoever they were—for a second. But if Taylor wasn't going to be with Brian, then why was she giving me back my necklace? Why didn't she stay to talk to me? What was she thinking?

Unless . . . she thought she was doing this for me.

Everything clicked into place. I saw everything through her logical, practical eyes. This was all for me. She probably thought she was being noble by stepping back. Letting me do whatever I wanted to do without being a burden. That noble idiot. I wouldn't even be here if it weren't for her. Have this chance. I needed her by my side, cheering me on and nagging me to be better.

The problem was, how would I change her mind? "What should I do now?"

With an irritated sigh, Mom marched over to sit on the edge of the bed. "You do whatever you have to and get her back! Why would you want to lose a girl who's so sweet, smart, beautiful, polite—"

"Stubborn, rude, nagging, and snarky," I finished.

Aaron snorted. "You two are so perfect for each other."

Mom had a smug grin plastered on her face. "You love her, don't you?"

"Yeah." There was no denying it. I loved her smile. I loved her sitting next to me, fidgeting with Rudy's stereo buttons. Heck, I even loved her complaining to me about my schoolwork. It was a Friday, and all my homework was finished because doing it made me feel closer to her.

And to think she was worried about her reputation before. My reputation was shot to hell because of her. See what I meant about Taylor screwing up my life?

Mom patted the top of my head like I was a kid again. "You're not too bad, either. You have my genes, so you're pretty handsome. And you're smart, even if you don't like to show it. Really lazy, though. Don't really think with your head much. Impulsive. And stubborn. God, you remember when you broke your arm on the jungle gym when you were eight? Or the second time two months later, because you wanted to show me your arm was fine when the doctor told you it wasn't?"

"Uh, are these insults supposed to help me feel better?"

She shook her head. "What I'm trying to say is that you're stubborn. And it was obvious earlier that she loves you, too. I could see it written all over her face. Now go get her back."

Mom was right. "So should I go over to her house? Get her flowers? Candy?" Pizza and blue cotton candy would probably be better.

Aaron cleared his throat. "Carly said you need to bring your A game. I mean, you really need to romance the crap out of her."

I snorted. Yeah, that sounded like her. "Then did she have something in mind?"

"Dunno. Something really big and grand to show her that you're not afraid of what anyone else thinks as long as she's with you. But still something that's personal and sweet so that she knows that you're thinking of her. How about skywriting over the school! Or a picnic in a hot-air balloon!"

"Taylor gets scared when we're on a bridge. I'm pretty sure she would die before getting in a hot-air balloon. A dead girl-friend really *isn't* what I'm aiming for right now." I felt a little dazed. I had *no* idea what to do. Big and grand but personal and sweet? Dude, what was I supposed to do with that?

His face fell, and he spun around in my chair. "Okay, maybe not that, then."

Mom leaned back on her elbows. "You know, when your dad asked me out, he took me to this fair in the next town. Or tried to. His truck broke down halfway there, and it started raining when he was fixing it, so we were both soaking wet. He had a blanket in the back, and—"

Oh god. I leaped to my feet. My arms crossed in an X in front of my face to try to make her stop. "Please don't finish that sentence." I didn't want to think about my parents in the back of any truck. I paced over to my desk. My fist lightly smacked against the back of the chair as I turned toward Aaron. "I'm surprised you had the guts to call Carly in the first place. Aren't you scared of her?"

Aaron snorted again. "Hell no. I'm on the football team. She's barely half my weight and—and I actually didn't *call* her. I texted her."

"Yeah, you sound really tough now." I held the necklace up in front of my face and watched it spin around. It caught the light and reflected like a real star. "Thanks, man. You, too, Mom. I really appreciate your help."

Mom beamed and reached out to give Aaron a high five. "Anything you need, sweetie. We're here for you."

He nodded. "You know we got your back."

28

{Taylor}

So did you and Evan really break up?"

Kimmy poked her head in my room, looking even tinier than usual in an oversize purple sweater. Her dark hair stuck out of the side of her ponytail, making her head look oddly shaped. She'd done her own hair this morning. At least she got an A for effort. I turned away from the bookcase, dropped the dust rag on the ground, and sat on the bed. "What are you doing? I thought you went to the store with Mom."

"She had too many errands to run, so I told her I'll just stay at home with you." Without an invitation, she came into my room and leaped on my bed, making me bounce a few times.

I didn't mind. I was happy for her company. Any company, really. I had talked to Carly a few times over the weekend, but she was always busy with something. And she said she could only take my moping in small doses. She promised to be back to lend a sympathetic ear tomorrow at school, but not a day sooner.

When Kimmy leaned her head toward me, I tugged at the pink scrunchie on her head and combed my fingers through her curly locks. Separating her hair in three sections, I braided it, concentrating on keeping each section even.

She fiddled with the strands on my quilt. "So did you? Mom told Dad that you did, but I didn't believe her."

My hands paused at the nape of her neck. "Yeah. I did."

"Oh."

The room got quiet as she rocked back and forth on the bed, waiting for me to finish. I took my time tucking in each of the strands that tried to escape until the braid was perfectly trailing down the center of her back. I finished the braid and tied off the end.

She scratched the bottom of her chin with the end of her braid. "Was it his fault?"

"No, not really. It was—we couldn't—" How was I supposed to explain our relationship to a nine-year-old? Heck, I didn't understand why we couldn't be together. I mean, I knew the reasons, but I couldn't help thinking they were stupid now. I was stupid. "It's complicated."

"Did you want to break up?"

"No," I admitted, unable to lie to her.

Her lips puckered into a pout. "Then it has to be his fault."

I couldn't argue with that logic. "Maybe."

She leaned back against my chest and let me hug her. "Taylor?"

"Yeah?"

"I miss him. He was nice. I don't think any other guys would let me put makeup on them."

I laid my chin on the top of her soft head and closed my eyes. "I miss him, too."

After Kimmy left to watch TV, I finished rearranging my bookcase by genre and favorite authors and dove into the closet next. I'd already divided the clothes that I would bring to college, the ones I'd leave behind, and the ones I'd give to charity, but there was no harm in double-checking. Maybe there was something I was missing. Something I'd need in the future.

And that's why I was partially buried in T-shirts and sweaters when Dad came in with a plateful of cookies. "Do you want to take a break for a minute?"

"Sure." I carefully maneuvered around the piles and came over to sit with him on the bed. "Do you have—" Without waiting for me to finish, he slipped two extra plates from beneath the plate of cookies and handed one to me with a grin. "Thanks, Dad."

"No problem. Wouldn't want any crumbs to fall on your immaculate carpet, now would we?" he asked, leaning backward against my pillow. "Who taught you to be so clean?"

I stifled a laugh. He was such a dork sometimes. "That would be you. Remember? As soon as you married Mom, you taught me that organization and structured plans were the key to happiness."

"Yeah, I forget how brilliant I am sometimes."

I laughed and was about to pop the cookie into my mouth when I realized that it was homemade. "Uh, where did this come from? Did Mom bake?" I asked, sniffing the cookie. It looked safe enough. And it was my favorite—oatmeal chocolate chip.

Dad grabbed one for himself and set it on his plate. "Good

god, no. Do you hear the smoke detectors buzzing? I think some-one gave a whole basketful to your mom. She didn't tell me who, though."

With a sigh of relief, I took a huge bite. It was delicious. Sweet and chewy. Within a minute, I had inhaled two more. I swear, I didn't even need to chew. I just blinked, and they were gone.

Chocolate really is the key to happiness. I was feeling better already, although the sugar crash would probably get me later. The cookies did make me feel kind of wistful. They reminded of the desserts Evan's mom used to make for me. And of course, that made me think of Evan, and *bam!* We were right back where we started.

Dad had a major sweet tooth, so I was surprised that he only ate two of the cookies. He dusted his hands over the plate before setting it aside on my nightstand. "So, are you ready to leave the ol' nest?"

I rolled my eyes and laughed. "Graduation's not for a while, Dad. And I'm not moving until the end of July. Believe me, there's plenty of time."

"It's one month, three weeks, and two days until graduation. I have a feeling time is going to fly by." Dad jabbed his thumb at the overflowing chaos on the floor. "Why are you packing so early if there's still 'plenty of time'? Are you that anxious to leave?"

"No, of course not. I just..." I shrugged. "I just didn't have anything else to do today."

He narrowed his eyes at me. "Is it because of that Evan boy?"

I shoved another cookie in my mouth to delay answering him. If I lied and told Dad no, he'd just interrogate me some more and find out the truth. But the thought of talking to him about boy problems made me want to throw up all the cookies I'd just eaten. This was one time where having a lawyer for a dad sucked.

Finally, I just nodded and kept my gaze down.

"I can't say that I'm sad that you two broke up. I mean, he seemed all right at first. But that was before you two—I'm not saying that you—hopefully you didn't. It's just that I know boys are into, hmmm..."

Oh god. Now I was considering deliberately throwing up to distract him. I'd never seen him stumble over his words so much. Not even when he accidentally ran over some lady's dog and ended up having to pay for the cremation.

Dad let out a sigh. "You're my little girl. To be honest, I don't think I want you dating anyone. Ever. At least, not while I'm still alive. Or while I can still see."

"Well, that's not really a problem now..."

"But I don't want you to be sad, either." He tugged on a strand of my hair. "I'm only going to say this once, so listen up. Organization and structured plans *aren't* the key to happiness and success. It might make life easier if things were perfect all the time, but they won't be. You can't plan everything. Things happen. And that's okay. You shouldn't do something just because it's easy and neat. Because sometimes messy isn't that bad."

My eyes widened, and I gaped at him. "Can you say that again? I think I need to record that as evidence that you've gone crazy." I dug out my phone and held it up.

"No way, I already told you I'm only saying it once." He

gathered up the plates and headed toward the door. "Besides, you know that in order to use the recorded conversation as evidence, both parties would have to consent, and I already said I wouldn't. Therefore, this conversation would be inadmissible in court."

I smiled sweetly up at him. "And *you* know that rule only pertains to certain states. And a good lawyer could always find a precedent in the conversation and obtain it as evidence if needed."

He laughed and shook his head. "I don't know if it's such a good idea for you to go to law school. God help me if you get any smarter than you already are. I'm just saying that if it's something or someone worth fighting for, you should fight for it. It's not called a fight because it's easy."

As usual, he was right. I munched on another cookie as I considered his words.

Dad paused at the doorway. "By the way, your mom wanted me to tell you that she bought more ingredients to make tuna. Should I tell her that you don't need it anymore?"

"Tell her to put it away. Maybe I'll need it later, but I'm good for now," I said with a smile. It was better to be prepared. There's no telling what would happen next. Life was unexpected like that.

29

{Taylor}

My eyes darted around the cafeteria at the booths and tables that were set up. A bunch of juniors and seniors wandered around to check out all the stuff. I let out a satisfied sigh. The first half of Career Day had gone according to plan and was awesome. Tons of people showed up (mainly because it got them out of class for the day) and got information about work-study programs and internships. The only thing left now was the presentation in the auditorium. All I had to do was start the slide show and introduce our guest speaker.

I shuffled through the papers in my arms, pretending to be busy looking for something so people wouldn't talk to me. I actually should have been practicing my speech, and I sort of was, but I couldn't help glancing up every time a blond guy walked in.

Where was Evan? He should have been here by now. The presentation was mandatory attendance for all seniors. Not that it had ever bothered him before. But still, he knew how much this meant to me. I thought he would at least show up.

"Ms. Simmons."

I plastered a bright smile on my face when Mr. Peters came up to me with a pretty Asian woman in a simple yellow dress. "This is Mrs. Ann Nguyen. She's the special speaker for today. She graduated—"

"Top of her class at Columbia, and not only is she the youngest partner at Ludwin, Pennington, and Nguyen—where all the partners are women—but her dream is to someday be on the Supreme Court. Something that she's clearly on the right track for," I recited, a little in awe that I was actually talking to Ann Nguyen. *The* Ann Nguyen. She was my idol. She even edged out Dad on my hero list (although I would never tell him that).

"I think I only mentioned the Supreme Court dream once in a university article when I first started law school." Ms. Nguyen gave me an admiring smile. "I'm surprised you found that."

"Well, Taylor has always been on top of everything. This entire fair was planned and organized by her," Mr. Peters said with a hint of a smile. "Someone told me before that there's nothing that she can't do, and he was right."

Looking at him in surprise, I beamed with his praise. It was almost indirectly admitting that he was wrong about me. Not exactly an apology, but I'd take it.

There was a bit of shouting on the other side of the cafeteria. His head jerked up, and the familiar frown crossed his face as he excused himself.

Grateful as I was for his compliment, I let out an inward sigh of relief when he walked off. He was nice (sort of) and all, but with all the stress of the past couple of weeks, I definitely wasn't going to be missing *him* when high school was over.

Ms. Nguyen took a few steps closer to me. "So I heard that you'll be heading to Columbia next fall."

I stared at her. "I just found out this past weekend. How did you know that?"

Her index finger rose to her lips, and she winked. "You're not the only one who's good at research."

I just blinked. This would have been a perfect time to show off my wit and charm, but nothing came to mind. At all. "You look a lot younger than I thought you would," I blurted out, inwardly wincing. Yeah, maybe I should have just stayed quiet.

"It's the genes. People thought I was twenty-one all through law school. It was annoying back then when I couldn't get into clubs, but now it's not so bad."

Okay, she just kept getting more and more awesome. Any type of small talk that I had planned evaporated with each second that I spent with her. Thank god the cafeteria lights started flickering on and off, signaling the beginning of the presentation, before I had asked her about her dog or something and she figured out I was a stalker and a complete idiot.

She smoothed at the nonexistent wrinkles in her dress. "Are you ready?"

"Of course! I . . ." A familiar greenish-gray car zoomed right by the window in front of us, momentarily distracting me.

Rudy.

My feet automatically raced forward, and I leaned out the window just in time to see Rudy park right outside the auditorium entrance down the street. I could sort of see Evan's shadowy form inside the car, but he didn't move. He just kept sitting there, drumming his hands against the steering wheel.

Why wasn't he moving?

A light hand touched my shoulder, bringing me back to reality. "Is everything okay?"

I nodded but couldn't help peering out the window again in case he disappeared. My heart leaped at the sight of that rusty old car. And the person inside it.

Ms. Nguyen glanced toward the window and gave me a small smile, like she understood. "You can go if you have something to do."

"But your introduction—"

"Someone else can do it. Heck, even I can do it. Who knows me better than me? And, well, you," she joked with a wave of her hand. "Go."

With a grateful smile, I stacked all the papers and notecards together. My stomach was bouncing with a different type of anticipation now. Looking around, I spotted Lin standing on the side with a scowl as she peered at everyone walking around. "Here, Lin, you can do the speech."

Her mouth dropped, and she stared down at the pile in her hands like it was a ticking time bomb. "What are you—I can't— I'm not ready..."

"Look, the slideshow is already loaded and set. Just click Play and read off the notecards." My hands waved in wide circles as I explained, already backing away toward the stairs. A twinge of regret and disappointment hit me for missing the presentation and for all my wasted work, but I shoved it deep down. It wasn't as important. There was somewhere else I needed to be.

Someone I needed to be with. "Give the speech and take all the credit. You know you want to." Before she could respond, I spun on my heels and left her sputtering.

Mr. Peters's mouth dropped open as I ran past him. "Taylor! Where do you think you're going? You need to start the presentation! You can't just leave before it even starts!"

His stern words made me want to pause. Especially because he was so loud that everyone turned to stare at me. But I forced myself to just think of Evan and run even faster. The pointing and whispering followed me out the door and down the hall, but for once I didn't care, because I knew that Evan was just outside, and he was the only one who mattered right now.

I ran down the sidewalk toward him just as he got of the car. I skidded to a halt behind him, barely able to stop before I smacked into his butt as he bent over the backseat to get something.

My eyes widened as I soaked in the sight of him. When I spotted him through the window, I couldn't actually *see* him that well. He was standing on the sidewalk next to Rudy in a handsome suit. I repeat, in a *suit*. Black suit. White shirt. Black tie. Simple and classic.

Oh. My. God. My heart started slamming in my chest, and the suit was only part of the reason. I'd been waiting, yearning, to see him for days, and now that he was finally here, I barely knew what to say. I wanted to apologize. I wanted to congratulate him. I wanted tell him how proud I was of him, but only three words kept running over and over through my mind.

I loved him.

30

-Evan-

I shoved the heart-shaped balloons down in Rudy's backseat just as Taylor showed up. Even if I hadn't heard her heaving and panting down the stairs, I felt her presence. Like the Force. Or Patrick Swayze in that old movie Taylor made me watch with her.

She skidded to a stop a few feet away, bent over at the waist. Her face was red, and her damp ponytail stuck to the back of her neck.

"What are you doing?"

Taylor waved her hand in the air while the other rested on her stomach. Her blue blouse scrunched together beneath her fingers. I'd never seen her look so disheveled. Taylor let out a loud whoosh of air and straightened. "I was in the cafeteria, and I saw you." *Pant. Pant.* "I had to jump over a lot of people to get out here. I might have accidentally kicked a couple kids, too, but I had to see you." Large inhalation of breath. "So you're leaving?"

"Yeah, I am . . ." The sight of her distracted me from what I was going to say. She was in front of me. Here. Now. I mean, I was thrilled to see her, but this wasn't part of the plan. "Aren't you supposed to be giving a speech right now?"

"Oh." She looked a little flustered. "I decided to skip it."

My eyebrows shot up. She had been preparing for this thing for as long as we'd been "dating." Hell, she even made me help her with it. And now she was skipping it? Just like that? "Why?"

Her eyes twinkled at me. "I told you. I had to see you."

Damn, not to sound sappy or anything, but I swear my heart melted at her words. I had this whole elaborate setup planned to win her over, and she ruined everything with five simple words. And I didn't care.

She was good. She was really good.

I moved toward her in one fluid movement and swept her into my arms. It felt so good to hold her. Like everything was suddenly right again. "God, I've been wanting to do that all weekend."

Taylor leaned into my embrace. "Why didn't you? Why'd you have to wait this long?"

"Because I'm a stupid moron."

Her lips curved into a smile against my arm. "That can't be your excuse all the time, though."

I kissed her cheek. "I know." Kissed the other one. "But I'm also an ass." Kissed her forehead. "And annoyingly wrong and confused." Kissed the tip of her nose. "And naive, while you're so understanding."

She clamped her hand over her mouth before I could kiss

there and looked down at our feet. "Flattery and kisses aren't going to work on me."

I laughed. "I forgot how stubborn you are. One of the many reasons I love you."

Her head snapped up so quickly that she almost clipped me in the jaw, like she had that morning in my room. Luckily, I dodged her in time by jumping out of the way. My reflexes were sharpened from all the injuries she'd caused. Her eyes brightened, and she beamed up at me. "You love me?"

My hand brushed against her cheek, and I lightly pinched it with my fingers. "I thought that was obvious."

Her brown eyes grew big and watery like she was about to cry. Instead, she took me by surprise and jumped on me. Literally jumped on me. Her feet left the ground. Her arms wrapped around my neck and hung on for dear life as she kissed me. Her soft, sweet lips crushed against mine.

And it was the hottest thing I'd ever experienced.

I couldn't keep myself from kissing her back with everything I felt.

"That's one hell of a kiss," I managed to comment when I was able to catch my breath again. My heart thundered in my ears.

"Well, I do aim to please," she said with a grin. "By the way, why are you wearing a suit?"

My hand smacked my forehead. "It's all your fault! I had this big surprise—I was going to show up in front of everyone after your presentation with flowers and balloons—"

Frantic barking filled the air, interrupting me. Taylor pulled away just as Oreo started bouncing up and down on the passenger seat, even though I had put him in the backseat. The navy bow tie I'd clipped on his collar was already falling off. He must have climbed up front somehow. He got more excited when he spotted Taylor and struggled to climb through the window.

"—and I even brought Oreo along," I finished with a sigh. All that weekend brainstorming and prepping with Carly and Aaron was ruined now.

Taylor tried to smother her laughter against her hand as she hugged me close. "It's so cheesy. Did you plan fireworks and skywriting, too?"

I waved my hand behind her head, hoping that Aaron and Carly understood to cancel the final plan. If she thought this was already cheesy, I didn't need her to know the rest. "No, that would be going overboard. What kind of guy do you think I am?"

"You're my guy."

"I am." With a grin, I brushed her bangs out of her face. "So about me moving to Florida—"

Her arms tightened around me even more. "We can make it work. We can video chat and call each other all the time. And we can even coordinate our visits back to North Carolina so we could see our parents and each other, and it would be cheaper. We could just meet halfway."

She took the words right out of my mouth. "You're brilliant, as usual. What made you change your mind?"

"Just that I realized you're worth fighting for." Suddenly, she leaned back a little and punched my shoulder. "Why didn't you tell me about your dad and college sooner? I'm so proud of you I could cry!"

"I wanted to, but I got distracted with all the Brian stuff."

"Oh." She bit her lip and looked down. "I'm sorry. I didn't mean—"

I pinched her lips together with my index finger and thumb—not enough to hurt, but enough for her to stop talking. "It's my turn to talk now, and I'm telling you that it's okay. You don't have to explain anything. I understand." My hand moved beneath her chin to push her face upward. With a sigh, I wiped at the tear on her cheek. "Let me guess, more allergies?"

"Yeah, spring really does suck." She laughed and wiped at her tears. "So let's just forget about everything, okay? Today could be a fresh start for the both of us. No apologies, no contracts. Just us."

"So you want to start over?"

"Yep."

"Seems like a waste, though." I leaned in until my lips were right by her ear again. "I've been starting to get more of my memories from that night, and believe me, there are just some things I'd rather not forget."

Her blush spread straight to her roots. "Wouldn't you rather make new memories instead? I guarantee that you'll never forget these, even if you tried."

"Oh really?" My eyebrow rose with interest. "Are you having dirty thoughts again?"

"I don't know what you're talking about."

"Sounds tempting. I think I'll have to take you up on that challenge." I dipped my head down until our lips were barely touching. "Let's get started, shall we?"

Just as we were about to kiss, bubbles suddenly surrounded us. Hundreds of them floated down to us, swirling in the wind to create a fairy-tale atmosphere. Or at least what Carly thought was one. Distracted, Taylor pulled away. Her eyes were round and amazed as she stared around us. "What's going on?"

Guess they hadn't gotten my hint. I closed my eyes and let out a defeated sigh. "Look up."

She did and suddenly burst out with laughter. Aaron and Carly were hovering out of the auditorium windows above us, armed with a bubble gun in each hand as they fired all the bubbles in our direction. They must have been hanging out on the balcony this whole time.

Carly stopped and blew on the top of one of her guns like it was smoking.

"Don't mind us. Just keep kissing!" Aaron yelled down at us.

Clenching her stomach from laughing so hard, Taylor peered up at me. Her eyes were shining again. "I thought you weren't a cheesy guy?"

Pulling out the coin necklace from my pocket, I slipped it around her neck. When it was secure in its rightful place, I looped an arm around her waist. "I wasn't until you made me one. I used to be cool. And now I'm just a moping idiot without you. And since you effectively ruined *my* reputation, I think you have to make it up to me. Starting now." I held out my hand for her, wiggling my fingers. "Deal?"

Her hand wrapped around mine, and she held on tight. "Deal."

BEFORE

-Evan-

Taylor caught my attention as soon as I spotted her at the party. She drifted through the crowd with a drink in her hand. Her other hand swept her dark hair out of her eyes as she bobbed her head to the loud music.

I don't really know why I noticed her in the first place. She was a little more dressed up than usual, but there were a lot of other pretty girls wearing tighter, more revealing clothes. Especially the one on my lap. I think her name was Abby? Annie?

My fingers traced along Abby/Annie's collarbone and shoulders. "So, are you having fun?"

She smirked and leaned in closer to nuzzle against my neck. "Especially now that you're here."

"Back at you." I tried to concentrate, but my eyes kept flickering back to Taylor. This time she was swaying to herself by the fireplace. Her hand was braced against the brick mantel. There were a couple of guys looking at her, but no one came close. Probably because they didn't want to get rejected by the Ice Queen, as everyone called her.

Giving up, I finally gave Abby/Annie a kiss on the cheek and stood up. She slid off my lap with a squeak. "I'll be back later." I turned away from her outraged face and slipped through the crowd to get to Taylor. She didn't notice me. Not even when I was standing directly behind her. "Hey."

She spun around and peered at me. "Oh, it's you."

Well, that was a pretty cool greeting. I was beginning to understand why everyone called her the Ice Queen. I leaned against the fireplace to face her, study her. "Uh, yeah. Are you okay? You don't look so great."

"I'm fine. Terrific. Stupendous." Taylor suddenly let out a small burp and covered her mouth. "And a little flatulent."

Snorting with laughter, I shook my head, too surprised by what was happening to know what to say. "Maybe you shouldn't be drinking so much if you're such a lightweight."

"What's a lightweight?"

"Someone who can't handle her drink." *Like you*, I added silently.

Her face beamed, and she leaned in toward me, patting my arm. "Then that's not me. I had two! And I'm perfectly fine."

"Oh yeah?" I held up three fingers. "How many is this?"

She rolled her eyes. "Three. If you want to see if I'm drunk, you've got to use a better method than that. I've been counting since I was fourteen months old." She fumbled in her pocket and pulled out a pen. Flicking off the top of the pen, she started writing on her own arm. "Look, I can still write perfectly. Drunk people can't write, can they?"

I took her arm and examined it. She did write her name really neat. With lots of swirls. *Taylor Simmons.* Since her handwriting was so perfect, it almost looked like a tattoo. I unconsciously caressed my thumb along the inside of her wrist. It was soft and warm. "Anybody can write their own name."

"Fine, then I'll write yours."

"Don't you need to know my name first?"

She grabbed my arm and rubbed her palm against the surface of my skin. Liking the way she was touching me, I took another step toward her. "Oh, everyone knows who you are, Evan."

Feeling a little flattered, I watched as she drew out my name. With her tongue sticking out a little bit, she concentrated on each letter. Finally curling the *y* like a lightning bolt, she tossed the pen over her head. It hit some dude's shoulder. "Done." Her hand slid down to grasp my hand.

"Nice. Now that I know you're not drunk, I think I should get you a drink." Still holding her hand, I wrapped my other arm around her waist and guided her through the crowd toward the beer keg and bottles of liquor on the kitchen counter. A giant blue cooler full of Cokes and other soda was on the ground.

Taylor followed me with a little skip in her step. "How do I know *you're* not drunk?"

"Oh, believe me, I can drink better than anyone here."

Looking very interested, her dark eyes flashed dangerously. She leaned against the counter and pointed a finger at me. "Oh yeah? That sounds like a pretty big dare. Why don't we test that out? For every shot that I drink, then you have to drink three."

Really? Was she really trying to challenge me? I didn't regret coming over to Taylor at all. The party had been getting a little boring, but this conversation with her was worth making out with five girls. Snickering to myself, I handed her a small stack of white plastic shot cups. "Deal."

With a grin of triumph, she grabbed a bottle of tequila and poured shots into them. She concentrated on getting the same amount in each one until there were three cups in front of her. I thought she was only going to drink one, but she let out a deep breath and grabbed them all, one by one. My jaw dropped as she downed three cups in a row before grabbing a can of Coke to chug.

Wiping at her chin, she shoved the bottle at me. "I had three, so that means nine more for you, Mr. Big Shot."

I gave her an admiring look. Damn, she was tough. A lot tougher than I'd originally thought. My pride was yelling at me to do it, while my head told me to just let it go. As usual, my pride won. Oh, I was definitely going to regret this in the morning, but I couldn't turn down her challenge. I splashed tequila in the cups she'd just used.

Here goes nothing. I took each shot before I could back down. After the ninth shot, I couldn't help gagging. I was a good drinker, but I'd already had a few drinks. Not to mention, I hated tequila. Dark liquor flowed down much smoother. I waved the last empty cup at Taylor in triumph. The room was already starting to spin a little bit, but determined not to embarrass myself, I kept my feet firmly planted on the ground. "Happy?"

"Awesome. Let's have another one."

I had to pry her away from the counter when she tried to lunge for the bottle again. Pride or no pride, I wasn't planning to get shitfaced at the party tonight, and I knew I was already at my limit. "Let's dance instead."

The crowd in the living room parted a bit when we came in. Or maybe we shoved through them. I don't know. I didn't really notice. I didn't notice anyone but the fascinating girl in my arms.

We danced to a few songs before someone turned on a slow one. Without any hesitation, Taylor wrapped her arms around my shoulders. Her face tilted back, and she bobbed to the music with her eyes closed. Tiny wisps of dark hair were plastered to her damp forehead.

My hands clasped both sides of her hips. Her tank top rolled up a little over her capris, and I could feel her soft skin. Just an inch or so. I rubbed it beneath my fingertips, back and forth until it started to warm up beneath my fingers. All the while watching her face as she swayed to the music. Her face was calm, but her cheeks were turning a pretty pink. I didn't know if it was because of my touch or because the alcohol was finally creeping up on her. Everything was already getting kind of blurry for me.

Taylor opened her eyes and stared up at me. Her dark eyes were wide and unwavering. For some reason, I froze. I couldn't look away. I just studied her face, from her small forehead to the little mole on her left cheekbone and sliding down to her rosy lips.

Suddenly, she licked her lower lip ever so slightly before leaning up on her tiptoes to kiss me. It was soft and hard. Hot and electrifying. Despite all the alcohol she'd just drunk, she tasted like candy. Sweet and addictive.

I wrapped my hands around her waist and pulled her tighter to my body. She fit perfectly in my arms, like she was made to be there. Belonged there. Her hands on my shoulders tightened like she heard me and agreed.

{Taylor}

With our hands linked together, we swayed in the empty street. My feet skipped to the music from the party still ringing in my ears. "Is it just me or is it really foggy tonight? Everything's all fuzzy. The stars, the trees..." I squinted up at the sky and frowned. "Why are there two moons?"

Instead of looking up, Evan just pointed a finger at me and snorted. "You're so drunk."

"No way." He had to be lying. I didn't feel any different. I did feel happy, though. And light. Unburdened. Just in case, I let go of him and paced back and forth in a straight line. Perfectly straight. It couldn't be any better if I had a ruler. I twirled in place. Once. Twice. "Maybe you're the one who's drunk."

"Oh, I definitely am. I'm still better than you."

I jabbed a finger in his direction. "No one is ever better than me—whoops." My phone fell out of my pocket and hit the street with a loud crack. I stooped over to pick it up. "Oh crap."

Evan bent over to peer at my phone. His blond, spiky hair tickled my nose. "What's wrong?"

"Carly called and texted me a couple of times." Blink. Blink. "Okay, more than a couple." My fingers fumbled on the tiny screen as I tried to text back that I was fine. Why was it so hard? The buttons were tiny! Autocorrect kept putting in funny words and commas, making me erase the entire thing and start over. *Concentrate, Taylor. You can do this.*

When I was on my tenth try, Evan's hand reached out and grabbed the phone from me. "Oh god, let me do it."

"It's not my fault my autocorrect is stupid." I tried to grab it back, but he held it straight over his head as he typed. All I succeeded in doing was smacking the top of my boob into his shoulder. *Owww.* "Make sure you use correct grammar! I hate incorrect texts."

"Okay, Grammar Nazi. Done." He stuck the phone into his pocket and reached for my hand. "Let's go."

My happy grin turned into a grimace. There was a weird buildup in my chest that made me sick. "I think I'm going to hurl."

His eyes widened, and he pulled back. With both hands on my shoulders, Evan ushered me off the street and toward a bush on the edge of someone's curb. I held my hair back from my face and threw up. Or at least tried to. The only thing that came up was some really bitter liquid. Once I started, though, it was like I couldn't stop. Shuddering from the taste, I kept trying and trying, but nothing else came up. Evan rubbed my back the whole time.

Finally, when it was clear that I was done, he handed me a

napkin. I finished wiping before realizing that it wasn't a napkin at all. It was the edge of his blue T-shirt. And now it was stained a darkish color. "Ew, you're dirty now."

"Because of you," he said with a snort. "You're welcome, by the way." He grabbed my hand and tugged me along the street again. A little slower. His other arm wrapped around my shoulders.

After a while, I started to feel a little better. Letting go of him, I twirled in the street. Once. Twice. My arms stretched over my head like a ballerina's. Evan grinned and did the moonwalk toward me. Even his arms moved up and down as he hummed a funny, upbeat tune.

I don't know how long we danced in the street, but I swear I just blinked and we were standing in his room. Like we had apparated.

The first thing I did was rush into his bathroom to brush my teeth and get the icky taste out of my mouth. When I came out, Evan was still standing, scratching the top of his head like he didn't know where he was. Like a cute, confused monkey.

I snorted. "So much for being good at drinking."

Evan leaned his back against the wall and slid down to the ground. "Tonight's not my best moment. But do you want to see what else I'm good at?"

Humming to myself, I stumbled over to his desk. "Not cleaning, that's for sure. Look at all this stuff." There was a pile of junk scattered on top. Magazines, comic books, keys, pens, and wires. With one hand, I shoved some of the boring stuff onto the floor.

"Gee, that's not helping. And watch out for that *Spider-Man* comic!" he complained with a yelp as he unsteadily climbed to his feet. "That's the one with the Human Torch appearance. It's probably worth about seventeen grand in mint condition."

I eyed the tattered copy in my hands. "This isn't mint condition."

"Well, no, that's a pretty bad one, but it's still worth about fifty bucks."

Boys. I'll never understand them. Still, I set the comic book back on the desk. Ahh, this looked interesting. I picked up a stack of pictures and shuffled through them. "Oh, she's pretty. I like her hair. It's really shiny and curly. Do you know what kind of conditioner she uses?"

"Sorry, we didn't do much talking that day," he said with a devilish grin as he crossed his arms. "But I'll ask her the next time I see her."

I snorted. "I doubt you even remember who she is." Before he could respond, I got distracted by the slightly dull turquoise surfboard propped against the side of the desk.

Dropping the pictures on the ground, I slid my fingers over the edge of the board, curving around the tip. Pretty. Was this the legendary board? So many nicks and scratches on the surface. There was no way he'd hooked up with this many girls. I didn't even know if there were this many girls in Wilmington.

I'd always wanted to try surfing. Well, there was a lot of stuff I'd always wanted to try. Like people say, there's no time like the present! I propped the surfboard on the ground and hopped on.

Well, I tried to. The darn thing was slippery or something. I couldn't stand straight.

Evan chuckled and reached out to steady me. His left hand

curved around my waist until I wasn't going to fall over any-more. My arms flung out on either side of me like I was on a tightrope.

He grinned. "Remind me to take you to the beach someday."

"Because I look like I'm a natural surfer?"

"No, because I want to see the look on your face when you wipe out and get dumped into the ocean by the first wave you catch."

I scowled at him, but his grin only grew wider. What did he know? *I never fail at anything. Never, never, never.*

God, my feet hurt. Stupid fancy shoes. I hopped off the board, yanked them off, and chucked them into the small space beneath his desk. They smacked against the wall with a satisfy-ing clunk. "Two points!"

He took off his shirt and tossed it at me. "Jeez, not only are you really chatty, but you're a loud drunk, too."

"I told you, I'm not drunk. I'm just happy." My eyes squinted, and I tried to focus on the half-naked guy in front of me. But he kept fading in and out of focus, like he was a mirage. Was any of this real? Maybe this whole night wasn't real. I reached out and poked the left side of his chest and then the right. Hmm, nice and firm.

He glanced down at my hands still on his bare chest. "If you wanted to feel me up, you should have just asked."

"Don't be cocky. No one wants to feel you up. I'm just mak-ing sure this isn't a dream." Backing up, I stumbled on some clothes on the ground. My legs wobbled, and I couldn't move. My feet were stuck! What kind of magic was this? I lunged forward and would have landed smack on the carpet if Evan hadn't grabbed me.

To my surprise, he didn't let go. His hands drifted down from my shoulders to tug on my hands. "Sit down before you hurt yourself."

I giggled and flopped down at the foot of the bed. "Yes, Daddy."

He snorted with laughter. "You don't know how dirty that sounds."

"I do. Why do you think I said it?" I kicked my feet out and wiggled my toes. "I usually never get to say what I'm really thinking, though. It'll ruin my reputation."

"What will?"

"When people find out that I'm not perfect and proper. I'm snarky and sarcastic and rude. I'm a horrible person. A real closet witch." I waved both arms in the air like I was confessing all my secrets to the world, and I accidentally smacked his cheek. It just felt so free to finally say what I wanted. Even if it was just to Evan. I tapped the side of my head with my index finger and gave him a cheeky grin. "And inappropriate dirty thoughts pop in and out of here. But I can't admit to any of it. No, I can't."

"Uh." He gave me an intimate look and leaned in closer to me. "So, your inappropriate dirty thoughts. Are they about me?"

"Don't you want to know?"

Evan laughed. "You're right. I do. Way too much." He wrapped an arm around my shoulders. "Why don't you just rest a bit?"

I wanted to argue, but my head suddenly felt heavy. Very, very heavy. I did need to rest. So tired. I climbed onto the bed and snuggled against the cool, fresh pillow. My hand smacked the pillow beside me. "Come. Lie down."

When he finally did, I scooted forward and lay against his bare shoulder. Hmmm. Despite all his muscles, it was soft and squishy like cotton candy. God, I would kill to have some cotton candy right now. Sweet and fluffy and melts in your mouth. I only eat the pink cotton candy. The blue would dye my lips.

That's stupid, though. Why? WHY? Nobody's going to judge me if my mouth is a little blue. Nobody would care. Except me. But I couldn't force myself to change. I can't.

"Why can't I?" I raised my head and stared up at Evan, our faces only inches away from each other. I never noticed he had a faint smear of freckles on his nose. They practically blended in with his dark tan. I didn't know if they were natural or from the hours he spent in the sun.

Evan swallowed and pulled back an inch. "Now what are you talking about?"

"What I want to do right now."

His voice got husky, and his eyes flickered down to my lips. "Well, what do you want to do?"

"Eat cotton candy. Blue cotton candy."

He blinked at me in shock. That was definitely not the answer he was expecting. Evan bit his lip and turned his face away. But by the way his shoulders were shaking, I knew he was laughing at me.

I didn't care. Well, I did a little, but not that much.

Evan wrapped an arm around my shoulders, pushed my head down, and rested his chin against the top of my head. "I'll get you some cotton candy tomorrow. Let's just sleep for now."

Something was weird and wrong about this. But it took too much energy to focus on anything, so I gave up. Hopefully it wasn't anything important. Nothing was important now.

I closed my eyes and leaned against his chest, cushioning my head in the nook beneath his chin. I was safe and warm. And this felt perfect. Nothing else mattered.

ACKNOWLEDGMENTS

First I want to give a special thanks to you, the reader. You read my book all the way to the end! Or, at least, I hope you read it instead of just skipping to the end. Not that there's anything wrong with reading it that way. ☺ You're the reason I write and why I'll continue to write. I love you!

My deepest appreciation goes to my publisher, Jean Feiwel, for giving *The Way to Game the Walk of Shame* the chance to be published. I really don't know what would have happened to my book if I hadn't submitted it to Swoon Reads, but I do know that it could not be in better hands anywhere else. Thank you for taking a chance on Evan and Taylor!

Holly, is there any way to get you nominated for the Best Editor Award? We really should look into that because you are just amazing! I didn't really know what to expect working with an editor, but you exceeded any expectation I could ever have. Your comments and insight are incredible and spot on. I consider myself so lucky to be able to work with you.

A huge thanks to Lauren, Emily, Rich, KB, and everyone on the Swoon Reads team for making *The Way to Game the Walk of Shame* shine as brightly as it does on the inside and outside. I never could have imagined my novel could be so incredible, and it's because of all your hard work. And a huge

HUG to the whole Swoon Reads community for all their reading, rating, and reviewing.

So much love for my writing buddies, Shayda, Rachel, and Ashley. Seriously, thank you for being there through all the querying, submissions, and meltdowns. For patting me on the shoulder and telling me everything will be okay. For reading and critiquing *The Way to Game* when it was still *The Love Contract*. For the late-night chats and brainstorming. And just being the most incredible cheerleaders anyone could ever ask for. I'm so glad to have met you guys. We'll have our dream writers' retreat one day!

My earliest writing started on a Harry Potter fan site. Specifically HE—Hogwarts Experience. There were countless hours of working on projects, writing fan fiction, and roleplaying with the best group of people. And I can't bring up roleplaying without giving a special shout-out to Elana, Lifey, and Veronica. Thank you for helping me learn the importance of character bios and honing my guy voice. Or rather, *Evan* thanks you!

To my wonderful family and friends. It took me ages to tell anyone that I wanted to be a writer. And even longer to admit that I'd written an actual book. Even now, it's hard to say that I'm an author because it still doesn't feel real. There are times when all the doubts and fears still come creeping in. But then I hear the pride and joy in your voice when *you* tell people that I'm an author, and it makes all this worth it. Thank you for supporting me all these years. Even if you didn't know you were.

I always tell people that I started reading in the first place because my sisters didn't want to play with me when we were growing up and there was nothing else to do. (Which is totally true.) So in a way, Thuc, Quynh, and Kien, you guys are the *true* reason this book exists. ☺ But to be honest, you taught me so many things in life and you were always there for me. Whether I wanted you to be or not. And even though you nearly chased Quynh off on prom night, there's no harm done now since we're married. And it makes for a hilarious story. Not to sound overly mushy, but you really are the *best* sisters anybody could hope for.

To my wonderful parents. I barely know what to say to even show an ounce of how much I appreciate and love you. There could be an entire new book dedicated to you and it still wouldn't be enough. I wouldn't be here without your support and care. I wouldn't even *be* here without you. Mom, nothing makes me happier than hanging out with you, watching Asian dramas all night. You always listen to me talk and ramble about everything and anything with a smile on your face. And, Dad, one of my fondest memories as a kid is when you brought home a boxful of books that you picked up at a yard sale or consignment shop for me. Even though you're not with me anymore, I know that you're still here to guide me with everything I do, every word that I write. I don't know how I lucked out in having you both as my parents. ☺ Thank you both for raising me, teaching me the value of hard work, and pushing me to go for my dreams.

To Quynh, my husband, the true owner of the REAL Rudy. The first thing you ever fed me was pizza on April 28, 2003. Even though it didn't have enough mushrooms, it was still one of the best things I've ever eaten. And we've eaten together A LOT since then. But that pizza will always be special to me because it was the first meal we had together. The beginning of our relationship and the start of my happily-ever-after. Thank you for being here for me. For the hundred trips to Barnes just so I can look at the books and get inspiration. For taking care of me while I struggle with edits. This book wouldn't be a book without you. *I* wouldn't be me without you. ♥

Turn the page for some

Sw♥♥nworthy

Extras...

List of reasons why Evan should be my fake boyfriend

• Improved reputation among everyone, teachers and adults. They love me (perfect grades and attendance, extracurricular activities which include Honor Society, student council, tutoring, yearbook, etc.) and the love will spill over to Evan.

• Help with homework/improve grades (although that shouldn't be too hard, anything is better than his grades now).

• Help with college applications (probably too late because applications have been due for a while now). Community college?

• Research colleges with late acceptances.

• Find out if Evan has a pet.
Offer to walk/wash it.

• Promise to clean his room three times a
week. Or scrub his surfboard. Wax?

• Free legal work for the three years after
graduation from Columbia.

• Bribe him with rare comic books. Note to
self: Look up rare comic books

• Protection from girls?

• ~~Because he actually likes me?~~ IMPOSSIBLE

The Contract

In light of the recent events, henceforth the aftermath of The Party That Shall Not Be Mentioned (TPTSNBM), it has been brilliantly determined that in order to salvage what's left of our reputations, a fake relationship shall be made between the two parties listed below along with the guidelines and stipulations that will be required of this "relationship."

This agreement executed on the _____ day of _____ 2016, between <u>Taylor Elizabeth Simmons</u> and <u>Evan McKinley</u> is a binding contract that will ~~curse~~ penalize the offending party when he breaks one of the rules. Punishments and penalty fines may be added to the contract later on if needed. Once a satisfying result has been reached and agreed upon, the two parties will amicably break up in public to officially sever the ties and dissolve this contract. Until then, they will abide by the rules listed below.

find out Evan's middle name?

Section 1: Relationship requirements in public eye

1.1 Public Displays of Affection. Hand holding and kisses on the cheek are acceptable in public at school. Anything more has to be discussed and agreed upon by both parties.

SwoonReads

1.2 Pet Names. Pet names aren't required
unless in extremely romantic situations.
Ex. Valentine's Day or a birthday. Even
then, they only need to be used when
within hearing distance of other people.

1.3 Dates. At least once a week, both
parties will go on a proper date to show
that they're in a real relationship. Ex.
Movies, dinner, or even library study
dates will work.

Section 2: Prohibited

2.1 While in this relationship,
neither party will date nor have any
inappropriate interactions with the
opposite sex unless approved by the
other party. This includes flirting in
person, texting, or online.

2.2 Obviously any mention of this contract
to anyone will violate this entire
agreement and the Ultimate Punishment
will be enforced. (Ultimate Punishment
will be decided upon later.)

-This rule excludes Carly because
she basically came up with this idea
and is privy to any and all secrets.
Not to mention, she'll find out about
this anyway with her secret snooping
powers.

Section 3: Miscellaneous

3.1 If asked by anyone, the evolution of our relationship/"love" is explained in detail in the following pages. The short version is below. Also note that our relationship was already official and underway when the events of "TPTSNBM" happened.

"Although Evan and Taylor already knew each other, they never actually officially met until a fateful afternoon at Starbucks two months ago. They both ordered a mocha latte, but Evan's had skim milk, which the waitress accidentally gave to Taylor. After exchanging the lattes, Evan was so occupied watching Taylor walk away that he stepped into the street and nearly got run over by a black SUV. Luckily, her warning shout made him jump back on the curb in the nick of time. After Taylor checked on him to make sure he was okay, Evan asked her out to dinner to thank her for saving him. At first, Taylor declined since he wasn't exactly her type, but he persisted by showing up at her house with a fresh mocha latte every single morning before school until she accepted.

Since then, they talked on the phone and went on dates for over two months before

officially going out. The party was
their way of debuting their relationship
to the world."

Both parties will agree to all the terms and
conditions upon signing of the contract.

Sign name _____

Sign name _____

*Note to self: When typing up the final draft,
make it sound more legal and fierce to freak
Evan into signing. Intimidation for the win!

Also borrow Dad's legal stationery. The one with
the ivory letterhead.

Should I get it laminated afterward?

A Coffee Date

with author Jenn P. Nguyen and her editor, Holly West

"About the Author"

Holly West (HW): What was the very first romance novel that you ever read?

Jenn P. Nguyen (JN): I think the first romance novel I ever read was in sixth grade. I don't remember the author or the title or anything, probably because I was trying to hide in the cafeteria when I was reading it. But it was a medieval story about two feuding families, and for some reason the youngest and only girl was masquerading as a boy. I don't know why. And then the other family had a guy who met her and fell in love with her. And they got married even though she didn't really like him. Probably because he was cocky. They're usually cocky. And they just got better. I don't remember the ending, but I do remember that much.

HW: That feels very familiar to me. It sounds like a Johanna Lindsey book, but I don't remember the title either.

JN: I've read a lot of Johanna Lindsey books and I haven't seen it. So I don't think it's hers because I read her books. But I always wanted to know what that book was.

HW: I'm curious now, too! Maybe one of your readers will know and can send a tweet to @JennP_Nguyen and @Holliambria to solve the puzzle.

JN: It was like 15 years ago, if that helps.

Swoon Reads

HW: Keeping with our romantic theme, do you have an OTP (One True Pairing)? A favorite fictional couple?

JN: That's really hard. I'm kind of a serial fan where I like all types of couples as long as I'm reading them. I like all the couples in Stephanie Perkins, I like Jessica and Marcus in *The Sloppy Firsts*, the Jessica Darling books. Of course, everyone has to like Elizabeth and Darcy, but I actually like—I might get yelled at for this—I like the Lizzie and Darcy from *The Lizzie Bennett Diaries* on YouTube better. And technically that's a book now, so it's still literary. I mean, I even shipped Edward and Bella at one point. So just anybody, really.

HW: That's fine. I tend to pick an OTP in everything that I read. Or if I'm watching shows I'll be like, "I'm going to ship THIS couple in this show."

JN: Oh, don't get me started on shows. It would be a while.

HW: And my personal favorite question: If you were a superhero, what would your superpower be?

JN: I would like to be able to teleport places, because then I could visit wherever I wanted, and also eat anything I wanted whenever I wanted it. Croissants from France, sushi from Japan, definitely pizza from Italy—and not have to worry about the plane and security lines and all of that.

"The Swoon Reads Experience"

HW: How did you first hear about Swoon Reads?

JN: I learned about it at Romantic Times 2014 because I danced the Swoon-ba to get a free tote! I didn't even know what Swoon

Reads was, but I wanted the tote bag! Then I looked it up after-ward just to see a little bit.

HW: What made you decide to put your manuscript up on the site?

JN: It was actually Sandy Hall's book. Because I found it at Barnes & Noble randomly, and I read it, and I really liked it. I thought, "This is a sweet, fun romance. And if this was chosen, maybe I have a chance?" So I went and posted.

HW: What was your experience like on the site before you were chosen?

JN: They always have those contests online where if you do the best, then you win a publishing contract or something. And I never really wanted to do that because it seemed like a popularity contest. But with Sandy Hall I could see Swoon Reads wasn't that. People genuinely liked it and they gave really good comments. It was awesome to get comments like, "I love it!" or "Great book!" but I also got great comments about the characters, and I could tell the readers had put a lot of thought into it and they wanted to help make it better. That was awesome.

"The Writing Life"

HW: Do you have any writing rituals, like do you have to write in a specific place?

JN: Not a specific place. I really could write anywhere. Now usually I write at home. I used to write at cafes, Barnes & Noble, libraries . . . I think my very first novel I wrote on little Subway napkins when I was working at Subway. I think I still have it. As for rituals, I always

have to have music on. If it's too quiet, I can't concentrate. And I like to print out my outline and have it next to me, so whenever I write something I can check it off and it always makes me feel good. If I don't have the printout, I can't write.

HW: What is your writing process? You just mentioned you have an outline. How does that work for you?
JN: Usually when I have a general idea, then I think of names and pictures. I have to have names and pictures. Maybe so when I plot I see their faces in my head? Then I plot out a detailed chapter outline so that when I finish a chapter I can check it off.

HW: What was it like to get the edit letter?
JN: It was nerve-racking because I didn't know what to expect. We had talked a little before about what changes we wanted to do, but it was a little more specific. I remember opening it up and it was like 17 pages. I freaked out a little bit. But it was good. I read through it a couple times and I could see everything and understand, so it wasn't that bad at all. Not as bad as I thought.

HW: How does the revision process work for you?
JN: When I got the notes, I wrote a new outline with "Things to Change" at the top. Change Lauren, take out a character, strengthen these relationships, have Aaron show up more, etc. And then I wrote for each chapter a brief outline of what happens and then what needed to be changed. Sometimes it was no changes, sometimes it was small tweaks, and sometimes it was scrapped completely and rewrite. And then I go through my list.

HW: What is the very best writing advice you've ever heard?

JN: It's one that I think everyone's heard and repeated over and over, but "Write what you want to write." Write what you love. Don't write what you expect other people want to read or what's popular right now. I've tried doing that. I've added drama and tension and a lot of issues just because that's what people say they want. And it just never worked out well. I was never happy with it, and if you want to get it published, you have to work with it a lot and reread a lot. And if you're not happy with it, then it's just going to be really hard.

From the author of *How to Say I Love You Out Loud* . . .

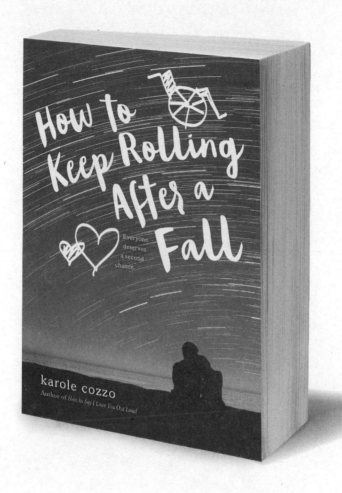

After taking the fall for a cyberbullying incident, former mean girl Nikki Baylor thinks her life is over. Then she meets Pax, a hot wheelchair rugby player who shows her that everyone deserves a second chance.

Coming August 2, 2016

Chapter 1

As I park in the lot of the Harborview Nursing and Rehabilitation Center, I realize that, for the first time ever, I'm actually excited to be there. I'm working a short, three-hour shift, and the shift itself won't be so bad, since I'm filling in on the orthopedics wing, where Jeremiah's been assigned.

After work, the two of us have plans to check out the end-of-summer party that spans the length of Ocean Isle's boardwalk. Since I've seen it in those mailers that started showing up after the Fourth of July, the phrase *end-of-summer* has stirred feelings of anxiety, loss, and sadness. But tonight it means it's time for a party. One final opportunity to eat handfuls of hot caramel corn with the salty breeze blowing across my face. One night to forget about everything else going on, in a crowd large and chaotic enough to get lost in.

I lift my butt off the seat and scrunch my hair as I look in the rearview mirror. Once upon a time, I was a shoo-in for "Best Hair" in the senior superlatives—it's long and wildly curly, with natural highlights. All summer long I've tucked it under a baseball cap with the brim pulled down anytime I've been forced to leave my house. But not tonight. I made an effort to look good for Jeremiah. And I want to pretend I'm the girl I used to be.

Walking across the parking lot, I decide this place would be a lot more appealing if there was, you know, an *actual* view of the harbor. Instead, it's located miles inland, in the middle of a bleak field. The builders tried to spruce it up with the usual gazebos and flower beds, but the name is still a bold-faced lie. It's a depressing place to be, for all of us who are here because we have no choice in the matter.

But not tonight! I think, breezing through the automatic doors with renewed energy as I picture Jeremiah's face. *Tonight, it's a good place to be.* I head toward the nurses' station to clock in, but when I catch a glimpse of Jeremiah through the glass-paneled cafeteria walls, I make a detour, a sudden diet Dr Pepper craving developing.

I feel giddy as I walk in his direction. We've been flirting for the past two weeks, since I started my stint at the rehab center. Jeremiah's a sophomore at Rutgers University, with a long-term plan for med school and a specialty in orthopedics—as he explained it to me, "I want to break some bones and fix 'em up again." Jeremiah's got it all worked out, but his plans are on hold at the moment. He's taking a semester off to help out with some family issues. He hasn't said what kind of issues, and I haven't felt right asking; I assume he'll tell me eventually.

In the meantime, I'm content with the flirting. Jeremiah's really hot—Abercrombie model hot, with the cool hair, and the scruff, and the smirk. He even looks good in scrubs. "One day women are going to be falling down the stairs on purpose just to end up in your waiting room," I've teased him.

He's sweet, too, taking the mop out of my hands and pushing it himself, and one time walking me to my car under an umbrella from the lost and found when it started pouring without warning. Then two nights ago, he snatched my phone and programmed his number. "So call me tonight," he'd said all coolly as he tossed it back. I had, and now we have a date.

Jeremiah turns away from the register and slides his wallet into the back pocket of his scrubs, and his eyes meet mine. I smile and wave and wait for him to smile back.

But he doesn't smile. He glowers instead, his brown eyes ignited with a fury that turns them amber.

"I know who you are." He's not discreet; he's loud, pointing his index finger in my direction. "And you can go straight to hell."

The blood drains from my face and runs cold. I want to vanish, but I can't move. My feet feel as if they're stuck in the wet sand left behind when a wave recedes, weighted down and useless.

A few trays clatter against steel, and then the room is deathly quiet. Workers stop serving, midscoops of mashed potatoes. Residents stop talking. The scene unfolds before me in slow motion as people who have had strokes and people in wheelchairs struggle to turn their heads in my direction.

"Nice try, *Nicole*." He says my full name, the one I'd used to introduce myself, like an accusation. "Nikki Baylor, right? I know who you are. You forgot your ID badge yesterday. Now let me tell you who *I* am." Jeremiah approaches and thrusts his right hand toward me with such force it jams against my rib cage. It's almost a shove. "Jeremiah Jordan. Taylor Jordan's my sister. My baby sister, for that matter."

I hang my head and clench my fists at the same time, the mention of her name evoking the usual combination of shame and regret and a desire to run and hide. Except my feet are still stuck in the damn sand.

He folds his arms across his chest. "Guess it's my bad. You should really find out a person's last name before asking her out." Jeremiah doesn't say anything else and I look up, but it turns out he was saving one final zinger. "But now I know. And now it makes me sick to look at your face."

Tears form in my eyes at once. It sort of makes me sick to look at my face now, too, but Jeremiah had changed that for a few weeks. Before I actually start crying, thankfully, whatever's holding me in place loosens and I run from the room. I dart through the side door and into the central courtyard, the late-afternoon sun glaring down on me like the harsh lights inside the questioning room of the police station.

I choke back my tears, bending over and grabbing onto

my knees for support. I'll never escape this. This is going to follow me forever. I can pretend to be someone I'm not—I can pretend to be the person I *used* to be—but it's nothing more than playing a part.

I shake my head back and forth and wipe my eyes with the back of my hand, struggling to wrap my head around what just happened, feeling like I have whiplash. Jeremiah had come and gone so fast. The prospect of happiness had been so fleeting. I walked in the door envisioning the warmth of his smile; now all I can remember is the cold hatred in his eyes.

What the hell just happened?

"That was pretty harsh."

I straighten and turn around . . . then look down. The boy is in a wheelchair more lightweight than most I see around here, and he can't be much older than me. But he has a more mature look about him, something about his deep-set hazel eyes and square jaw that makes him look more like a young man and less like a boy. His light-brown hair falls to his chin, and the muscular build of his upper body makes me think he might've been a badass at one point.

I square my shoulders and lift my chin. "I probably deserve it."

"Highly doubt that." He wheels a bit closer, shaking his head. "That was a bad scene back there."

"Well, you don't know what you're talking about." I stare into the distance and blow out the breath I realize I've been holding. "If you did, you probably would've stood up and applauded him."

"Nah, I don't think so." A hint of a smile plays on his bow-shaped lips.

"Trust me, you would've."

"No, I don't think so," he repeats. He taps his knuckles against the wheels of his chair. "Standing ovations, not really my thing."

I cringe and want to die. "Oh my God. I'm really sorry."

"No apology necessary. I'm not easily offended."

"Still. I'm sorry."

He nods once in acknowledgment. "'S okay." Then he tilts his head and studies me. "Anyway, I've seen you around here a couple of times. And I think you have a really nice face. I have a hard time figuring why it makes that dude want to puke."

I smile in spite of everything, just for a second. Then reality sets in again, and I cover my eyes with my hand. "Today officially sucks. And I need to clock in. Like, five minutes ago." I take a deep breath, trying to imagine how I can possibly make myself go back inside. "But I can't go back in there."

"I can have your back if you want," wheelchair guy offers. "Give you an escort."

I look at him, asking why without saying the question out loud.

He shrugs. "I'm old-school like that. A guy shouldn't lash out at a girl, and he really had no business putting his hands on you. Just because of a fight or whatever."

"It wasn't a fight," I mumble. "Not his fight, anyway. You certainly don't have to make it yours."

But he doesn't go anywhere, and I don't ask him to leave.

READ YOUR HEART OUT

Join the hottest community of Young Adult readers and writers online now at swoonreads.com

© Anh Tran

Jenn P. Nguyen fell in love with books in the third grade and spent the rest of her school years reading through lunchtime and giving up recess to organize the school library. She has a degree in business administration from the University of New Orleans and still lives in the city with her husband. Jenn spends her days reading, dreaming up YA romances, and binge-watching Korean dramas all in the name of "research." *The Way to Game the Walk of Shame* is her debut novel. Find her on Twitter at @JennP_Nguyen.